# The Porches of Holly

**Traci A. Vanderbush**

T. Ann Publishing

Special thanks to my husband, Bill Vanderbush, for recognizing and empowering the things in me that I often overlook or consider to be lacking. Thank you for encouraging me to write, and valuing the time that I've spent being creative. Twenty-three years with you has taught me more about love, grace and the power of union beyond what I could have imagined possible. Here's to many years of the front-porch rocking that we've dreamed about.

This book is dedicated to every person who thinks themselves to be in a hopeless situation. There is always hope. Redemption is always possible. May the goodness of God become a reality to you right where you are.

# The Porches of Holly

## Prologue

It was a quiet night in the southern town of Holly. The wind whispered its way through bare, winter trees and whistled through creaky, old homes that held the sleeping people lying inside. Quaint porches stood peacefully, displaying their rocking chairs and swings that swayed gently with the air. The sounds of soft, clinking chains and wood rocking on wood, released stories of those who lived and dreamed in their presence. Porches. Where life happened. Where connections took place. Where babies were rocked, kisses were given, tears were shed, and old stories repeated.

Shared victories, triumphs and tragedies had been experienced by the community, and a supernatural force awakened the hearts and spirits of those threatened by destruction. The trials of life chose their victims at random. Addiction, lies and betrayal knew no boundaries. And neither did the grace of God. It was this grace that breathed over Holly, the tiny town of 3,000 that longed for the return of its lost perfection.

Jackson Sawyer, a handsome, local newspaper reporter had come to understand the power of words. Dylan Vanberg, the local pastor, came to realize the power of grace. Now the sleeping town lay silent as an invisible presence began to reveal itself on a deeper level. The winds knew what was coming and the soil was conscious of what was about to emerge. Some hearts still remained cold, but an unseen presence pursued the resurrection of the dead. The breath of life was coming to the porches of Holly.

## Chapter One

Dylan Vanberg lay in bed, contemplating the last five years of his life. Loneliness hung over him, threatening to steal the hope he had preached about for so long. He stared at the ceiling, tracing every crack with his eyes. *Foundations aren't always secure*, he thought. *Solid ground doesn't promise perfection.* Dylan considered the miraculous fact that he was still alive and breathing after his life was forever changed by the choices of those he loved.

The irony of being made strong in weakness filled his mind. *How does one find the faith to believe in goodness again when their dreams and deepest desires are stripped away? And how is it possible that loss can bring new sight...even strength?* He turned his attention to the clock, wishing he could convince his brain to sleep. Four o'clock in the morning was certainly the worst time to be thinking about the weightiness of life. Dylan sat up and placed his feet on the cold, wood floors. He stood up and walked to the window that overlooked the home of his best friend, Jackson Sawyer. *My God, if it wasn't for Jackson, I'd probably be a dead man.* He smiled, remembering the kindness the young man lavished on him during the darkest day of his life.

## The Dream

Across the street, Jackson lay sleeping, falling quickly into a dream world. As Jackson drifted into another dimension, he carefully stepped on the fallen leaves beneath his feet, trying to be quiet as he inched forward to find where the voice originated. As the sky began to darken, the woods seemed to embrace him, inviting him to come further. Red, yellow and brown leaves cracked as he walked into a small, circular clearing, and his eyes fell upon an unusual sight. A shaft of golden light pierced through the scraggly, tall pines, creating what looked like a spotlight on the ground. Inside the light stood the one whose voice Jackson had heard. The man's back was turned to Jackson. He studied the man from head-to-toe. Shoulder-length, brown hair flowed out from underneath the black beret on his head, and he wore a long-sleeved shirt which appeared like multi-colored, stained glass. Black suspenders held onto his khaki pants that were tucked into black combat boots.

The man faced an unusually large artist's canvas that rested on a wooden easel. The canvas held a glorious picture of majestic, colorful mountains towering above a crystal-clear river that flowed into a breathtaking waterfall. The waters poured into a multi-colored stream of liquid. Its colors reflected in the sky above.

The man reached his hand toward the canvas and uttered words that Jackson couldn't understand. At the sound of his voice, colors swirled upon the canvas and the picture shifted and changed. Jackson held his breath, in awe. *Is this man actually painting with mere words?*

Jackson continued watching as the man spoke and created. After a minute or two, the man stepped back and crossed his arms as he studied his creation. "Yes," he uttered. "It is good...very good!" He tilted his head back and began to laugh. He looked at his painting with sincere admiration. "You are absolutely perfect! You are mine and I am yours. How beautiful you are, my love." The man slowly stepped toward his painting. Leaning forward, he placed his hands on his knees, bent toward the canvas and breathed on it. Stepping back, he laughed with pure pleasure.

Instantly, the painting began to move. Everything on the canvas became fully alive and three-dimensional...breathing, moving, and pulsing with life. The man was glad. He began to spin around, arms spread wide, and face tilted upward, as he declared, "In our image and after our likeness!" Jackson couldn't see his face clearly, but he knew the man was smiling as he spun. "All of this is yours," he spoke to the painting.

Beautiful, bright colors shot out from the canvas, swirling into multiple rainbows which began to take form and stretch into the woods. Sounds of rushing waters rustled through the trees and jewels of many colors appeared, covering every inch of the forest floor. The pine trees seemed to awaken. The dirt seemed to breathe beneath the glimmering beauty. Everything was alive and aware of another realm.

The man stood, surrounded by living color that erupted from his painting. Jackson remained behind a tree, peering out at the spectacle, breathless with excitement. A flood of peace filled him with joy! He placed his hand over his mouth to hide the laughter that was erupting from his lips. What was this bliss?

Amidst the ecstasy, a screech pierced through the air. Jackson grabbed his ears, trying to protect himself from the painful sound. The screeching continued for a few seconds, leaving his heart and his head pounding. Terror struck his heart as he watched the swirling rainbows transform into blackness. First gray and then black. Everything within the painting began to fade as it pulled the gray into itself. Seemingly reaching for darkness, inviting it in, the canvas heaved like a monster, sucking everything back into itself. The multi-dimensional life was now trapped inside the canvas, pulsing slowly, like a dying heart.

The artist stood firm, reaching his hands toward the canvas. He spoke gently. "Don't leave me, my love. I will never forsake you." The man turned his body slightly. Jackson could see tears falling from his cheek. The man fell to his knees, keeping his eyes locked on his creation. "All you are is all of me. The darkness is not part of us. Why do you hide?"

The painting appeared to struggle for breath as tornadoes of gray and black twisted inside of it. The edges oozed black, like grease and oil, falling onto the ground. The colorful gemstones and majestic mountains were hidden by the darkness. The dirt became lifeless. The sky darkened, and there was stillness…and heaving.

"Just be still and know…" the man uttered. Jackson couldn't hear everything he whispered at the painting, but he felt the man's longing for his creation. Jackson's heart was overwhelmed with grief. He continued to watch. The man and his creation sat, staring at each other. Jackson believed he was watching Love itself face a seething serpent. The canvas was bitten and now infused with anger, resentment, and hatred.

As the black venom continued spilling out, the dirt, trees and rocks crackled with a sizzling sound as they burned away beneath the poison. Jackson realized the painting was killing the forest, and if it continued flowing out, everything would die. He jumped out from behind the tree and yelled at the artist, "Do something! Destroy it before it destroys us!" But the artist remained still and quiet.

"You have to do something now!" Jackson's bright, blue eyes were filled with fear, and he was losing his breath to the threat. "Listen to me! Can't you hear me?" Jackson ran in front of the man and knelt before him. As he looked into his eyes, he was instantly captivated by immense pools of peace that engulfed him with love. Jackson began to weep, overcome by the light that filled his heart. In that moment, everything was perfect. Everything was good. The disappointment that he knew in his twenty-eight short years was completely gone.

The man placed his hands on Jackson's cheeks and he pressed his forehead to Jackson's forehead. Face-to-face. "What is this?"

Jackson asked. "What are you doing to me?" He wept tears of relief that he couldn't understand.

The man said, "This is the way."

As waves of wholeness melted into Jackson's heart, he found himself on his back, lying on the forest floor, peering into the gray sky above. He was losing his focus on the artist and canvas as the world around him became narrow and hazy. His attention was drawn to the heavens. He felt himself lifting into them, far above the earth, yet somehow, still attached to the life he had always known.

As he ascended, he was aware of an indescribable presence. It was a tangible power…the most joyful, perfect love he'd ever felt. His body trembled in its presence, not from fear, but from being absorbed in an invisible substance beyond understanding. And this substance was unlike anything he'd ever experienced. It was love. Pure, perfect love.

The pain of recent years diminished into light. The demons that were once so overwhelming in size and scale were now eliminated. The roar of rage became a faint cry. The churning turmoil that existed in his soul became a gentle river.

Jackson became aware of three beings leaning over him, peering into his soul. He felt their warmth and heard their voices and laughter, yet he couldn't see their faces clearly. Their hazy forms were encircled by brightness. Jackson sensed the world far behind him, and it seemed tiny in comparison to this new realm in which he was enveloped. The voices were talking about love, and about Jackson. Although he lacked clarity, lost in a dream world, he knew that he was being celebrated. His arrival brought joy to the beings that surrounded him with honor.

For a brief moment, he remembered the pain that lay below him on the spinning globe, but the memory of it was wiped away as a hand gently entered his chest. "Watch this," a voice said. The sound of a fast-moving river surrounded his head and warm waters purged his heart. There was no pain. Just peace. "Heart surgery…" Jackson whispered to himself. The waters flowed, bringing relief and healing. Occasionally, a painful memory would thrust its way into his mind and heart, but as quickly as it came, the waters washed it away. The debris and marks of life's disappointments became light as a feather.

Waves of love swept away things that he didn't know existed within him. Claps of thunder sounded as anger's bite broke its hold. Tentacles of bitterness slowly shriveled away, unlocking their grip on his bones. Immense love filled his entire being, saturating the deepest places of his heart. A rush of life shot through Jackson's veins, awakening his spirit to the reality of a life that he never imagined existed.

As healing waters rushed through his heart, every battle scar of his soul vanished and the broken shards of betrayal were pushed out, leaving his body vibrating with light. Like waking from anesthesia, his awareness painted a blurry picture of three people laughing hysterically.

Jackson felt his body descending back into the forest. He slowly opened his eyes and found himself face-to-face with the odd artist who was still pressing his forehead to Jackson's forehead. "This is the way," the man said, and he breathed on Jackson's face. The artist stepped away and faced his raging canvas that had been consumed by darkness.

Jackson sat up slowly, watching in awe, while fighting fear that threatened to rise inside of him. The canvas, still swirling like an angry hurricane, moved toward the artist, blowing venom at its creator. The man threw his arms wide, and with an embrace, he surrendered to the painting, allowing it to devour him completely. "No! No!" Jackson screamed, with tears pouring from his eyes.

Like a ball of fire and rage, the painting poured out its wrath on the man who gave it breath. Jackson wept as he watched him succumb to the darkness. The ball of fire expanded. Black liquid poured from the angry sphere. As it wrapped its arms around the man's body, suddenly, a flash of light illuminated the whole forest. Jackson blinked his eyes, waiting for his sight to return.

Soon, Jackson's eyes adjusted and he watched as the man's hands became red with blood. Droplets of red fell from his forehead. The artist, breathing hard, grabbed each side of the canvas with his hands and pulled the painting into his chest until it disappeared. As the artist became one with his creation, the leaves on the forest floor swirled around them, the trees swayed, and the ground shook.

The air shifted as silence penetrated the forest. Jackson directed his attention to the man who barely moved beneath the weight of the painting he had drawn into himself. The man opened his arms, revealing the canvas. It became quiet and still. The man sat up, running his hands over every inch of the painting, admiring the textures and designs that he made. As he touched the canvas, beauty returned. Darkness began to fade, color returned, and it morphed into its original form. The artist inhaled, pulling the violence from it, into his lungs. Light was in his mouth as he spoke, "You have died with me. Now you are raised with me."

In an instant, peace rested like a blanket over the landscape. A towering pine tree stood before him. It opened its arms like an easel, and the man rested the painting there. "Now, you and I are one," the man said. Once again, life and beauty were living and moving, breathing within and from the canvas as it took its place in the forest.

Birds of every kind filled the trees. Jackson heard sounds coming from the woods that surrounded them. He turned to see what it was. Moving quietly through the forest, animals approached the scene in joyful awe of the man and his painting. "This is unbelievable," Jackson mumbled to himself. All of nature seemed to celebrate what had just happened.

The scene began to fade away from Jackson's vision. He felt himself being pulled backwards, into oblivion, he thought. He wanted nothing more than to stay in this place...the place where the artist lived in the forest, but he was carried away by a force that he couldn't resist. Blurry shapes appeared to move as he fought to make his eyes focus. As his vision cleared, his bedroom ceiling came into view. No forest. No artist. *Dear God, what an intense dream!*

## Chapter Two

As morning dawned, Jackson spent several minutes trying to convince his eyes to open. Deep sleep, he thought, was like a drug that connected him to another world, and at times the trip was delightful. This dream world captivated him and he wondered how his subconscious self had experienced the things it did. Who were the people he encountered and where did these crazy ideas come from?

As he sat up in bed, rubbing his eyes, he peered outside his window at the old house across the street. He studied the red shutters that were still hanging by one hinge, and the screen door that woke him every morning as Dylan Vanberg left for work. "Is he ever going to fix those shutters," he mumbled to himself. The house seemed to stare back at him, threatening to remind him of the disappointments of the past. His friend, Dylan, lived there, but it wasn't the same as it was in the beginning. The house was once full of life.

The whole neighborhood used to call it "The Christmas House," and every year, they waited anxiously to see the creative light display that would go up after Thanksgiving. Dylan and Lynette Vanberg, young twenty-somethings who slightly resembled Ken and Barbie, not only owned the house, but also pastored Hope Fellowship on Main Street. The quiet, southern community of Holly, with its population of three thousand always gathered in full support of the choir concerts and plays that made the holidays come to life. Even those who weren't "religious" churchgoers pitched in to help with special events.

Dylan and Lynette were like a lighthouse, mysteriously drawing in wounded souls lost at sea. Their eyes smiled before their mouths did. Their warmth was genuine and they loved their community, whether the people attended church or not. Sure, there were those who gawked at them as if they carried some rare disease. After all, religious folks can be quite strange and often controlling…or so they thought.

Christmastime was the Vanbergs' time to open their home to the down-and-out. Hundreds of lights enveloped the house in sparkles, and the huge bay window in the front displayed a colorful tree that glistened with silver and gold. Christmas music was heard by passersby. For several nights in a row, the Vanbergs would invite less fortunate families from the community to gather around their table for a feast and they would present them with gifts, honoring their roles in the community.

Occasionally, members of the congregation would volunteer their time and livestock to do a live nativity scene in the Vanbergs' front yard. A choir would surround the holy family, singing beautiful songs about the Christ child. Theirs was the only house with a massive star on the roof. There was no question where the Christ-child was to be found.

Here it was, the first of December, and Jackson thought about what happened five years ago at the Christmas House. "I can't believe it...five years ago," he muttered to himself. He began to relive that day in his mind.

### Five Years Ago

It was a Sunday morning. Eight o'clock in the morning. Jackson was awakened by the sound of Dylan yelling, "How could you? How could you? What were you thinking?" He heard Lynette sobbing, "You just don't understand! I didn't plan to...you're just never there for me, Dylan!"

There was more yelling and crying, but Jackson couldn't understand all that was being said, deciphering only a few words here and there.

"What about the church?" Dylan cried.

"Exactly!" Lynette angrily shot back. "The church! The church! That's all you ever care about, Dylan!" Lynette yelled. "Now you can give **all** of your time to the church! I'm setting you free."

The noisy, old screen door slammed shut and Jackson gently moved the curtains aside with his fingers so he could see what was happening. He was surprised that the thick, old windows and doors failed to hide the sounds of the turmoil across the street. Whatever was going on, the Vanbergs weren't trying to hide it.

He watched as Lynette ran to the car, crying as she jumped into their Ford Expedition. Dylan came running out of the house, clearing all four steps of the front porch as he dove toward the driveway. "Lynette!! Lynette! Please stop!! Wait!" She threw the car in reverse and sped out of the driveway before he could reach her.

Dylan dropped to his knees as he watched her leave. He doubled over, wrapping his arms around himself as he sobbed loudly. Neighbors peered out of their windows at the sight, but no one dared to approach the "man of God." After a minute or two, Dylan stood up, still sobbing, and slowly walked into the house. The old screen door slammed shut behind him. Like a judge's gavel smashing into wood, the sound declared guilt, shame and brokenness. And Jackson's heart shuddered at the sound.

Later that day, Jackson went to Annie's Cafe as churchgoers began pouring in for lunch. "Hey, Jackson. How are you today?" asked the waitress. Her brilliant smile always caught his attention.

"Oh, hey, Lucy," Jackson replied. "I'm good. I'll have Annie's chicken potpie today." He patted his stomach. "I've been thinkin' about it all week."

"You and about twenty other people already today. I think we have a few left. What would you like to drink?"

"I'll have water. With lemon."

Lucy waited. "Seriously? Is that it?" Lucy peered at him with a grin, tapping the pen on her notepad.

Jackson smiled. "You know me too well, Lucy. Bring a glass of sweet tea as well."

"Boy, I knew that glass of water wasn't going to be sufficient." Lucy smiled.

While Jackson waited for his water and tea to arrive, he thumbed through Facebook on his iPhone. He thanked God this town worshipped wifi and had a cell tower nearby. Trying to push the morning's drama out of mind was easier with social media to serve as a distraction. A chicken potpie, a sweet tea, and the company of Lucy would definitely help him forget about the soap opera that took place at the Christmas House. Jackson admired Lucy. The twenty-two-year-old waitress with silky black hair and blue eyes was quirky, yet wise beyond her years.

As Jackson tried to lull himself into a happier world, he heard Mike's voice booming nearby. "Well, that was a hell of a Sunday morning at church, eh? It ain't everyday that your pastor's wife dumps him right before service. Dang! I wonder what happened," said Mike.

Mike's loud, grating voice could be heard by everyone within a mile, it seemed. Either the man suffered major hearing loss or he was starved for the attention of the whole community. Jackson wasn't sure which was the case. But he wished Mike would close his mouth, because Jackson could smell his dirty breath from behind him.

Curt grinned and slapped his beer belly with both hands, "Well, that woman is so fine, it won't take her long to get snatched up by another guy. A purty blonde pastor's wife like that won't be alone for long."

"You dip wad, she probably done got snatched up already. Are you really that blind?" Mike shook his head.

The burly, unkempt pair snickered at their collaborative humor. No one could understand why Mike and Curt attended church. Most likely for entertainment and material to enhance the gossip of the week.

Lucy returned to Jackson's table with tea and water in hand. "Here you go. Your lunch should be out in a few minutes. Can I get you anything else?"

"No, thank you. This is perfect."

Lucy hesitated to leave the table. "Jackson, are you hearing what people are saying about Pastor Dylan and Lynette?"

He nodded his head. "I haven't really talked to anyone yet, but I heard a fight across the street this morning. Pastor Dylan is my neighbor, you know?" Jackson's gaze fell to the table as his nervous hand grasped the napkin. "I never went to their church much, but I've been to their Christmas parties. Nice people. Always kind. I don't know what's going on, but it sounds really bad."

A tear rolled down Lucy's cheek. "I'm alive because of them."

Jackson looked up, surprised by her emotion. "What do you mean?" Jackson asked.

"They gave me back my will to live. And I don't want anything to happen to them." A soft sob escaped her strong demeanor and she placed her hands over her mouth in an attempt to stop it. Her pained eyes released a flood of tears.

Jackson touched her arm. "Lucy, I'm so sorry. I don't know what to say."

"Jackson, just pray. Really pray."

Lucy turned quickly, and disappeared into the kitchen.

As the lunch crowd grew in the cafe, mutterings and gossip began to escalate. Some seemed amused while others sat tearfully as if in mourning. The town of Holly hadn't experienced this much energy since Edward Statley accidentally knocked over a lit artillery shell at last year's Fourth of July celebration. People had talked about his clumsy failure for months.

Jackson listened to Mrs. McKinley's conversation as she spoke to her friend. "Pastor Dylan brought groceries to our house after Allen lost his job. He came every week to make sure we had food...even paid our electric bill a couple of times. Lord knows we wouldn't have made it without his help."

"Yeah, I know. Us, too. When Phillip went to rehab last year, Pastor Dylan and Lynette were there for me. They prayed and encouraged me not to give up on him. Our life together is better than ever now...and just to think that I almost threw in the towel...makes my stomach turn just thinkin' about what might have happened. Dylan was there for Phillip when he hit rock bottom and he walked him back to the top." She shook her head. "I just hope the Vanbergs will be okay."

Jackson shifted his attention to the booth in front of him where Preston Richland sat in his white, starched shirt underneath a navy blazer. "Precocious little turd," Jackson muttered under his breath. A slim, blonde woman that looked like she was fresh off a New York fashion runway, slinked her way out of the bathroom and sat across from Preston. Jackson thought to himself how ridiculous it was to wear high heels, short skirts and ruby-red lipstick in this cow town.

Lucy interrupted Jackson's thought. "Sorry about the wait. Here's your potpie. Can I get you anything else?"

"How about a vacation from this town?" Jackson grinned.

"Yeah. You and me, too," Lucy replied.

Jackson discreetly pointed towards Preston. "So, is that his girlfriend? Or just a business partner?"

Lucy leaned down near his ear in an attempt to not be overheard. "She's been in here with him every week. It's obvious there's something going on. He takes these trips into Holly, trying to take over John Clark's feed business, you know? He has a wife and kids in the city. Poor woman. I wonder if she has a clue? I whisper a prayer for her everyday." Lucy patted his shoulder and walked away.

Jackson's curiosity peaked, so he pressed in to listen to the conversation in front of him. "…whole town's all upset over that sorry preacher man. I don't know what they expected. A preacher is a preacher, and a preacher sins like everyone else.

They just hide their sins and enjoy judging everyone else for theirs."

The woman sitting with Preston sipped her water and cleared her throat. She tilted her head and smirked in a seductive manner asking, "So, what great sins did he judge you for, Mr. Richland?"

"That self-righteous jerk pulled me aside last week in the grocery store...telling me this is wrong. What is it about preachers that make them think everyone else's business is theirs?" Preston reached across the table and touched her hand.

The woman leaned her head to the side, smiling. "So, is this wrong, Preston?"

He grinned. "All I know is this feels really right. And I'm enjoying every minute of it. If I'm a bad man for doing what makes me happy, then so be it. The life that Christians expect people to live is boring and stuffy."

"Speaking of boring," the woman replied, "did you tell your wife yet?"

Several seconds passed quietly before Preston answered. "Listen, Fay. I'm happy with things the way they are. I have you. I don't want to hurt Kat...or my kids. Just wait awhile before we make a change."

In a hushed, agitated tone, Fay responded, "Look, Preston. You tell me you see a future with us together, so we need to make a plan now. I'm ready. Let's be free together. She'll be upset, but she'll get over it and your kids won't hate you. They adore you. And I'll be good to them."

"It's not that easy, Fay. You don't just turn nine years of marriage and two kids upside down without causing all kinds of issues. Frankly, I don't want to deal with the stress of it. I want to enjoy now. I want to enjoy us. Nobody back home knows and I want to keep it that way."

Her face reddened as her voice began to rise. "So, you're ashamed of me?"

"Fay, keep your voice down! Don't make a scene."

"Preston Richland, I've known you for fifteen years, and I know you better than you know yourself. I can make you happy. Just because you chose this marriage doesn't mean you have to stick with it. People divorce all the time. People get over it and move on. You and I have a connection and we shouldn't have to hide it because of what people might think."

Jackson's stomach felt sick over this conversation. He stared at his potpie, poking at it with his fork, but he couldn't bring himself to eat. He wondered why the world seemed to be falling apart today, and he wondered why he was chosen to witness it all.

"Dang it, Fay. Just give me time. Let's just be."

Fay spoke forcefully, "Listen. I drive an hour-and-a-half one way to get here every week to be with you. The phone calls are good. Emails and texts are hot, but seeing you just once or twice a week isn't enough. I want to be with you. And I've had to give up our Tuesday nights since you have to babysit your kids while your wife leads that religious women's group. Why should our connection suffer just because you're afraid to cut off the relationship that keeps you so limited? If you're going to succeed, it's going to be with me. C'mon, Preston. Release yourself from this prison."

Jackson motioned for Lucy. "What can I get for you?" Jackson looked up at her, revealing a nauseated look. "Will you please pack this up to go? I can't eat right now." Lucy knelt down beside him and peered into his eyes. "Are you okay?" Jackson slowly shook his head. "No, I'm not. I need to go."

**Chapter Three**

As Jackson walked home from the cafe, tears filled his eyes. His mind tried piecing together the chaos of the morning. Thoughts swirled crazily in his head. The fight between Dylan and Lynette, the slamming screen door, people talking, speculating, praising and cursing the man who had a bad morning. An affair. A cheating wife. And the cheating husband at the cafe. It was barely 1:30pm and he was already worn out by his surroundings. *If this is the kind of crap that Dylan and Lynette deal with all the time, it's no wonder they're having trouble.*

He entered his house and put his lunch in the refrigerator. Staring into the depths of the fridge, not really knowing what he was looking for, he finally closed the door. Jackson stood, hand still on the refrigerator door and sighed deeply. Thoughts of Pastor Dylan began to nag at him. *What's a neighbor supposed to do? It's a private matter. What do I do? Just walk over and knock...hey, what's up?* He thought to himself, debating with what his heart was telling him to do.

Sighing once more, Jackson headed out the door and across the street. As he approached Dylan's porch, he felt odd walking over the spot where the man of God had been sobbing on his knees. Climbing the porch steps softly, as if walking on sacred ground, his heart pounded in his chest. He whispered to himself, "What do I say?" He managed to knock on the door. *Oh, man.*

As seconds passed with no answer, he decided Dylan must not want to come to the door. As he took a step backwards, the doorknob rattled and his heart skipped a beat.

Slowly, Dylan opened the door and peered at Jackson with swollen eyes. "Hi, Jackson," the pastor muttered.

"Pastor Dylan, I'm sorry to bother you. I was just worried, and wanted to check on you."

Dylan leaned his head on the doorframe and began to cry. Jackson's heart was pained to see such suffering.

"I'm so sorry. I don't mean to upset you." Jackson placed his hand on Dylan's shoulder.

"No, please. Come in." The pastor led Jackson into the house and shut the door. Jackson saw the Christmas tree standing in the corner next to the fireplace that displayed a beautiful portrait of the couple on the mantle. Smiles. They looked happy. A velvet throw lay across the couch next to three empty boxes of Kleenex. This was where Dylan had spent his last few hours. Sadness filled the house.

"I'm glad you came. I don't feel like talking to anyone, but I feel so alone. I guess you heard…all the noise this morning?" The pastor seemed embarrassed.

"Yes."

The pastor dropped his head, looking at the floor as tears fell from his cheeks.

"Pastor Dylan, I'm so sorry. I don't know what happened, but if there's anything I can do, please let me know." Jackson became sharply aware of the oddity of consoling the preacher man. He always thought of ministers as being superhuman. Perfect, and always on top of the world.

"It's my fault," Dylan said. "Lynette has asked me all year to take art classes with her. I told her I was too busy with the church, so she's been taking the class by herself. And she's been ready to have children for the last three years and I keep putting her off. I just didn't feel like I could give attention to children. I'm so used to giving everything to the congregation and trying to do everything right." Dylan looked down. "I've spent all these years trying to do everything right…and I ended up doing it all wrong. And I think I've lost what's most important to me." They sat in painful silence for a minute. "She met someone." With those words, the tears began to flow again.

"Pastor Dylan, I'm so sorry."

"Please. Just call me Dylan. The word "pastor" makes me sick right now. What a joke. What a fool I am! My God! A blind, ignorant fool!" Dylan slammed his fist into his own chest and his body shook with rage. His face contorted with disgust at himself. "Everything I've taught…everything I've done…it all seems like a lie! I teach people how to do life…how to be a good husband, and look at me! An idiot!"

Jackson cringed as he watched this all-American, young, picture-perfect pastor crumple into a ball of turmoil and shame. "Dylan, listen. It's not a lie. You've helped so many people and you've made their lives better. I've heard people talk about the good you've done, and you know…the Christmas gatherings and the way you help others…you have given lonely people a place to go, and given hurting people a chance to smile again. It gives them hope." Jackson struggled for the right words that would ease Dylan's pain.

"But any hope I've given them is meaningless now. If my life is screwed up, how does that give them hope for their own families? What if someone turns from God because my life just imploded?" Dylan lowered himself onto the couch, leaning forward and dropping his forehead into his palms.

Jackson thought for a moment. "You know, I'm not much of a churchgoing guy, and I'm sorry for that. It was nothing against you and Lynette. I've never been one for doing the church thing. I don't know much, but it seems to me that if someone loses a relationship with God because you're going through hell, they didn't have much of a relationship to begin with. And after all, it's not like you're supposed to dictate what others believe. People are supposed to look to God, not to the pastor."

Dylan looked up at Jackson with a slight smile. "Jackson Sawyer, for someone who never goes to church, it sounds like you know a lot more than some who do. Where have you been all this time? Hiding out across the street?"

Jackson chuckled. "I guess."

"You'd think I'd have some support right now from my board, but…" As Dylan searched for words, his chin trembled. "I had to call them this morning after Lynette left. I mean, it's

Sunday, for Pete's sake. I called to tell the head elder what happened. His words to me were, 'We'll get this worked out. I'll talk to you later.' And I haven't gotten one phone call today. No one came over, until you came. I'm sick to my stomach just wondering what's going on. What are they saying about us? And I wonder what's going to happen. I've poured everything into those people, and yet, here I am…alone."

Dylan stood and walked to the dining table. He sighed deeply as he picked up a man's black leather watch. "This morning, we were getting ready for church, and I realized I left my briefcase in the car. I couldn't find my car keys anywhere, so while Lynette was in the shower, I looked in her purse for the keys. And I found this." He turned the watch over, reading the engraving on the back. "Brothers always. To Owen from Pastor Dylan."

Jackson's face filled with shock. "Owen Smith?"

Dylan nodded. "Yes. Deacon Owen. One of my best friends. My confidant. I gave him this watch at an appreciation dinner last month. It turns out, he was taking the art class with Lynette over the last year. While I was tending to church business, Owen was tending to my wife." Dylan's jaw tightened. "When Lynette got out of the shower this morning, I asked her why his watch was in her purse. There was no hiding it. Everything came out, like a flood." Dylan's chin shook. "They've been seeing each other for five months. And…and the worst part…" Dylan looked down, then dropped his face into his hands and began sobbing once again. Between sobs, he spoke, "…the worst part…she says they're in love."

Jackson sat with his head hung low, his mind swirling with the events of the day. Owen Smith had been his football coach in high school several years ago. Owen had been an encouragement to Jackson and built his confidence during a time when his father was absent. He wondered how a great man could do such a horrible thing to the preacher man. He remembered that Owen had divorced last year, so he thought maybe that explained how the man could be vulnerable. *But still…the pastor's wife?*

A light knocking on the door echoed through the house. "Would you like me to get it?" Jackson asked. Dylan tried to compose himself. "I've got it." Dylan stood and slowly peered out the window to see who it was, but he couldn't see anyone. He opened the door and his stomach jumped as his eyes fell upon the harsh disciplinarian face of Elder David.

"Dylan, may I come in?" David appeared as usual in his "it's-all-business" facade. The look always bothered Dylan, but especially today, he found it to be repulsive. "Of course, David. Come in."

Clearing his throat, David began, "Dylan, the board met this afternoon and it was given to me to deliver the news of our decision. Firstly, we'd like to express our sorrow over the situation. I know it's a difficult time for you." Dylan nodded. "Secondly, we have decided it would be best to obtain your immediate resignation. We will address the congregation regarding the situation."

Dylan's heart broke for the second time that day. First, losing his wife. Now, losing his church. Those two things made up everything he knew and loved. "David, I can understand a resignation, but please let me speak to the congregation. They're my family and they deserve to hear from me."

"Dylan, I think it's best that you disappear for awhile. There's too much confusion and I don't find it to be healthy for people to see you."

Dylan's voice rose. "Disappear? What do you mean?"

"Listen, I know you're committed to this church, but it's very clear that you couldn't keep your own home in order. If your own home isn't in order, you have no business trying to continue keeping the church in order."

Jackson stood to his feet, "Excuse me, sir! This man has given himself to this church and community for years, and you just expect him to walk away from it without any explanation? Why are you punishing him for something he didn't do?"

David glared at Jackson. "Young man, you don't even attend the church regularly, so you have no business poking your nose in where it doesn't belong. This board has served the church for decades and we know what's best."

Dylan interrupted, "David, I need to talk with the congregation."

"Absolutely not. We will not permit it. There will be a meeting with the congregation this evening and we'll tell them what's happened. In the meantime, you stay put and begin getting your business in order. I voted to give you one month's severance pay, however, the rest of the board insisted on at least four months. You have four months to find yourself some income…and a new church to attend. We ask that you do not speak to congregants. We can't afford the confusion they'll feel and we need to maintain their attention within the church."

Dylan's eyes filled with tears. "I've just lost my wife…to a deacon of all people! My entire world is in the people of Hope Fellowship. Why do you insist on taking everything away from me? I've done nothing but serve you and give in to your recommendations and I've bent my will to do what you wanted. I've been there for your families, and you're coming into my home now to strip away everyone that I care for."

David stood expressionless. Stone cold. "Well, then I suggest you find some new people in your life. Perhaps, consider moving back to the city, where the rest of your family lives. It's just not healthy for you to be here. It would only remind people of the failure." David turned and headed towards the door. He turned to look back at Dylan. "I'm sorry, young man, but someday you'll understand." As he opened the door, Jackson spoke through gritted teeth, "You sorry, no good, son-of-a…" David loudly interrupted him, "And that nasty mouth is exactly why you need to be in church! Don't you cast your judgment on me, young man." He slammed the door.

"I can't believe this!" Jackson kicked a Kleenex box across the room. "This is so wrong!"

"Jackson, it's okay. Let it go." Dylan sat back on the couch and sighed.

"How can you just let it go?"

Dylan dropped his face into his hands. "I don't know. But just do it."

## Chapter Four

Hope Fellowship was packed. The call for an evening meeting for congregation members attracted more than church members. It seemed that the entire town of Holly suddenly had a free night to attend church despite games and activities that had already been planned. Jackson decided to be among the crowd who came to hear the news. Since his time with Pastor Dylan that day, and after witnessing the unfair treatment delivered to him by Elder David, he felt commissioned to be a guardian angel for Dylan. Being one of the local newspaper reporters often left him feeling the need to protect people that other reporters were determined to tear down in the public eye. Why reporters felt the need to destroy, he'd never know.

He sat in the back corner, listening and observing.

"I heard that he beat her and that's why she left."

"What? Nah. I heard she was always flirtatious. Such a pretty woman with a husband stuck in church business all the time, she probably made the rounds behind the scene." Laughter.

"This town needed something to liven it up a bit. Gotta have some drama every now and then, and ain't nothing better than a church sex scandal." More laughter.

Jackson wondered who these people were and why they were here. There were those who had obviously been crying. *That's good. Some actually care.* The first few rows were dotted with sweet, old ladies with fake birds and berries on their hats. Most were widows, but a few lucky ones still had a husband by their side. The aisle displayed a couple of walkers, complete with tennis balls on the feet. Across the aisle were several young couples that sat quietly as they awaited confirmation of the news that had robbed them of hope for their own marriages. Opinions of sorrow and sadness, and judgment and criticism clashed in the air, meeting an inexplicable grace.

Tears were being wiped away while others appeared to enjoy the entertainment. A few stared at the empty pulpit that seemed to scream at them in mockery of their optimism and belief in a good future.

"If this stuff happens in church, what hope do we have?" Jackson listened to the whispers around him. "We're all just human, my boy. Everyone is prone to fall." Jackson closed his eyes as he thought of the questions that his readers would be asking. He had a deep appreciation for Dylan and Lynette Vanberg, and the thought of the community indulging in rumors and ripping them apart caused his heart to ache. He wondered why people put others on a pedestal. And he wondered why he never had.

Jackson supposed that living across the street from the highly revered man of God had taught him that people are people. Dylan and Lynette mowed the grass, dug in the dirt, took out their trash, and drank coffee on their porch swing in their bath robes like everyone else did. They were simple people, doing life. And he knew that's what had drawn him to the Christmas House.

## At the Christmas House

Dylan stared out the window, taking note of how many driveways were emptied. It appeared that most of the town was at Hope Fellowship tonight to hear about his failure as a husband. A lump came up in his throat as he imagined the faces of faithful friends and families that sat under his teaching every week. Worried thoughts overpowered his mind. *Will they be angry with me? Will they be sad? What will they think of Lynette?* Many of these people had sat at Dylan's dining table and shared their fears, dreams, and hopes. They had prayed, laughed and cried together.

Dylan turned toward the living room. *How empty and lifeless.* Beautifully framed wedding photos stared back at him, mockingly. He stared at pictures of himself and wondered who that brown-haired, happy man was. Who was he now? The man in the pictures was dead and gone. He felt himself locked in a realm he could never escape from, and he wanted desperately for it to be a nightmare from which he would awaken.

He absent-mindedly wandered through the house, peeking into each room as if it were a foreign place. The bathroom in the hallway was perfectly clean and ready for guests. Lynette lived with the philosophy that the home should always be ready for unexpected company, and that it should be a comfortable place that made people feel valued. As he stared at the perfection, he realized he had never appreciated her hard work. He couldn't recall a time when he ever thanked her for cleaning the toilets and scrubbing sinks and bathtubs. He was sure he hadn't.

His office was lifeless and silent, except for the ticking of the grandfather clock that stood in the corner. His big, black Bible sat on the desk next to his notepad. "What a crock…" he muttered. He pondered how many hours he spent in that chair, studying and preparing sermons, all while his wife was with Owen.

Dylan walked to their bedroom and stood in the doorway. The king-sized, wooden, four-poster bed was beautiful, made for a king and queen. Before Lynette had stepped into the shower that morning, she made up the bed like usual. Ornate, modern-Victorian flare. He always teased her about the ten pillows that had to be placed just so. He thought of numerous intimate moments they shared in that bed and the conversations they shared about their hopes and dreams for the future.

A horrifying reality flooded Dylan's mind. Owen. His wife had been with Owen. "My God," he said, as his eyes began to burn with another scourge of salty tears. How much could a man cry without dying? How much heartbreak could he endure? Dylan crumpled to his knees, leaning his head on the doorframe, as he worked hard to stop a flood of images of his wife touching another man…another man touching his wife.

## At Hope Fellowship

7:00pm

It was time for the meeting to begin. Jackson glanced at his watch and looked up just as Preston Richland made his way into a pew. Jackson's face grew hot as he thought about the typical onlookers who would be taking the news into the city and broadcasting twisted information to make matters worse. And Preston himself was a cheater. *How does he dare to show his face in here?*

Elder David approached the pulpit and began: "Thank you for coming out on a cold night. There are many faces here that we don't normally see, but we welcome you as part of the community and hope that you will handle tonight's news with sensitivity. Obviously, many have already heard the news that, sadly, Lynette Vanberg has chosen to separate from Pastor Dylan. This came as a shock to Dylan. We ask that everyone be considerate and give him space to heal and get his personal business in order. Hope Fellowship will continue services as planned, with the help of guest speakers and members of the board filling the pulpit until further decisions have been made. The special holiday events that were scheduled to be held at the Vanberg home are cancelled. We ask that the community be sensitive to the Vanbergs during this time. This concludes this brief meeting. We will not be taking questions tonight. Thank you."

People began to whisper, "That's it?" Mary Elliott, 88-years-old, slipped her hand into the air. "Mrs. Elliott," David responded, "I said we will not be taking questions tonight." Mary stood with boldness, "Excuse me, David, but I feel it's our duty as a church body to pray together for the Vanberg family. After all, they have served us for several years." David tried to hide the sting of shame and humiliation he felt after being corrected by an old woman. "Of course. Everyone stand and let's pray."

### At the Christmas House

Fear of the future gripped Dylan's heart. *What will happen next? Will I really lose my wife?* He moved from his knees into a fetal position at the foot of their bed. A groan arose from a place deep within him, and it surprised him. Who was this soul that wailed so deeply? Surely, it couldn't be the preacher who had everything together. Surely, it couldn't be the man who taught everyone else how to live. Dylan felt a separation in his soul, and he pondered how he could feel connected to God, yet terribly far away from Him at the same time.

"Dylan." Her voice caught his attention. "Dylan, please stop crying." Lynette stood in the doorway. He sat up and faced her. "Lynette? You're here." For a brief moment, relief flooded his heart. "You came back." She sighed, then headed to her dresser and began taking her clothes out and collecting her belongings. He approached her. "Lynette, why?" She kept herself busy, barely looking at his face. "I don't want you to leave. Let's work this out."

"Listen, Dylan. Please don't make this any harder than it has to be. I need you to understand. You've always been good at understanding people's decisions. Now it's your turn to understand mine. I'm moving in with Owen and I just need to pick up some of my things. I'll have to come get the rest later this week."

Her words pierced his soul. "Lynette…but I love you. I really don't want to lose you." Tears fell from Dylan's eyes as his body shook.

Lynette refused to look at him. She continued folding her clothes into a bag. Dylan reached to push her blonde hair aside, hoping for a connection that would change everything. Glaring, she directed her fury at him. "How interesting. Now you decide you don't want to lose me? For over a year, Dylan, I haven't felt loved by you at all…for over a year, I've felt like a nuisance to you. I was just in your way…something to be juggled with all your pastoral duties." The disdain and coldness in her voice made him shudder.

"Lynette, I am so sorry. You're the most important person in my life. I've been so blind, and I'm sorry. Please give me a chance."

"A chance? Do you remember how many times I asked you to take the art class with me? Do you remember how many times I asked you to take me out on a date? Or take me out of this town?

You always have an excuse, and the church always comes first. You've had many chances, Dylan. And if people accuse me of being a sinful, horrible human being for having an affair, they need to realize you're the one that had an affair first! Not with one person, but with the entire church! That church is your 'woman.' And, as for Owen…they'd better not judge him, either. He loves me. He listens to me and he knows what I'm feeling. He can read me like a book. That's something you haven't even tried to do."

Dylan's pulse raced as her words cut into his heart like a knife. "How can you even defend the man who betrayed me? He was my friend. I trusted him with everything, yet he steals my wife?"

Lynette glared at Dylan. "Stole your wife? You practically gave me to him. Besides, I don't want to be a pastor's wife anymore. Everything I do is analyzed and scrutinized and misjudged. I want to be a real person again."

"Why didn't you tell me these things?" Dylan began to weep.

"I'm sorry, Dylan. It would be wrong of me to prolong this…to keep playing this game. You're a good guy and you'll find someone else who can be the woman you want."

"My God, Lynette…you're everything I ever wanted! I was just…I was blind. I lost sight. I just forgot."

"I'm that easy to forget about, Dylan?"

"That's not what I meant, Lynette."

" I can't. I just can't. I'm committed to Owen now. We have a connection that I wanted with you. You and I lost ours a long time ago, and I don't think it can ever be found. I've waited long enough."

With that, Lynette picked up her bag and headed to the front door.

"Lynette. Wait. Please listen." She turned to look at Dylan. "Whatever happens, I'll wait for you. Don't forget our Dream Door, under the porch. Promise me?"

Her chin quivered as a tear escaped her hardened visage as she nodded a 'yes.' She opened the door and let herself out. The screen door slammed shut. Dylan placed his hand on the screen as he watched her leave. "Please, God."

## Chapter Five

Jackson sat at his desk in deep thought, tapping his cheek with a pen. His part-time job for the Holly Herald provided an actual office which boosted his pride and gave him confidence around his old schoolmates that had moved on to greater things. Though the desk was dilapidated and the walls, floors and ceiling screamed of 1954, it was his own office and he was determined to make something of himself.

The sounds of people hammering away at their computer keyboards and carrying on one-sided phone conversations filled the room with purpose. The Holly Herald was a weekly publication that was started by a local family in the 50's when the town of Holly was thriving. Young families were building new businesses and popping out babies left and right. In the last decade, however, Holly's population was diminishing as people began moving into the cities for better jobs and other opportunities.

Jackson was loyal to the town of Holly and he was convinced that he would be part of its resurrection. His love for journalism fueled his passion to bring the community to life through his writing. When he first began writing for the Holly Herald, he made the mistake of causing pain to several residents through his lack of consideration. He learned his lesson.

He was young and in a hurry to write up juicy stories and to be the first to deliver details of car accidents, public meetings, house fires and any tragic situation that might grab the attention of the people. After Mayor O'Donnell committed suicide over a year ago due to false accusations that were printed in the paper, Jackson was shaken. He was awakened to the human heart and the power of words. At the mayor's funeral, Jackson promised himself that he would only write things in a way that would give life and hope to people. Never again would he play a part in the destruction of another human being.

"What to write…what to write," he muttered to himself. He had requested that he be the one to deliver the main story of Hope Fellowship's latest announcement. People all over town were gossiping about the Vanbergs and speculating as to what would happen next. Some had taken the opportunity to rake Dylan over the coals. Jackson wanted to make sure that whatever he wrote would be honorable to his neighbor across the street. His heart was moved with compassion as he remembered seeing Pastor Dylan, on his knees, crying his heart out in his front yard. The image haunted Jackson daily.

"Jackson, how long are you going to sit there staring at that computer screen?" asked Amber. "Just write it already. Put it out there. We have deadlines around here, you know?" He sighed. "Seriously, what's so difficult about it? It's not like you're reporting something that's news to everyone. The whole town already knows."

He peered up at Amber, the town sweetheart in her pink sweater, black slacks, and stilettos. He was annoyed by her coldness. *And to think that I used to want her*, he thought to himself.

Jackson stood up from his desk. "I'm going home to write this article. I can't do it here. I'll be back later." With a nod of approval from the editor, he walked out.

As he drove through town, pondering how he could write the story without bringing shame to Dylan and Lynette, he thought about what people would be expecting. *They just can't wait to get their hands on this so they have something to gossip about.* He wondered what it was about human nature that made people avid devourers. *I refuse to feed their sickness.*

Driving past the courthouse, an idea came to Jackson. He parked his car and began going from business to business, from house to house, interviewing everyone who had interaction with Dylan and Lynette. His opening question: "How did Pastor Dylan and Lynette touch your life?"

### That Evening at Annie's Cafe

"Hey, Lucy."

Upon seeing Preston, Lucy appeared agitated, but she worked hard to hide her disgust. "Hi Preston. What can I get for you?"

"Start me off with coffee, please. Cream and sugar."

Lucy went to the kitchen and immediately began complaining to the staff. "That pompous Preston drags his butt in here, expecting us to serve him after he brings his mistress in here to be served! It's nearly the end of the day and he should be at home with his wife and kids. I'm sure that nasty woman will be dragging herself in here any minute. By God, if I were evil, I'd spit in his coffee…or better yet, pour it in his face. God, help me."

She stormed back into the restaurant, carrying his coffee, cream and sugar. Trying to calm herself down, she sat it on the table in front of him. "Wow. Why are you shaking so bad?" asked Preston.

Her face was growing redder by the second. "If you want to know the truth…" she paused. "I just don't understand, Preston."

"Understand what?" He sat in his usual confident way.

"I know you're married. And you have kids." Lucy's eyes began to moisten. "How can you do this to them?"

"Look, Lucy. It's not your place to get involved. You don't know what's going on in my life, so don't judge me." Preston poured his cream into the coffee.

"How can you be so casual about this, like it's not a big deal?" Lucy's breathing increased as she tried not to cry.

Preston looked up at her. "Why is this bothering you so much? You don't even know me…or my wife. Stop taking this personally."

Lucy slammed her fist on the table and leaned in, trying to keep her voice down. "Listen to me. You have no idea the pain that you'll cause your children. You have no idea how you'll break your wife's heart. Please, Preston. Please, stop it now, while you can. Make things right. I beg you." Tears streamed down her cheeks as she stood and walked back to the kitchen.

Preston sat in stunned silence, staring into his coffee.

"Well, hello handsome." Fay slid into the booth across from Preston. "What are you thinking so deeply about?"

"Hi, Fay." He continued looking at his coffee as he poured in the sugar. Stirring, and staring into oblivion.

"Uh, should we do this over again? This greeting thing? What's gotten into you?" Fay was annoyed.

"I'm sorry. I'm just...I don't know. Hard day. I'm just kinda tired."

"Preston, you're with me now, so lighten up." Fay reached across the table and lifted his chin up. "See? All better."

Preston smiled softly. He tried to shake off the weight of Lucy's words and jump back into his fantasy world.

Lucy returned to the table, pen and paper in hand. Trying to maintain a business-like demeanor, she looked at Fay. "Well, hello. What can I get for you to drink?"

Fay replied, "Coffee. No cream. No sugar. Just plain black."

Lucy glared into her eyes and repeated her order, "Coffee. No cream. No sugar. Just. Plain. Black. Yes?" Fay looked confused by Lucy's strange demeanor. Lucy turned to look at Preston and asked, "Anything else for you?" He shook his head "no," as if to tell her 'no more, please.'

As Lucy paced into the kitchen, she muttered to herself, "Just plain black. She likes her coffee the way she likes her soul."

"What's gotten into that girl?" asked Fay. "I always thought she was odd."

"Oh? Why's that?" asked Preston.

"Well, look at that cheap haircut and lipstick. She's like a character off of some goofy sitcom. She's like a whimsical modern, trying to fit into classical Victorian."

Preston looked amused, yet disturbed. "And what's so wrong with her style? I'd just say she's eclectic."

Fay looked offended. "Oh, you like it do you? Since when do you have a soft spot for the weird little waitress?"

"I don't have a soft spot. I just think she might be a decent person."

"No decent person does their hair and make up like that," Fay said with pride.

"Fay, just because you were privileged to grow up with the best of things, you don't have to put down people who didn't. She's a small town girl."

For the first time ever, Preston saw something in Fay that turned him off.

The bell on the cafe door clattered, announcing Jackson's arrival. Lucy immediately came toward him. "Hey, Jackson! Welcome. Where would you like to sit?"

"Hi, Lucy. I'll just take this table. How are you today?"

She glanced down and shrugged her shoulders.

"Is everything okay?" Jackson asked. Lucy tilted her head to the right, motioning his attention toward Preston and Fay. He understood that she was disturbed by their presence. "I see," he said.

"What can I get you to drink, Sir Jackson?" She quickly jumped back into her role as professional waitress, with a twist of her typical 'Lucy humor.'

Jackson smiled at her. "Just a sweet tea, please. And, when you come back, do you have a minute to let me interview you for an article I'm writing for the paper?"

Lucy looked delighted. "Of course! Right after I serve King Preston over there." She rolled her eyes and walked away.

Lucy managed to be civil as she took Preston and Fay's orders. As she walked back to the kitchen, she muttered to herself, "Be loving. Be loving."

Delivering Jackson's tea to him, she sat down. "I have a couple of minutes. What's this interview about?"

Jackson pulled out his computer. "I have the job of writing the news about what's happening at Hope Fellowship. You mentioned before that Pastor Dylan and Lynette saved your life. Can you tell me more about that?"

"Oh, man. That's a loaded question. I honestly can't answer that here. Can I meet you tomorrow morning?"

"I actually have to turn this article in by midnight tonight for printing. What time do you get off work?"

"I get off at nine o'clock. Can we meet then?" Lucy seemed excited.

Jackson nodded. "Sure. Can you meet me at my place when you're done?"

"Sure thing."

### The Interview

Lucy had long held a secret crush on Jackson, and here she was, on his doorstep. "Hi, Lucy. Come on in." Lucy admired the cleanliness and order of his bachelor pad. *The perfect old house for a young, small-town boy*, she thought to herself. "I'm impressed, Jackson."

"Thanks. I like it here. It's nice having my own place. Well, I rent, but you know what I mean. My deadline is up at midnight. Can we get started right away?"

"Sure thing." Lucy sat on the sofa.

Jackson sat next to her and opened his computer. "You said Dylan and Lynette saved your life. Can you tell me more about that?"

Lucy sighed. "Sure. About two years ago, I lost my best friend, Cynthia, to suicide. We were best friends since fourth grade. We did everything together."

"Oh my gosh, Lucy. I'm so sorry."

"It was a huge shock. She was always the life of the party and she didn't know a stranger…just sweet as anyone could be. Her parents went through a horrible divorce that devastated her, and she was already dealing with depression." Lucy's chin trembled. "After a nasty battle, joint custody was settled and she realized she would be going back and forth between her parents. I guess she decided she couldn't handle it. Her parents were so bitter toward each other. It was just awful. She was supposed to go to her dad's for the weekend. She left a suicide note for her parents that basically said she was sorry. She…I'm sorry, Jackson. I don't want to relive the whole story." A tear fell down Lucy's cheek.

"Lucy, I'm so sorry."

She continued, "So after losing Cynthia, I got really depressed for awhile. My parents were arguing a lot during that time and I guess my mind got away from me, thinking my family was going to fall apart, too. I saw myself going down the same path as Cynthia. I really struggled with cutting myself. My parents kinda woke up to what was going on with me and they called Hope Fellowship to ask for help. Pastor Dylan and Lynette met with my family and they walked with us through the process for several months. I learned so much about life and love from them, and about my worth and value in this world. They also helped my parents with their relationship. My mom and dad worked through their issues and we've become an incredibly close family."

Lucy looked down at her hands, clasped together, thumbs twirling. "And I just don't understand why Lynette left. But what I do know is that she's forgotten who she really is. I know this isn't her. Dylan and Lynette taught me about how everyone has a life journey. They go through a process to become who they're meant to be. Dylan once told me that, sometimes, because of confusion, fear, doubt, or just plain selfishness, people lose their way for awhile. But we can't mark them by their moments of being lost. We have to love them through it and help them remember what's true. I suppose Lynette got blinded."

Jackson was intrigued. "Wow. That's such great insight. I never thought of it that way. Everyone's on a journey." He jotted down notes in his computer.

Lucy stood up and continued talking as she paced back and forth. "Cynthia lost sight of who she was, partly because her parents forgot who they were. It's crazy how our lives affect each other. Her death makes me think about every decision that I make and how it will affect someone else. We're all connected."

Jackson clicked away on his computer keyboard. "I suppose this world would be a much better place if we all did that…thinking of others above ourselves. Tell me more about how Dylan and Lynette influenced you."

"Gosh. There are so many things I could tell you. I've learned respect for people. I'm not always good at it, though. God knows I struggle with respecting Preston and Fay. But I've got to hope for the best for their lives. There are times when I just want to smack the tar out of them!"

Jackson laughed at her choice of words. "That sounds like something my grandma would've said."

Lucy continued, "Dylan talked a lot about some Bible verse that says, 'Love covers a multitude of sins.' When we love someone, we cover them while they're too blind to walk the right path. Love opens the door for them to see correctly again. Dylan said that love removes blinders. And he said the kindness of God leads to repentance. Our kindness draws people to the heart of God." Lucy looked down at her lap and nodded her head. "Yeah. That's what they taught me."

"Thank you for sharing your story, Lucy. And no worries. I won't write about the loss of your friend in the article, but I'm going to include the things you learned from the Vanbergs and how they affected your life positively."

Lucy smiled. "You're doing what Pastor Dylan taught."

"What's that?" asked Jackson.

"You're loving. You're covering a multitude of sins by focusing on the good things. People can do many things right, but one wrong move, and they get devoured by others and marked by what they did wrong. Shouldn't it be that the good outweighs the bad? Shouldn't we know people according to what they've done right? I love the way you're bringing the good things to the forefront."

Jackson looked at Lucy in awe. "How old are you?" He grinned. "If only everyone thought like you, we'd all be in good company."

She shrugged her shoulders, smiling. "Maybe."

## Chapter Six

Jackson hadn't seen Dylan around town for a couple of days. He became worried, but figured that Dylan was keeping to himself to avoid the stares and judgments of the community. *But what if he's dead?* He thought about knocking on Dylan's door several times, but he was afraid of being too intrusive. The thought of Dylan lying in a pool of blood or possibly hanging from a ceiling beam finally pushed him to run across the street and bang on the door.

Imagined horrors caused his heart to pound. The doorknob turned. *Thank God.* "Jackson. I'm so glad to see you. Please, come in." Dylan seemed delighted to have company.

Jackson reigned in his fears, displaying a calm relief. "I hope you don't mind me stopping by unannounced, but I wanted to check in and see how things are going."

"I'm glad you did. Man, I can't thank you enough for your article." Dylan's eyes filled with tears. He hugged Jackson tightly. "I don't know what to say. I was sure Lynette and I would be publicly ripped to shreds. I was afraid to read the paper, but I just had to. What you did…I have no words to thank you."

Jackson's face glowed with joy. He had accomplished what he set out to do. One more soul saved from public humiliation by the media. This is what Jackson lived for. "Dylan, you've touched so many lives in this community. It would be a sin for people not to know. Someone I know told me that people should be remembered for the things they did right, and you've certainly done a lot right. You and Lynette both."

Jackson's attention was drawn to a stack of canvasses and painting supplies in the corner. "Are you working on a project?"

Dylan walked over to his supplies. "Yep. I've never done anything like this before." He picked up a canvas. "Lynette wanted me to paint with her. I decided to take some time to learn and give it a shot. You might want to pray for me because I only know how to draw stick people." He chuckled.

"Are you taking a class?"

"Well, I can't exactly sign up for the local art class. Lynette and Owen go there. Too awkward, so I'm taking private lessons from Mrs. Elliott. She's 88-years-old and she's an incredible artist. She did the murals in our fellowship hall. And you've probably seen the mural in the grocery store. She did that one many years ago."

Jackson looked delighted. "I'm glad you're trying something new. Good for you, Dylan! Hey, by the way, have you had dinner?"

Dylan shook his head. "I didn't even think of it until now. I haven't eaten anything today."

"Dude, that's not good. I'd really like to take you to dinner. Would you join me at the cafe?"

Dylan looked unsure. "I would love to, but…"

"But what?"

"I haven't shown my face in Holly since Lynette left. The only trip I made was to the city to get art supplies, and hardly anyone there knows who I am. I don't know. I don't think I'm ready to see people." Dylan picked at his fingers.

Jackson noticed Dylan's shaky hands. "Look. You've got to get out sometime, and you can't sit here and starve. You need to eat. C'mon, man." Jackson grabbed Dylan's coat from the rack. "It's looking a bit dusty. Better wear it out and get some fresh air." Jackson grinned.

"Well. I guess I have to face it eventually. You talked me into it."

"Great! I'll go warm up my car. You can ride with me." Jackson headed across the street.

### At Annie's Cafe

Walking into the cafe, Jackson turned back to look at Dylan who was following slowly. "You like it out here in the cold?" he asked sarcastically.

Dylan grinned. "Nope. I'm just afraid it might be colder inside, if you know what I mean."

"Man, have a little faith in the people. They love you."

The bell jingled on the door as they entered. Lucy turned and saw them. "Pastor Dylan!" She ran toward him with arms wide open. "Oh, Dylan. I'm so happy to see you!" She stepped back and wiped her tears away.

"It's good to see you, too, Lucy."

"I've got a table just for you. How about this little booth in the corner where you can have some privacy?"

"Thanks, Lucy. That's perfect." Dylan was thankful for her warmth and consideration.

As they settled into their seats, a couple of congregation members approached Dylan and thanked him for his service, and expressed their sorrow over the situation. "Thank you, I really appreciate your kindness." What else could he say? He felt awkward. Everything felt so final, like it was his own funeral, and he had died unexpectedly, far too soon. He struggled to cling to the positive attitude that gave him strength to enter the cafe, but the reality of his circumstances was threatening his peace.

Jackson sensed his struggle. "What looks good to you tonight? The dinner special is roasted chicken, garlic mashed potatoes and green beans. Sounds pretty good to me." He hoped the art of distraction would succeed in redirecting Dylan's thoughts. His face revealed the conflict that lingered inside of him. He had been used to many years of visiting the cafe with friends…with Lynette. It was always a place of laughter, connection and celebration. Everyone knew Dylan and Lynette. They were lavished with respect and happy greetings by those who surrounded them.

Now, it was all different. Dylan hated this new feeling, and he especially hated that he couldn't escape it. *How can this possibly be my life?* He longed for the past, when things were good.

Sitting in this new atmosphere that was now his life, drained him of hope.

Dylan sighed. "Jackson? I'm sorry, but would you mind if we order to go? I'm not feeling up to being out. Can we eat at my place?"

"We just got here, but, yeah…if that's what you want to do, that's perfectly fine with me." Jackson was gracious.

They placed their orders and began grasping for lighter subjects to focus on. "So, explain this newspaper process. When did you start working for the Holly Herald and how did you get into reporting?"

As Jackson answered his questions, Dylan couldn't help but notice loud-mouthed Mike walking in. He had always been patient with Mike. He tolerated his gruff attitude and figured he was just a man in need of genuine acceptance. Mike's eyes met Dylan's. No words. Just a genuine look of sadness that flashed in Mike's eyes. Dylan was surprised that he witnessed tenderness in the vile man.

Shaking the distraction, he attempted to return his attention to Jackson once again. "All I can say is that I'm glad you're the one that reported the news about me and Lynette…and the circus that is now Hope Fellowship. There needs to be more reporters like you."

"Thank you." Jackson smiled.

"So, what are you going to paint on all those new canvasses of yours?"

"I'm not sure yet. A strange thing's been happening. Since Lynette left, I've had tons of dreams where I'm painting. I don't dream very often. I guess it's my guilty conscience wishing I had taken those classes with her. I keep having this one, particular dream about a canvas in a forest, and I'm painting a tree on it. That's as far as the dream goes. I felt compelled to buy supplies and see what happens. I called Mrs. Elliott and asked if she'd give me a few lessons. She's the coolest old woman I've ever met." Dylan smiled. "She's always been supportive of us. I value her kindness now more than I ever have. I was thinking about it…how easy it is to brush off the elderly, but as you experience life, you start to appreciate them more. They're like old vessels with hidden treasure buried inside."

"Yeah. Mrs. Elliott is one tough woman. I remember her being around since I was a little kid. She's definitely been through a lot…losing her son in that accident, fighting the lawsuit that almost destroyed her husband's business, and then losing him. I can only hope to be as strong as her. She just keeps going." Jackson ran his finger around the rim of his glass. "If life was just as smooth as the rim of this glass…"

Dylan interrupted. "It'd be one boring journey if it only went in circles like that glass. Never going anywhere."

Jackson grinned. "Unless the journey leads you to something refreshing inside. Like, if it contains ice-cold, sweet tea, it'd be the perfect life for me."

Dylan chuckled at his friend. He thought for a moment as he looked at the rim of glass.

"Hmm. Jackson, maybe you're onto something. We're used to looking at life in a linear fashion. One long line. Our past is at the beginning of the line and we strive to make it to the end with something good to show for the journey. Most people end up labeling their entire life based on the stuff that happened in the past."

Jackson nodded. "That's for sure."

Dylan continued, "What if life is really a circle of sorts? If it's a circle, and we fall, then we have the chance to come back around again and set things right. My life stinks right now. I can only hope that God will do what He says. 'I make all things work together for good to those who love Me.' If that's true, then there's hope that things will be set right. I have no choice but to believe that. If it's a lie, then I'm doomed."

"Man, Dylan. That's deep."

The two sat still for a moment. Dylan grinned. "You know, here I am with my life in shambles, and I'm being all philosophical." They laughed. "Let's go back to your tea addiction. What the heck is up with you and your obsession with tea? I'm surprised you're not a beer kind of guy."

Jackson wrinkled his nose. "Beer? Nah. I drank for awhile but it never really appealed to me. It's an acquired taste that I never fully acquired. I finally decided that if something had to be an acquired taste, it wasn't worth tasting to begin with. It smells like dog pee to me, anyway."

Dylan laughed. "Dog pee? I never thought of it that way. Maybe like soggy, old bread, but not pee. I actually appreciate a good, German beer every now and then. American beer isn't really beer in my book."

"Here you go, guys." Lucy sat their to-go order on the table. "It's on the house. Someone wanted to cover you tonight."

"Oh, wow! Who?" Jackson inquired.

"Anonymous," Lucy smiled.

Tears filled Dylan's eyes. Kindness was like life to his weary heart. He had never been so vulnerable to simple acts of goodness. "Thank you, Lucy. Please tell them thank you."

Jackson and Dylan got in the car. Dylan fastened his seatbelt and stared at the cafe, relishing the good memories. It had never felt this way leaving the cafe…never with a sense of sorrow. He pondered the odd way that a place can feel like an old friend, bringing comfort when it's needed the most. It was good to be there, and at the same time, it was hard to be there. He realized the cafe could either be his friend, or become his enemy. An enemy, because it served to mock him with memories of what used to be. A friend, because it reminded him of what used to be. How ironic.

He spoke up. "Hey, man. Could we take a ride past the church on our way home, if you don't mind?"

"Sure. No problem." Jackson hoped this was an idea that Dylan wouldn't regret.

The ride was silent. Jackson tried to think of ways to break the silence, but they both understood the gravity of the moment, and neither one could think of an appropriate way to break the ice.

Hope Fellowship came into view. Dylan managed to speak. "This is so weird. I feel like I'm supposed to be there. All those years of going in nearly everyday…this was our life." He stared at the front doors of the church. "Well, for the last year, it's been **my** life. So weird having everything change, literally in one day. One moment, I'm getting ready to preach, and the next moment, it's all gone. The church, my wife, the relationships. I don't know what to do with myself." Dylan motioned toward the building. "Just pull up in the parking lot for a second."

Jackson struggled to find the right words. "I don't know what to say. I can't imagine how hard this is for you."

"You know, what's blatantly clear now is how much I love Lynette and how blind I was…wrapped up in this bubble I created. I feel like I've been awakened, but unfortunately I'm waking up in a nightmare, and I have no idea how to fix it. Part of me feels hopeless and I can't see a future. But part of me knows I have hope because surely God wouldn't abandon me." His face tightened. "And there's a part of me that's madder than hell. I mean, I'm caught in this craziness of trusting God and not trusting God. Sometimes I feel angry at Him. I don't understand how He could let this happen while I was giving everything for Him. But then I realize I was just doing the things I thought I was supposed to do, and maybe I wasn't really listening to Him, but more to my own ego."

Jackson sat speechless.

Dylan continued, "And then part of me knows that God is the only faithful being in the universe. Who else can I trust?"

"Yeah. I suppose He's the only one we can truly rely on. The difficulty is in not allowing the failures of people to reflect on the One that made them."

Dylan sighed. "You got that right. Let's go eat this food. I'm starving."

As they stepped onto Dylan's front porch, he turned to Jackson with sincerity in his eyes. "Jackson? I don't know how to thank you enough for being here. You're a lifesaver."

Jackson patted Dylan's shoulder. "It's my honor."

As Dylan opened the screen door, a crumpled paper fell to the ground. "What's this?" He leaned down to pick it up, then unlocked the door and went inside. Setting the food on the table, he smoothed out the paper and read the words written in thick, black ink:

**"FALLEN FROM GRACE. JUST LIKE THE REST OF THEM."**

Dylan sighed.

"Dylan, what is it?"

He handed the note to Jackson.

Jackson's jaw clenched as he read the note. "What the heck is wrong with people? This is sick!"

Dylan shook his head. "Who can blame them?"

Jackson fumed, "But they have no idea what happened. How can anyone be so cruel?"

"It's probably a person who's been hurt or disappointed by somebody they'd put on a pedestal. It's hard being on a pedestal. Maybe it's a good thing I fell off of it." Dylan tried to shake it off.

"But you don't deserve this. You didn't do anything wrong. All you've done is love this community." Jackson was frustrated beyond belief.

"Look. Let's just eat this food before it gets ice-cold." Trying to inject some humor into the situation, Dylan spoke with a British accent, "Come, my friend, and dine with me in my sorrow and misery."

Jackson grinned, shaking his head.

## Chapter Seven

*Fallen from grace. Just like the rest of them.* As Dylan lay in bed, trying to fall asleep, the phrase wouldn't stop ringing through his mind. He sat up, dropped his face into his hands and began to weep. "Oh God. Help me." His body began to shake as it heaved all the sorrow it could bear.

Dylan thought about his prayer when he began his life as a minister. He promised God that he would always live to honor Him and he promised he wouldn't be one of "those" preachers who brought reproach on the name of God. He had his life mapped out and nothing was going to interfere with his perfect path. He promised he would be faithful and true. And he had been.

"God, I failed. I failed You. It wasn't me that cheated, but I know I hurt Lynette by ignoring her and not loving her the way I should have. Please forgive me for not loving my wife as You love the church. I didn't give my life for her." Dylan realized his lack. "I gave of myself for myself. Forgive me for trying to be everything to the church when You're the One who is everything. Oh, God. I've misled people. Without knowing what I was doing, I taught them to rely on me and not You. Please forgive me for making ministry about myself. I've always said it's all about You, but it wasn't." He sobbed. "If it was about You, I would have paid more attention to my wife."

The bed shook as his body wrenched with the release of deep pain. "And please, please, forgive my wife. Lynette. Oh, Lynnie. I forgive you. I love you. God, please let her know how much I love her. Rescue her. And forgive me for hating Owen. God, I have a hard time not hating him! Such a liar. All of that time, right behind my back. Why would You let him get away with this? I don't understand." He pressed his fists into his chest, wishing he could rip his heart out to ease the pain.

The sobbing continued over an hour and Dylan felt as if he might die. He was surprised his heart hadn't stopped from the anguish. He quieted down and curled up in a fetal position, staring at the wall. *Is this what I've been reduced to? What's happening to me?* His eyes fell upon one of Lynette's paintings of a tree by a river. It read, "Your grace is sufficient."

Delirious, Dylan spoke out loud, "Yeah, but apparently I've fallen from grace." Immediately, he heard a man's voice, "You have not fallen from grace. You've fallen into grace." Dylan sat up, stunned. He wondered if he had imagined it, yet it was so clear.

He got out of bed and walked into his office. He picked up his computer and brought it back to bed. Sitting in the dark, his face lit by the light of his laptop, he searched "fallen from grace." Galatians 5:4 popped up.

*You have become estranged from Christ,*
*you who attempt to be justified by law;*

*you have fallen from grace.*

**"You who attempt to be justified by law**." Dylan pondered the thought for a moment as he let it roll off his lips. He thought about his life as a believer and how he had lived with pride in his own strength to maintain righteousness and overcome sin. If anyone lived to be justified by the law, it was Dylan. And having a body like a Ken doll fed his ego and self-image of absolute perfection. **"You who attempt to be justified by law, you have fallen from grace."** He mouthed the words, hoping to unravel the riddle.

Dylan dropped his head into his palms. "Oh, my God. All along, I was fallen from grace, and I didn't even know it." He chuckled hysterically at his delusion. Swollen eyes now poured tears of laughter. He wasn't sure what was happening to him, but he highly suspected insanity. He was certain that the exposure of just one more lie would drive him into the ground, and when a man is being crushed to death, what more can he do but laugh?

Dylan thought about the words that he heard. "You have not fallen *from* grace. You've fallen *into* grace." He began to weep again. He knew he wasn't alone and he had never felt so loved before. Here he was, considered a failure by his wife, Elder David and most likely, the whole town, yet God was comforting him with His love and grace. *Your grace is sufficient.* Dylan held his pillow to his face and let his heart melt in the presence of His creator.

## Waking Up

The moment Dylan sat up in bed, he was looking forward to his art lesson with Mrs. Elliott later that day. He longed for a good distraction. Though it was cold outside, the sun cast a brilliant gold in his bedroom. As he peered out the window, he whispered to himself, "The sun rises to remind me of His love." He grabbed his clothes for the day and headed to the shower.

As he stepped into the shower, his cell phone rang. He quickly jumped out and picked it up from the bathroom countertop. "Lynette." He shut off the shower and answered. "Hi, Lynette."

"Hey. I need to stop by to gather some more of my things. I need about an hour." Her voice was firm. Familiar, yet strange.

"Okay."

"Dylan, I'd like to be there alone. I can't handle seeing you right now. Will you give me an hour and then I'll get out?"

He was hurt. Was he something to be 'handled?'

"Sure." Practicing patience and understanding, he agreed. "I can leave here at ten o'clock. Won't come back until noon, so you can have more time."

"Thanks." Awkward silence lingered between them.

"I wish I could see you, Lynette."

"Listen, Dylan. We need to talk about Christmas. I know we planned to go to your parent's house. Have you told them yet, that I won't be there?"

"Yes, unfortunately."

They sat quietly for a moment.

"Needless to say, they're devastated. Everyone is having a hard time." Dylan tried not to lay into her with harsh words. He wondered how she could hurt so many people. "You know they love you like their own daughter."

A few seconds passed by. "Yeah."

Dylan hesitated, "So, is this temporary? Do you have long-term plans?" Dylan's gut wrenched. He wasn't sure he wanted to hear her answer.

"Owen and I want to be together. He's ready to move on with life. Marriage. Children. You know…all the things that are important to me. He and I are both ready for more."

Her words assaulted his heart. His eyes burned. "Lynette, I want children, too. I want a future with you. Please don't make any rash decisions. This is so fresh. Can we go to counseling? Maybe give it some time?"

"Dylan, honestly, I don't ever want to be in ministry again. I'm done with that life."

Dylan understood. "I don't care about ministry right now, either. I don't know what I was thinking all these years. I totally overlooked the most important person in my life. If I could do it all over again…"

Lynette caught her breath, trying to hide the emotions that were welling up inside of her. She thought, *My God…why couldn't he have been like this before?* She placed her hand over her mouth.

"Lynette, I love you."

She hung up the phone before the pain escaped. She still loved Dylan, and she realized then that she had never stopped loving him, but she couldn't resist her connection with Owen. He seemed to know everything she was feeling, he complimented her and believed in her. Owen lavished her with goodness, and she didn't have to perform for him. Being a pastor's wife meant she had an endless list of people to please, but with Owen, it was only him and no one else. Lynette's heart was torn in two. *I'm in love with two different men. How did this happen?*

Dylan stepped into the shower and leaned his head against the wall. He thought he was all cried out, but tears continued to make their appearance. "What's going to happen?" He stood there for a long time, allowing the water to wash it all away. "God, what's going to happen?" His mind raced with numerous thoughts that overwhelmed him, from rage to sadness, from hopelessness to hope. He imagined showing up at Owen's door with a shotgun. *No, that would be too easy...too painless.* He imagined grabbing Owen by the throat and dragging him into his house where he'd tie him up, and slowly cut his body a thousand times as he described his own pain to Owen. Horrendous ideas of gruesome torture washed over his mind. These were thoughts he had never entertained. Where were they coming from? How could he get Owen to feel the kind of pain that he was causing him? *These thoughts are so wicked! Maybe I'm more evil than I ever knew.*

"God, help me." He hammered his fists against the tile wall. "Forgive me, Lord." Dylan tried hard to shake off the evil thoughts and extend forgiveness toward Owen. He wondered if Owen even cared. *God, he was my friend.* Dylan gritted his teeth together. "How could he do this to me?" The question of the unthinkable nearly crushed him into the ground. His entire being ached beyond belief as he remembered months of worshipping with and praying next to the very man who was sleeping with his wife. Dylan beat his fists on the wall, "God! God! What the hell?" He pounded his fists harder. "What the hell?"

He couldn't comprehend such two-faced wickedness and he was angry at God for merely standing by as it unfolded. "Why? Where were You? Did it never occur to You to strike him dead in Your presence? Was it too difficult for You to intervene and stop it from happening?" He recalled the appreciation dinner just one month ago and how he honored Owen as his trusted friend. "My God!" He continued beating his fists on the wall. "And in the church! Church is supposed to be a refuge! How could You let this happen?"

What was this freakish roller coaster of emotion that drove him into a ball on the shower floor? He was beginning to feel like two different people. One that wanted to love and forgive…and one that wanted to hate and torture. Dylan feared he was losing himself to hell, giving in to a darkness that he never knew existed inside of him.

After an hour of sitting underneath the cold waters of the shower, Dylan managed to pull himself up. The sound of the water shutting off brought him back to a quiet, empty reality. He dried off and looked at the man in the mirror who looked like he crawled out of a ditch after three years of heroin abuse. He was appalled at who he was becoming…appalled at where life had taken him. As he stared into the mirror, he sneered at himself, "Well, hello, Pastor. Whose life are you going to save today? Pathetic." He shook his head.

Once he got dressed, he went into the living room and moved the art supplies into his office closet. He didn't want Lynette to know he was starting art lessons. She'd probably be angry at him for taking so long to take an interest.

Glancing at the clock, it was now 9:40am. He made his way out to the old, blue Volvo. *I guess she'll be keeping the SUV.* He wasn't sure where he was heading. About 20 miles outside of Holly, he pulled over near a worn path that went down to the river. The raging pain that swirled inside his heart pressed him to run down the path, and he hoped it would never end. If he could just keep running until he was dead, that would be a dream come true.

Lynette pulled up in their driveway, thankful to see that his Volvo was gone. She was afraid he might have stayed and she wasn't in the mood for talking. She sat in the car for a minute and stared at the old front porch, eyeing the swing that they used to spend their mornings and evenings on. She had fond memories of their times out there. She determined to shut her heart off and enter the house. "Just get this over with."

Jackson heard a car door. He pushed his curtains aside to see who was across the street. He was surprised to see Lynette going into her house. After spending time with Dylan and getting to know him, Jackson wanted more than anything to run across the street and shake some sense into her. *Doesn't she realize how much pain she's causing?*

Lynette walked into the living room and stood still for a moment, staring into the place she once called 'home.' The Christmas tree in the corner held their precious ornaments and keepsakes. *First Christmas Together*, read one ornament. And another: *Dylan and Lynette*. Her eyes turned to the mantle that held their wedding portrait. It was unreal to her…how life had shifted. "New chapter," she muttered to herself.

She stepped into the kitchen, hoping that Dylan hadn't consumed her Starbucks bottled frappuccino. It was there, unopened. "Thank God." She picked it up, twisted the cap, and guzzled it down.

Lynette headed to the bedroom to begin going through her things. She noticed empty boxes of Kleenex strewn on the floor. The crumpled bed spoke of hellish nights. A tinge of guilt punched her in the gut. The room was filled with sadness. She tried to distract herself with the job of gathering her clothes and accessories.

She reached for the top shelf of her closet, stretching to grab a box of important items. As she pulled it out, a music box came tumbling down. It landed in a pile of clothes, unbroken. The first few notes of a melody chimed. Dylan had bought it for her on their first anniversary. Beauty and the Beast. She adored that movie and always told Dylan that someday they'd own a castle with a massive library. She would tease him about being the Beast. She looked at the music box and pondered how she had become the beast.

"What am I doing?" She spoke out loud to herself. Lynette had become afraid to talk to God. She supposed she stopped talking with Him several months ago. She had gone through a phase of pleading with Him to make her husband listen to her. She prayed for change. She hoped he would back away from the needs of the congregation. Sure, she cared about people's needs, too, but she was overwhelmed at how their life had become completely intertwined with the church.

She and Dylan couldn't go on dates anymore without running into people who wanted to talk about their situations. Or they would approach Dylan with a request and leave him carrying an expectation that he couldn't stop thinking about all evening. If they decided to take a trip or spend money on something special, people would analyze their purchases and judge their decisions. Dylan seemed oblivious to it, but the ladies talked, so it always got around to Lynette. Eventually, it came to the point where intimate moments were interrupted by phone calls and Dylan had a hard time ignoring them. Church went from being a refuge to being a prison. There was no escape. Even in her own home, she swore that every wall was glass, and she was a spectacle to be studied.

In desperation for a break, Lynette began taking the art class. She had always been creative, and creativity brought her peace. She hoped Dylan would join her. Lynette had envisioned moments with her husband, sitting side by side at their canvasses in an open field creating together on a glorious morning. She was a romantic at heart.

When she showed up for her first class, she was deeply disappointed that Dylan decided not to come. Owen walked in that night and his face lit up when he noticed Lynette. After his divorce, he was seeking a distraction for himself. He found a newspaper ad about the class, and decided it was time to stir up his love for art. Owen asked Lynette to keep his new adventure a secret so his manly buddies wouldn't tease him about being a "pansy."

Lynette didn't dare tell the church ladies that she joined the class. She knew they would sign up, too, and that was the last thing she needed. This was going to be her time with Dylan…so she hoped. Now, as she sat in the closet, remembering the beginning of her relationship with Owen, she recalled something that Dylan once told a couple in counseling. *You're only as sick as your secrets. In the beginning, secrets seem innocent and we have a way of convincing ourselves that we're doing the right thing, but secrets are often the thing that destroys what we love the most.*

Where had young Dylan gained so much wisdom? His smarts were one of the things that she found attractive in the beginning. She marveled over what an incredibly intelligent person he was…definitely mature beyond his years.

Lynette stepped out of the closet and headed to her dresser to grab a few things she left behind. She noticed her painting of the tree on the wall. *Your grace is sufficient.* Lynette scoffed, "Yeah, well…let's hope so." It was her first painting from art class. She remembered thinking of the tree as being Dylan and she saw herself as the river. She longed to nourish him and thrive together, but she was afraid his roots weren't growing near her. When she painted it, she prayed that he would grow deep, into her.

Staring at the painting, she talked to the air, "Yeah, that'll never happen." Though she still loved Dylan, she believed she and Owen were a better fit. She had gone too far and there was no turning back. Her mother's often-repeated quote rang through her mind. *You made your bed. Now lie in it.*

## Chapter Eight
Two Months Later

Dylan headed into Marshall City for his job interview at Perry's Gym. He already interviewed with a computer software company, a restaurant, and the electric company, but being a pastor for so many years, he lacked the skills and experience they were looking for. Coming to the end of his money, he felt the pressure to find work and make a change.

He set his heart on staying in Holly despite the uncomfortable interactions with the locals and the painful ban on his attendance at Hope Fellowship. Elder David had convinced the board that Dylan needed to stay away from the church in order for people to move forward in accepting a new pastor and overcoming the stigma of Lynette's choices.

Dylan pulled into the parking lot and parked his car facing the entrance to Perry's Gym. He turned the car off and gripped the steering wheel with both hands. He sighed heavily, depressed by his current situation. Negative thoughts ate at his mind. *So, this is what my life has come to? Desperately hoping to get a job as a gym boy. Cleaning up sweaty mats and running a front desk. Brilliant.*

He walked in and immediately became aware of the smell of stale sweat. For a moment, he considered backing out, but he wasn't one to be a no-show. A jubilant, twenty-something male came bounding in behind the desk. The blue-eyed, blonde-haired, Arnold Schwarzenegger-bodied man excitedly introduced himself. "Welcome to Perry's! I'm Josh. And you must be Dylan?"

Dylan's eyes widened and he found himself smiling with amusement, wondering if the guy was on speed. He reached his hand out to shake Josh's hand. "Hello. It's nice to meet you."

"Let me start you off with a tour and then we'll head to my office to discuss details. We'll start in the instructional room. Here, we hold all kinds of classes like yoga, aerobics, zumba and a kickboxing class. The room to the right is kind of our 'chill out' room." Josh chuckled. "You'll notice that the walls are a nice, calming green. We have these comfortable reclining chairs for people to relax on and clear their heads before or after their workouts. Over there on the table, we always have water with fresh fruit in it. We encourage people to stay hydrated. And, hey…what do you think of the music? Peaceful, isn't it?"

Dylan was trying to keep up with Josh's energy. "It's nice. Love it."

Josh continued the tour. After they explored the weight room and cycling room, they headed to the office. "What do you think so far?"

"I think you've got a great place here. It's a great set up." Dylan tried his best to appear excited about the gym, even though gyms were never a draw for him. His idea of exercise was hiking or running outdoors, not being held captive inside a building, breathing controlled air. Everything within him wanted to leave. There was absolutely no attraction to being in this environment, but his desperation pressed him to submit to the torture.

"Basically, I need someone to be here Monday through Fridays from eight in the morning to three o'clock in the afternoon. We have other staff members that come in at three to take the evening shift. Pretty much, I'd need you at the front desk to greet people and make sure they sign in. Between people coming in, you would be cleaning mats and surfaces and restocking a few items. When you come in the mornings, the first thing to do is to make sure the restrooms and locker areas are ready to go." Josh threw his hands in the air excitedly. "So, would you like the job?"

Dylan was shocked by such a quick offer. He barely had time to accept the idea of working here. He wasn't sure how to say no to someone who appeared like a game show host who just offered a million bucks. "Yes. Of course. When do I start?" Saying yes when his entire being screamed, '*I don't want to be here*' was a difficult task, yet after losing Lynette, it was a welcomed change. And money was an absolute necessity.

Josh looked at a calendar on his desk. "How about next Monday?"

"Perfect. I'll be here."

They shook hands and Dylan turned to leave.

"Yo! I almost forgot." Josh tossed a *Perry's Gym* t-shirt at Dylan. "I have a couple more I'll give you when you come on

Monday. Just be sure to wear it to work. You can wear either black workout shorts or pants. And any New Balance tennis shoe is what we prefer. It's a family thing." Josh chuckled.

"Thanks. I'll see you on Monday."

Dylan headed to "Old Blue," the Volvo. Getting in the car was comforting, something familiar. All of this change was gut-wrenching for him, but he knew he had no choice. He picked up his phone and dialed Jackson. "Hey man. How are you?"

"Hi Dylan. I'm good. And you?"

"Well, I got a job here in Marshall City."

"Awesome! Where at?"

"Don't get too excited. I'm the new gym boy at Perry's Gym. I will be running the front desk and I have the great honor of cleaning people's nasty body fluids off of equipment. Loads of fun."

Jackson felt sad for Dylan. Watching a good man go from a place of influence to being a regular Joe pricked at his sense of justice. "I'm proud of you, man. You can do this. It may not seem like much, but you'll find something better later. It's only temporary."

"Thanks, man. You always cheer me up."

"Did you decide where you're going to live?"

"For now, I'll stay at my parent's house here in Marshall City during the week, and I'll spend weekends at home in Holly. I love my house. I don't want to let go of it…at least, not yet."

"I'm glad to hear that. I was afraid you wouldn't stick around. This way, we can keep our weekend breakfast date." Jackson laughed.

"Yes! It's a deal. All right. I'd better go. I'll be back this evening."

"See you then." Jackson cringed as he hung up the phone. *Poor Dylan. God, help him.*

Dylan was craving a hamburger. He ventured down the road until he found Red's Burgers. Floorboards creaked as he stepped into the old-fashioned joint decorated with red-checkered tablecloths and mason jars. He immediately began salivating as the smell of bison burgers hit his nose.

As he looked over the menu, he noticed a beautiful young woman sitting alone across from him. He couldn't help but notice her mysterious demeanor. She wore dark sunglasses and a long, tan trench coat. Her brown hair was pulled back in a ponytail. She was focused on her cell phone.

Soon, a large, black man in a high-powered suit approached her. Dylan thought he was built like "The Rock." The man reached his hand out and the woman shook it.

"Have a seat." She motioned across from her.

Dylan was intrigued with this odd meeting, so he worked hard to listen in on their conversation.

The woman sighed. "So, what do you have for me?" she asked.

The man let out a deep breath. "I think you already know, Kat. I'm sorry to tell you…your suspicions were right."

The woman nodded her head as she opened her purse and pulled out an envelope and some Kleenex. She dabbed her eyes underneath the sunglasses and handed the envelope to the man.

"I have pictures if you want them. Photos are included in my service fee. You just have to decide how much you want to know."

She nodded. "Yes. I'll take them."

The man looked concerned for her well-being as he handed her the brown envelope that contained the photographs. He looked down at the envelope she had given him. He proceeded to open it and count the money. "Here. I want to give you half of this. You're gonna need it." He placed the money in front of her. "You're a good woman. I wish you the best."

Kat mustered up a faint smile. "Thank you." She reached to shake his hand.

"You have my number, so be sure to contact me if you need anything else. And just so you know, there are many men and women in your shoes. You're not alone." With that, the man left.

Dylan watched Kat closely. She took a deep breath as she held the brown envelope. A tear rolled down her cheek, but she dabbed it away quickly. She suddenly stood up and stuffed the envelope into her purse, then turned like a soldier, strong and sure, eyes on the target, and marched to the front door.

Dylan left his seat to peer out the window. He made a mental note of her light blue Chrysler Town and Country van. His heart was beating fast as he considered running after her, but he didn't want to intrude or cause her more distress. He wrestled against his pastoral side that had always caused him to run to the rescue. For years, he strived to be all things to all people. As he watched her car exit the parking lot, he thought, *Who do I think I am anyway? A broke pastor whose wife left him for a deacon. What do I possibly have to offer? Well, God…I guess You'd better go help her Yourself.*

A unexpected rush of freedom swept over him. His thought was half-sarcastic, but he felt a purity in those words. *God, I guess You'd better help her Yourself.* He returned to his seat and pondered how God was much more powerful and able to intervene than he had ever been. He wondered if he had committed a disservice to his people. How ironic, he thought.

He had a habit of whispering to himself. It was a practice for preparing his sermons…a verbal processor, of sorts. "In trying to serve others and press them towards God, I managed to do a disservice in drawing them to myself." He shook his head as he thought of the monster he created. Dylan made himself into a 24/7 answer. The man who had all the answers. It was no wonder that Lynette finally snapped. Her husband was open-access to the community and he never had the wisdom to shut it off. While his wife's heart was breaking, he was busy fixing the broken hearts of other wives. While Lynette was recovering after a painful knee surgery, he stayed busy with hospital visitations and meetings to discuss trivial church matters. As Dylan thought about his blindness, his eyes burned with tears that he refused to release. The reality of his ignorance seared his heart with self-hatred. *What a fool I am.*

## Chapter Nine

Kat dropped the children off at the babysitter's house. She drove back home, making sure to put her car in the garage so no one would know she was home. The babysitter thought that Kat would be at a doctor's appointment and grocery shopping most of the day. *Good, I can be left alone. I need time to deal with this.* Preston was gone. That morning, when he told her he had business to take care of in Holly, she bit her lip and fought back tears. She couldn't let him know that she knew his secret…not yet.

She closed her car in the garage and went into the house, making sure all doors were locked. Slowly, she walked into their bedroom and locked the door to ensure privacy, just in case. Kat sat on the bed, staring down at the brown envelope. "Why am I doing this to myself?" She sighed. "But I have to know the whole truth." Picking up the envelope, she slowly began breaking the seal. She slipped her fingers into it, and feeling the photographs, she took a deep breath.

"God, help me." Kat was a woman of great faith and had always enjoyed leading women's groups and Bible studies. She thrived on being a good mother to her children. She considered parenting to be one of the greatest missions on earth. Being a part of raising up the next generation gave her incredible purpose. She always loved being a wife to Preston. Kat was well-known for praising her husband and his work, even when he failed to meet her needs. While some women verbally slaughtered their husbands for their lack of spirituality, Kat continued speaking well of Preston. Women were often jealous of her relationship with him.

"God, give me strength." She slid the photos out of the envelope. Upon looking at the first one, she gasped as she gripped her stomach. "Oh, my God. Oh, my God." She fought to keep breathing. "Fay." She recognized the 'other woman.'

Preston had introduced Kat to his old friend, Fay, when they were dating. In fact, Preston couldn't wait for Fay to meet his girlfriend. They all spent time together and Fay even helped them with their wedding plans. She was like a sister to Kat. Over the years, she communicated with Fay much less, simply due to her busy life, and because Fay lost interest as Kat became more involved with children, church, and God. Fay had asked her to leave the "God-stuff" out of their conversations. Eventually, their relationship drifted apart.

Kat crumpled the photographs in her hands and screamed. She threw them on the floor and buried her face in a pillow. Sobs erupted. "Oh, God! Why?" She normally felt like a strong woman, but this…this was too much to bear. Everything in the room seemed to mock her. All that she knew as faithful and true suddenly became a betrayer. *Is anything true and good?*

### At Annie's Café

Preston and Fay sat across from each other. The question that became more and more annoying to Preston arose at the start of their lunch. "Preston? What do I have to do to move you toward me? You need to be free so we can be together."

Preston sighed. "You always ask me that, and I wish you would stop. Can't you just be in the moment and enjoy it?"

She grimaced. "I feel like I've waited an eternity. I can't think about anything else. It's hard to focus at work. I just want to be with you. Don't you want to be with me?" Fay tilted her head to the side and tried to capture Preston's attention with her sad puppy eyes. It was a little trick she learned long ago. Manipulating her dad into meeting her desires was a full-time job for many years.

"You know I want to be with you, Fay. Otherwise, I wouldn't be here right now." He stared down at the table.

Fay reached for Preston's hand. "Just think how good life will be when everything is said and done. We'll be free to be us. We can go where we want and do what we want without having to hide."

"I wouldn't say that we're exactly hiding. We're sitting together in public now."

She let out an annoyed, "Hah."

"Well, we **are** in public, Fay." He pulled his hand away from hers.

"The town of Holly doesn't count, Preston! No one knows who we are here."

"Actually, with my business dealings here in town, more people are starting to know about me, so we're going to have to be a bit more discreet for awhile. I don't want word getting back to my wife…"

"Oh my gosh! Preston!" Fay fumed. "I **want** word to get back to your wife. I'm sick of hiding and I want out of this prison! You're letting her hold you back, and I want to set you free. Both of us free…together. And frankly, I'm tired of having to find places to be with you. Having sex in the back of your car is not exactly comfortable…and neither is the empty barn down the…"

Preston's jaw tightened. "Dang it, Fay! Lower your voice."

A new waitress, Ellie, came to the table. "I'm so sorry for the long wait. What can I get for you guys?"

Preston was glad for the interruption. "No problem. Water with lemon, please. You're new here, aren't you?" He desperately grasped for a distraction from the current conversation.

Ellie smiled. "Yes. My second day."

"Cool. Happy 'second day.' Is Lucy here?"

"It's her day off. The whole kitchen is talking about her hot date with the newspaper reporter, so apparently, she's having a pretty good day off." Ellie laughed.

Fay spoke up, "Coffee for me, please. Straight black."

"Got it."

After Ellie walked away, Fay put on her sad puppy face. "I'm sorry, Pres. I know you're under a lot of pressure and I don't want to add to it. I just have a hard time waiting, Baby. When you're away, I feel incomplete. Every chance I get to see you, it's like I have everything I need. And you know how my father treated me over the years. He rejects me and then he comes around long enough to give me a few minutes of attention...and a few gifts. Then he ignores me again. When you go home to your wife, that's what it feels like. I hate it. And I feel like I'm not good enough for you."

"That's not true, Fay."

### Kat

As Kat lay on the bed, curled into a ball of torment, she cried, "God, why am I not enough for him?" She thought back over the years and the way she kept their home meticulously clean, washed his laundry and ironed his shirts, scoured the internet for incredible recipes and prepared meals...and how she always made his birthdays special...surprise parties, secret get-aways...and the incredible sex. In her mind, she had taken good care of Preston and met every need he could possibly have, but somewhere along the way, she figured she completely missed it. *I must be the biggest fool on the planet.*

The scenarios that she imagined when piecing together Preston's whereabouts over the last few months weren't enough to prepare her for the photographs she saw. Seeing her husband holding another woman's hand and kissing her…her own husband's lips on another woman's lips…it tormented her entire being. She sobbed as she thought about how much she loved kissing him.

Her mind went to their anniversary one month ago. She thought back over their dinner that night. Preston had taken her to Charming's where they enjoyed a candlelight dinner near a roaring fireplace. Now that she thought about it, he seemed distant, yet he was trying to engage with her the best he could. Their conversation was somewhat lacking and basic. She felt it difficult to reach his heart. They ended the evening the way they always did on their anniversary. Making love. But that night, it seemed as if Preston's mind was somewhere else. She couldn't shake the feeling that he was conflicted, but when she asked what was wrong, he assured her that all was well, and that he was deeply in love with her.

*How could I be such a blind idiot?* The confusion and ripping of her soul nearly crushed her. *How could I be so blind?* As she thought about this man who lied to her and deceived her, she realized that somehow, she still cared about him deeply. She wondered how that was possible. The intensity of the deception challenged her to hate him, but she couldn't. More than anything, she longed for his soul…for his heart. That's all she ever wanted.

Kat composed herself enough to call her best friend, Paige.

"Hello? Paige?" Kat tried not to cry, but hearing her friend's voice on the other end of the line unleashed the tears.

"Kat? What's going on?"

"I...I...can you come over?"

"Yes. Kat, what's going on?"

"I just need to talk. I'll tell you when you get here."

"I can be there in twenty minutes. You hang in there, sweetie. Okay?"

"Okay. Thank you."


### Lucy and Jackson

The Elephant Room was the only upscale restaurant in Holly. At least for the town of Holly, it was considered upscale. The owner, Rose Reynolds, brought her love of Italy back home, and her husband agreed to fund her dream of owning an Italian restaurant. It was a good thing for the people of Holly. Romantic dining could happen without having to drive thirty or forty miles.

The rich, red carpet held the weight of antique tables, ornate chairs and statues of half-naked people. The crystal chandeliers sparkled, casting their light on the crystal candleholders that sat beneath them. A waterfall in the corner provided the peaceful sounds of a flowing river. Some guests thought it might fit better inside a Chinese restaurant, but everyone gladly waded through the overly gaudy atmosphere in order to taste Rose's amazing home-cooked, Italian dishes.

Lucy and Jackson sat at a small, round table, peering at each other in the candlelight. Lucy chose her red high heels, a blue pencil skirt and white shirt for this special outing. Jackson was used to seeing her in her cafe uniform. Tonight, he was captivated by Lucy.

"Jackson Ryan Sawyer," Lucy smiled as she said his name.

Jackson returned the gesture. "Lucinda Belle Flowers."

They giggled.

"Good Lord, Lucy. I'm so weird when I'm with you." Jackson laughed.

"Well, thanks a lot, Jackson! Could it be that you're just being the real you when you're with me?" Lucy's ruby red lips outlined her huge, perfect smile. Jackson's heart jumped.

"My gosh, you're beautiful. Do you even have a clue how scared I was three weeks ago when I asked you out? I was afraid you'd say no."

"Why would I say no to the only person in this town that makes me smile every time I see him?" Lucy placed her elbows on the table and clasped her hands together.

Jackson continued. "You inspire me. The things you say...you've taught me so much. It's like you have this incredible wisdom, but it's more than that. It's like wisdom, but all wrapped up in joy. You see life more deeply than most."

She smiled. "Thanks for saying that."

"It's true. I'm not making it up." Jackson reached across the table for her hand.

Lucy smiled as she placed her hand in his. "Jackson, you're truly the most incredible man I've ever met. You're a genuinely beautiful person, and I don't know that I've ever expressed this before, but what you did for Pastor Dylan...writing that article...was one of the most noble and kind things I've ever seen."

Jackson beamed. "Thank you, Lucy. You're an amazing person yourself. I can't imagine handling Dylan's situation any other way. He's a good man and has been a great friend to me." Jackson looked down at the table. "And I wasn't even an avid churchgoer. That's what I love about him. He treats everyone the same."

"What do you think will happen? I'm hoping they'll get back together."

"Dylan is determined to wait for Lynette to come back, but she's filed for divorce. I don't know what'll happen. I wish it would work out, but it's not looking good. I really admire Dylan. Gotta give him credit. All of this time has passed and he hasn't killed Owen or stirred up trouble. I'm not sure I'd be that good. Sometimes I wonder, though, if he's just torturing himself by holding onto their house and sticking it out in a town where half the people act like he's a leper."

Lucy nodded. "Yeah, I've seen that in the cafe. I overhear lots of conversations. Most people adore Dylan, but some still say horrible things. The crazy thing is that most of what they say isn't even true. I have a hard time biting my tongue."

Jackson agreed. "I know what you mean. Some of the staff at the Herald have managed to print a couple of things about the situation, for the sake of gossip. The longer I'm in the media world, I see how it works. You give people something to talk about and it keeps them looking for more. Especially if it's negative crap. Human nature, I guess."

"Gosh. I can't imagine how different things would be if you weren't reporting for the Herald. Dylan and Lynette would have been crushed, literally, forever in this community if it wasn't for you." Lucy's eyes filled with light. "Jackson, you're like grace incarnate. You've literally saved a life." Lucy leaned back in her chair, smiling at Jackson with delight.

"Grace incarnate, huh?" Jackson chuckled. "Nah. I wouldn't go that far."

Jackson and Lucy finished their drinks and dessert.

"Lucy? Can we do this again tomorrow night? I mean, maybe not the Elephant Room," he grinned, "but can we be together?"

Lucy smiled. "Sure thing. I'd love that."

## Chapter Ten

In Marshall City

Dylan was happy that it was Friday. He finished his duties at Perry's Gym and headed for Holly for the weekend. After several lessons from old Mary Elliott, it was time to begin the paintings he had seen in a series of dreams that visited him each night. He looked forward to weekends so he could spend time in his home…in his and Lynette's home. Each time he drove there, he envisioned her standing on the front porch, ready to hold him in her arms, but each time, his heart sank as he pulled into the empty driveway and saw that no one was there.

As he gripped the steering wheel of "Old Blue," his mind filled with the dream he had the night before. The dream was intensely memorable. Empty canvasses everywhere. His entire house was filled with canvasses. They were all blank except for one. The canvas that stood in their bedroom displayed a tall tree that appeared to be a cypress growing next to a winding river.

The dream began with Dylan standing in the living room. The only sound was his own breath. He slowly walked down the hallway, glancing at the empty canvasses along the walls. At the end of the hallway, he pushed the bedroom door open. Inside the room, canvasses stood on easels in a circular fashion, around the bed. At the foot of the bed was the canvas that displayed the river and tree. As Dylan reached out to run his fingers along the river, he heard a voice whisper, "Stepping into me."

When Dylan heard the voice, he turned quickly to look behind him. No one was there, but the room had morphed into a lush, green forest. Wind blew through his hair and he heard the voice of a woman, "Stepping into me." The voice repeated several times as the wind increased. He turned quickly, looking in every direction. All around him, the voice repeated the phrase, but he couldn't find its source. It seemed the entire forest was speaking.

To his right, he heard cracking and popping. He set his eyes in that direction. The ground began lifting and rolling, finally giving way to a bubbling river that began to flow in his direction, engulfing his feet. The water and dirt mixed, creating mud that turned to a golden gel around his legs. "Stepping into me." Dylan bent over, drenching his hands in the golden substance. Electricity, like a bolt of lightning shot up his arms and into his chest. Dylan fell to the ground, shaking. Not in pain, but ecstasy. He felt every part of his brain become alive. Every cell in his body was fully awake. He knew things he had never known before, and he could see beyond the prison walls of the temporal world.

As his mind flipped through the scenes of the dream, he realized he was already crossing into Holly. "Holy cow! Already?" Dylan couldn't remember any points in between and he wondered if he had even stopped at the stop signs along his route. Then he thought about how Lynette used to laugh at him and his obsession with the phrase 'holy cow.'

He pulled into the cafe. "Popular spot tonight." It seemed the whole town was out seeking something to do, and the cafe was about the most exciting place to be. No movie theaters. No malls. And the shops all closed early. For the first time in quite awhile, it didn't feel so awkward facing the community of Holly. A tiny flame of joy flickered in his heart. It would be good to see familiar faces. This was home.

Opening the door to the cafe, as usual, his eyes were met by curious faces that turned to see who was entering the premises. Lucy quickly set a cup of coffee on a table and ran up to him, throwing her arms around him. "Pastor Dylan! It's so good to see you!"

Elder David was sitting with his wife, Marcy, and another board member in a booth near the door. He rolled his eyes and spoke so that others could hear, "**Pastor** Dylan? Oh, no, no, no. That has to stop. He's no longer a pastor and no one should place that title on someone who's in his situation." Looking at the other board member, John, he pointed his finger firmly, "We must get a new pastor soon and establish him at Hope Fellowship to rid of this confusion. In order for our church to move forward, we need to wash our hands of this mess and redirect the attention of people in this community. Have you received any resumes since our conversation with Mr. Pierce?"

John shook his head. "No, sir. We've had no interest. Our best bet at this point is to keep the board members and deacons in rotation at the pulpit on Sundays when we don't have a guest speaker. We're doing well on Wednesday nights with Mrs. Elliott's Bible study. There's something about that old lady that lights everyone up. She's like what I'd call 'aristocratic granny meets wild west granny.'" John chuckled. David was not amused. "I'd say we'd better hang onto her for Wednesday nights." David nodded in agreement.

Dylan's battle with anger and bitterness towards Elder David since Lynette's sin had been exposed, challenged him to no end. Not only did he suffer the loss of his wife and ministry and employment, but he suffered frequent battles with anger and rage that would emerge at unexpected times. Like ocean waves, it would come in layers. Some small and barely noticeable, and other times an unexpected tidal wave would carry him away and smash him into the shore of his ugly reality.

Lynette's lies. Owen's lies and deceit. David's self-righteous, uncaring, self-promotion at Dylan's expense. The whispers among the judgmental. Layer upon layer, it would come crashing in on him at the most inappropriate moments…at work, in the grocery store. His body would begin to shake as he fought hard to stop the breaking dam of emotion. But as Dylan walked past David's table, he was determined not to let the raging waves win.

"Well, hello, David. How are you?" Dylan knew the power of not forgiving. He had seen it rot many souls, as well as their bones. He was determined not to empower its talons in his own heart.

David lowered his coffee mug and looked up at Dylan. "Hello. I'm fine. And you?"

"Fair, considering the circumstances. The job is okay. I'm sure you've heard about my job at the gym?"

"Of course. I'm glad to see you've found something. I'm a bit surprised that you continue coming to Holly on the weekends. Are you considering selling your home? Or finding tenants?" David folded his hands together and straightened his posture in a confident manner.

Dylan felt the sting behind David's words. Certainly, he was hinting that Dylan needed to stay out of Holly and move on. "Holly is my home, David. This is where Lynette and I came to begin a new chapter and I'm not real keen on the idea of allowing that chapter to end poorly. I'll stay here until God tells me to get out."

David's wife, Marcy, quickly butted into the conversation before her husband had a chance to interject a snide remark. She had become a champion at tolerating his harshness, but she couldn't stand by and allow him to unleash it upon others, especially someone as kind as Dylan. "I admire you, Dylan. I think that's wonderful. We're so glad to see you around town. And just so you know, I take a glance at your place everyday when I drive by. I want to make sure your house is safe and protected." She winked. "I'll keep an eye out for you."

Dylan smiled. "Thank you, Marcy. That does my heart good."

Awkward silence swallowed a few seconds as Dylan debated asking the question that burned in his heart. "How is the congregation doing?"

David replied, "Doing well. Very well. Things are moving along."

Again, Marcy threw her two cents in. "Oh, Dylan. So many people miss you and are praying for you. To this day, when I walk in the door, I expect to see your face…and Lynette's."

David's face reddened. "But the church is doing well and we're getting along fine. And it's important that you continue keeping your distance from congregants so they can keep moving forward."

"David!" Marcy was humiliated by his attitude. "Dylan, I'm so sorry." She turned to David. "What's so wrong with letting him know how much he's missed? After all, he and Lynette poured their lives into this church for years. Why do you just write them off? I'm not willing to cast their sacrifice aside and dishonor them…and especially when they're going through hell!" She turned her attention back to Dylan. "I don't know what to say, Dylan." Her eyes filled with tears. "I've never understood his lack of grace and concern. Now, please excuse me." Marcy rose from the table and quickly made her way to the women's restroom.

Dylan felt sorry for her. He looked at David and shook his head as he walked away from the table. He found it to be ironic how a man could humiliate his wife numerous times, yet she faithfully stayed by his side.

"I got your booth in the corner." Lucy approached Dylan with her joyful smile.

"Thanks, Lucy. I hear rumors coming out of Holly, you know." He smiled at her. "Something about a newspaper guy?"

She giggled. "Oh, yeah. He's amazing! I just adore Jackson."

"I adore him, too. He's been an incredible friend. He's the best friend I've got. Can I expect to see him in here tonight?"

"Of course! Jackson will be here soon."

Dylan settled himself into his seat, still wrestling with the underlying desire to punch Elder David in the jaw. A strange mixture of vengeance and a desire to let it go warred within. *Wasn't the man miserable enough just being himself,* Dylan wondered. *Why should he be punished further?*

"Dylan." Marcy appeared at his side. "I can't apologize enough for my husband."

"Oh, Marcy. Don't worry about it. I've probably given him reason not to like me. We always butted heads in staff meetings. We couldn't agree on much." Dylan patted her hand.

"No. It's absolutely uncalled for." Tears began to stream down her cheeks. "You've done so much for this community. I constantly run into people who talk about how you helped them through their troubles. There's a lot of light in Holly because of you, and it's just not right for people to ignore it because of your situation. And, Dylan, I don't know if anyone talks to you about

Lynette or not, but I know she won't be happy for long. I know Owen's tendencies. Those two are just living in a fog…in an illusion. One day they're going to wake up. I promise you that Lynette isn't truly happy. She might think she is, but she's not. You're the best thing that ever happened to her."

Dylan's face softened. The rims of his eyes were moist. "I'm afraid that while I was helping everyone else, I let my own wife down. I really hurt my wife in ways that I couldn't see before, Marcy."

"Every marriage has its ups and downs. Everyone makes mistakes and we all get blinded from time to time, especially toward those closest to us. It's just that people get scared when they find themselves in that place, so they throw in the towel too soon. My Lord, there have been times when I wanted to quit with David. But I pushed through and endured. We broke down for a time, but it was in the brokenness that I actually learned why he acts the way he does. It doesn't mean that his actions are acceptable. It just means he needs more grace. And he's getting better. He's just a broken boy trying to be a man. And somehow I've learned to love him more."

Dylan smiled. "You're amazing, Marcy."

"Dylan, I'm praying for you and Lynette everyday. You hang in there. Okay?"

"I sure will. Thank you so much."

Marcy patted his back and headed to her table.

## Chapter Eleven

Friday nights were typically the obligatory date nights for Preston and Kat. After dealing with housework, cooking and two small children all week, Kat always looked forward to Friday. Going out on the town with Preston made her feel special, loved and beautiful. Pedicure, manicure, legs shaven, eyebrows plucked, make-up fully applied. She enjoyed preparing herself for her husband. Even though sex happened a couple of times throughout the week, Friday nights were certain to end with it. She looked forward to the intimacy and counted it an honor to please the man she loved.

This Friday night would be different. She worked hard to keep her broken heart in hiding. When he asked why her eyes were puffy, she made up a story about having bad PMS and a rude cashier at the grocery store.

"You about ready to go?" Preston asked as he entered their bedroom.

"Yep. And I have a new destination in mind." She picked up her purse and walked over to Preston. "Here's a map. It's marked with numbers for you to follow. We're going to play a game."

He raised his eyebrows. "This sounds interesting."

As Kat followed Preston to his black BMW, she wondered what she was doing exactly. She didn't really know. It was a plan she came up with in a moment of confusion and anxiety, but she was going with it anyway. In her mind, the night could end in several different ways. Upon revealing what she had learned, she thought they could perhaps end up in each other's arms as he cried and begged for her forgiveness, or perhaps he would deny everything. In that case, she would pull out the photos. The night could end in a huge, ugly fight. Maybe this was it. Maybe it would be the last night of their life together.

"So, where am I going?" he asked.

"Start with number one. Go to that location first." She was firm in her instructions.

Preston smiled, "I've never known you to do anything like this before. Should be fun."

"Well, I figured you might need some excitement in your life. With all of that hard work you've been doing…trips to Holly…you need to have some fun." Her own words bit at her heart. *Be strong, Kat. Be strong.*

Preston's stomach lurched when she mentioned the town of Holly. He felt compelled to talk about his business dealings there. "Yeah. I could use a break. Between Clark's Feed store, the new ethanol plant that's in the works, and dealing with the crop sprayers, I've got my hands full."

Kat looked out her window, biting her lip. "I'd say you do have your hands full. Amazing how you even find time to come home to your wife."

He detected a problem in her voice, but he didn't dare to ask what it was. The further he could stay away from uncomfortable conversation, the better.

"So, what did you do this week?"

"The typical. Cleaned house, fed the kids, washed the kids, drove the kids, Bible study. Same ole. Not nearly as exciting as your life."

Preston worked hard to drum up a topic. "So, what's your Bible study about this month? Don't you have like a monthly theme?"

Kat chuckled.

"What's so funny?"

"This month's theme is about being a Proverbs thirty-one woman. Have you heard of her?" Kat kept her gaze out the passenger's window.

"It sounds familiar, I guess. Who is she?" Preston had never been much of a Bible reader.

"Uh. Let's just say she's a woman that women think a man wants, but I'm not so sure that's the case. She's too perfect. I'm thinking that most men actually prefer unwholesome women. Someone more exciting."

Preston's tongue went numb with a metallic taste as adrenaline surged. "Uh...okay?" They rode in silence for a few minutes. "Well, it looks like we've reached our first destination. The Wine Dive?"

Kat stared at the front of the fancy restaurant where she used to work. "Yes. What's significant about this place? Do you remember, Preston?"

"Other than the fact that they have incredible fried chicken and collard greens, and the best wines, it's where I met this hot waitress named Kat." He smiled and looked at her.

She forced a smile. "I'm glad you remember."

"How could I forget? I married her eight months later."

"Do you remember what you said to me that night?"

Preston grinned. "Yes. I told you I wanted a nice red wine to go with my meal. You offered me a wine that was made in Fredericksburg, Texas. I'll never forget that because you mentioned that your German ancestors owned the land where it was made."

"And when I mentioned being German, you asked me if my name was…?"

Preston laughed. "Gertrude."

"It's a miracle that I accepted your request for a date after that." Kat smiled. She pulled out a bottle of red wine and two wine glasses from her tote bag. "Let's have a glass of wine to start the evening.

"Right here? In the car? So we're breaking the 'no open container' law?"

"Preston, since when do you care about not breaking laws?"

He shrugged off her comment. He had always been a law-abiding citizen.

She poured the wine and Kat tapped her glass to his. "Cheers. Here's to…well, I don't know…a long, happy life or something."

Preston took a few sips. "Are we going inside to eat?"

"Nope. Not here." She stared out the window.

Preston shifted in his seat. "Well, then. I suppose we'd better head to clue number two."

Kat appeared perturbed. "Why are you in such a hurry? Do you have to be somewhere?"

"No. Actually, I'm pretty hungry and I'm hoping this map will lead to food." Preston patted his stomach as he chuckled.

Clue number two took them to Britton Park. "Oh, I see," he said. "Uh, huh. This was our make out spot." He turned off the car and turned to face Kat. "So, do we get to play?"

"I don't know, Preston. Two kids, and over nine years of marriage. I didn't know if you'd still want me or not."

"Of course, I do, Kat. You're beautiful."

Her eyes began to water. "You really think so?"

"Yes. Any man would find you to be extremely attractive." Preston wondered what was brewing.

"But would I be good enough for any man? I mean, maybe I'd be boring to him after awhile." Her lip quivered.

"Look, Kat. I think PMS must be getting the best of you." He put his hand on her thigh. "Maybe we can make out and you'll feel better?" He grinned and tilted his head down, looking up at her in a seductive manner.

"I think we'd better go on to clue number three." She wiped away a tear.

"Already? We just got here! I thought you were bringing me here to relive some memories."

Kat stared out the window. "Preston, do you remember how you felt about me that night?"

"My gosh, Kat. How could I forget? I remember many times when we parked here." Preston pointed across the way. "And that tree over there…we laid on a blanket and kissed for hours." The memory struck Preston and pricked his heart for a moment. "Of course, I remember how I felt about you that night. I knew I loved you." He swallowed hard.

Still staring out the window, Kat asked, "Do you still love me?"

"Of course, I do!" What more could he say?

She turned to look at him. "Let's head to the next spot now."

He sighed. "All right. It's your call." Nervously filling in the awkward silence, "So, let's look at the map here. Number three. I know where that is." He tapped his finger on the paper map. "You're taking me to the church where we got married?"

She nodded.

The drive to First Christian Church was quiet as Kat tried to compose herself and not give away her discovery yet. She was certain that Preston was catching on.

As he drove the car, Preston thought about how difficult it was becoming to maintain two relationships with two needy women. It was exciting with Fay in the beginning, but it was quickly becoming a grueling task to keep her happy. He wondered if all relationships were about maintenance. He glanced over at Kat as a streetlight cast its shadow across her face. He was worried about what was going on inside of her.

"Are you hungry yet?" he asked. They hadn't had dinner.

She shook her head no. "I don't have much of an appetite."

"I think after this 'clue number three visit,' we need to head home and let you go to bed. Seems like you need a good night's sleep."

"I don't need to go to sleep, Preston." Her voice was tense.

"Well, I definitely need to eat. I'm starving. I know I don't feel right when I'm hungry. Can't think straight. You'd probably feel better if you ate something. I thought tonight was supposed to be fun, and you sure don't look like you're having any fun."

"Sorry. I guess I'm not feeling like myself anymore. I don't know who I am exactly."

"What the heck, Kat?"

She shrugged her shoulders.

Pulling into the parking lot of First Christian Church, Kat unbuckled her seat belt, opened the door, and walked up the steps to the old, arched doorway. Preston sat in the car, uneasy, and unwilling to face confrontation. He hoped that her mood didn't have anything to do with Fay. *No. There's no way she could know*, he thought.

Preston stepped out of the car and approached the church steps. "Kat, what are you doing?"

"Remembering." She stood facing the church, arms wrapped around herself.

"Yeah, I remember that day, too. It was the best day of my life, Kat."

Tears stung her eyes as she forbid them to fall. "Really? The best day of your life?"

"Yes." She couldn't believe his answer. *How can he be such a liar?* He reached to take her hand. "And you're still just as beautiful and amazing." He kissed her hand.

"But not enough," she said as tears made their escape.

"Of course, you are, Kat. Why do you think I chose you?" Preston looked into her eyes and his heart jumped. He felt something for his wife that he had forgotten long ago, and suddenly he was aware of the pain he was causing.

"Why aren't you choosing me now?" Kat pulled her hand from his.

"What are you talking about? I'm right here with you…right now." Preston appeared confused.

"Preston, when we came to this place over nine years ago to get married, I was sure. I believed with everything within me that you and I would be madly in love forever. I believed I'd be your one and only. And you'd be mine. I envisioned a full life with you, with a family. But your heart went somewhere else. I feel it." She tried to still her quivering chin.

"Kat, I don't know what you're talking about. You're talking like a crazy person. You need to pull yourself together."

"I'm the crazy person?" She turned away from him for a moment.

"Look. Why don't we call it a night? Get in the car and let's go home. Take a hot bath or something." Preston's heart was racing as he wondered if she could possibly know about Fay. He remembered Fay's words, *I want your wife to find out*! He wondered if Fay told Kat. His body felt clammy and the moment felt unreal.

"No, Preston!" Kat turned to face him. "No! I don't need a hot bath. I don't need to go home. I don't need you to tell me I'm crazy when you're the one that's crazy! Why, Preston? Why are you cheating on me?"

He threw his hands in front of him, "Whoa, whoa, whoa! Kat, I don't know what you're talking about. I'm not cheating on you."

Kat's eyes narrowed. "You're not cheating on me? You can honestly say you're not cheating on me?"

Looking her in the eyes, he repeated, "I am not cheating on you." In the back of his mind he thought there was no possible way that Kat could know and he didn't want to risk losing everything. The last few days left him feeling unsure and confused with Fay, and he certainly didn't want to lose his family. The affair was beginning to turn from a newfound happiness to something he struggled to manage.

Kat's eyes pierced right through him. "Preston James Richland. You mean, you aren't going to tell me about Fay?"

His heart pounded in his chest. His vision narrowed. He became lightheaded. "Kat. Fay and I have met in Holly just to catch up for lunch a couple of times. There's nothing going on. She's just a friend."

Kat's body stiffened as she tried to fathom the extent of his lies. "She's just a friend? She's just a friend. That's the winning phrase that never means what they say it means. A couple of lunches? That's it?" Her chest rose and fell with rapid breaths.

Preston worked to maintain a poker face, hoping there was a way to dig himself out of this moment. "Of course. I just never mentioned it because it wasn't even important. With everything else going on with the business, lunch with Fay was a detail that I forgot. How did you find out? Somebody saw us at the cafe together?"

Kat glared at him. "So that's it? An innocent lunch?" She was giving him every opportunity to tell the truth. "Did you hold her hand?"

"Why would I hold her hand?" Preston chuckled.

"Did you kiss her?"

"Kat, this is ridiculous."

"Preston, do you love her?"

He was losing the upper hand. "That's enough! I'm not playing these games. You want the truth? The truth is that I do care about Fay. She's a long-time friend. That's it! There's nothing else." Preston was exasperated and ready to bring this accusation to an end. He had to keep his cover until he figured out what to do. He couldn't afford having his wife pack up and leave with his kids. He wasn't ready for his family and reputation to fall apart.

Kat was caught between anger and sorrow. She was sure this flood of emotions was enough to carry her into the grave, immediately. "Why are you meeting with her? If it was nothing, you would have told me. She doesn't even live in Holly. A woman doesn't go that far out of her way to have lunch with a man unless there's something more."

"Fay had work meetings in Holly, too."

"Seriously, Preston? The tiny town of Holly is suddenly this up-and-coming boomtown, and everyone has business to do there? I may be naive, but I'm not that stupid! You need to tell me everything now, or I'm going to leave. I can't live like this."

Preston's heart surged in his throat. Panic mode set in. His judgment was clouded, but it had been for many months. "I'm telling you the truth. No handholding. No kissing. It was just lunch." He placed his hands on Kat's shoulders. "I love you, Kat."

Kat closed her eyes as a deep groan erupted from her chest. Tears poured like waterfalls over her cheeks. She turned away and walked toward the car, holding her arms around her stomach. Grief hit her like a wall and she nearly collapsed. *Be strong, Kat. Be strong*, she told herself.

"Kat, where are you going?"

"To get a gift out of the car. I brought you a present," she said through sobs.

Reaching into her tote bag, she pulled out the envelope of photographs taken by the private investigator. She thought about the first things that tipped her off to the possibility of an affair. Multiple trips to Holly. He was less focused. Less loving. He wasn't as affectionate. She watched the light in his eyes grow momentarily, but then it began fading. She remembered touching his chest one night, and the question she asked him. "Preston, I feel like I can't reach you. Like I can't get to your heart. What is this barrier?" He pretended it didn't exist.

Kat approached Preston and handed him the envelope. She sat on the church steps. His heart beat ferociously. "What is this?"

"Just open it." The tears continued flooding her soul.

Preston sat next to her. He thought he might have a heart attack. He feared what he might see. *Divorce papers?* His fingers fumbled with the seal. Finally, he pulled the photographs out. The first picture was all he had to see. It was him, kissing Fay. "Oh, God. Oh, God."

"Now you call out to Him?" Kat tried to calm herself. "Did you call His name when you were having sex with her?"

"My God. Kat." He dropped the envelope and leaned over the stone stair railing and vomited. Kat stared at the ground as she listened to Preston's heaving and gagging. She distracted herself by watching the pattern that her tears made on the concrete steps that were lit by the lampposts. She hoped this was a nightmare that she'd wake up from. The church steps reminded her of the time she walked upon them, filled with immense joy at the thought of her future with Preston. Now, the steps silently collected her tears as her world fell apart.

Preston returned to her side. "Kat? I don't know what to say."

"Neither do I. I hoped you would tell me the truth, but you didn't. I can't ever trust you again."

"I'm so sorry, Kat. I really am. You don't deserve to be hurt."

His words infuriated her. *What kind of twisted logic was this?* Her jaw tightened and she clenched her teeth. "Then, why?" The groaning rose up once again...an uncontrollable cry from a place that she didn't know existed. Like a small container trying to hold an ocean, she thought she might be shredded in two. "Why, Preston? What did I do wrong?"

His body shook. "You didn't do anything wrong. It's not about you. It's about me. I was selfish."

"Why did you need her? If you would have told me what you were needing, I could...I could have...oh, my God. How long was this going on?"

Preston gulped and closed his eyes as the guilt washed over. "I don't know. I don't keep track."

"Well, figure it out!"

He thought for a moment. "Around seven months ago. Just talking at first. Mostly just talking on the phone and email."

"When did the sex start?"

"Kat, please don't ask me these questions. Please."

"I have a right to ask these questions! I was being lied to. I was the one sleeping with you while you slept with someone else! I feel defiled! Disgusted!"

"Please, Kat. Stop."

She slapped his face twice. "No, **you** stop, Preston! Stop lying! Stop cheating! Stop treating me like a worthless piece of crap that exists to wash your clothes and clean your house. What am I? A maid with benefits? I want to know, when did the sex start?"

"It's hazy." Preston dropped his head into his palms. "I guess around three months ago."

"How many times? Where?"

"Please, Kat."

"Is she better than me? Does she kiss better?"

"Kat, why are you torturing yourself?"

"I'm more than tortured. I'm dead. I'm dead inside. Everything is numb."

"I don't want to leave you, Kat. I don't want to lose my family. Please."

"Why didn't you think of that before you unzipped your pants?"

"I don't know what I was thinking."

"So, are you going to marry her?"

"My God, no."

"So, she's a side thing?"

"No."

Kat heaved as a sob began to overwhelm her and tears spilled from her burning, puffy eyes. "Preston? Do you love her?"

He was overcome with grief as he watched the torrents of hellish pain engulf her. "I thought I did. But I don't think so anymore. I care about her life, but I don't feel for her like I did in the beginning."

He placed his hand on Kat's back, slightly. He didn't know if he should touch her or not. Kat sobbed, "What are we going to do? What about the kids?" As she thought of the kids, more tears came.

Preston was desperate. "Will you let me stay? Please don't make me leave."

Crying mixed with a half-amused chuckle, "Let you stay? I don't understand you. You want to live at home while you play with your girlfriend?"

Preston sighed. "I don't want to be with her."

"Does she know that?"

"Not yet. But I've been thinking about it."

"Did you have plans with her?"

"She wanted me to move in with her, but I didn't want to leave you. That became an issue. She was angry with me. I'm just so confused. It's a huge mess and I need to figure it out. But I know I don't want to leave you and the kids. I'm not going to be that kind of person."

Kat planted her face in her palms and groaned. "I don't know what to tell you, Preston. I can't live with a liar. My trust in you is so damaged. I just don't know. I need time to think. For the kids sake, come home tonight, but I need to think." They sat in silence for a few seconds, overwhelmed by the reality of their circumstances. "I wish I was enough for you."

"You are more than enough, Kat."

"Obviously not. I'm beginning to think it's impossible for men to be monogamous. All of these Christian books and marriage conferences...it's such a farce. Here I was being the perfect, little Christian wife with the perfect Christian husband, perfect kids, perfect house, with the church life...all perfectly packaged. Proper and neat. 'Look at us, aren't we perfect?' It's all so laughable. Wasn't it just last year we went to that marriage conference and did the whole corporate vow renewal thing? So freaking laughable! It's like we're all fooling ourselves, trying to create a perfect bubble for everyone to live in with the hopes that it will attract the rest of the world into our pretend world...until they see how screwed up we are, and then they bail. It's such a farce. And then they call us hypocrites. Well, I guess they're right. Because right now, I'm not sure what I believe."

"It's not a farce, Kat. It's real. And it's good."

"Ha! Really, Preston? It did us a lot of good, didn't it? You know what makes this even more ironic? I'm supposed to write an article for our church's next newsletter. What am I supposed to write about? "How to Hire a Private Investigator to Find Your

Husband's Mistress?" Or how about "How to Be a Dumb, Naive Bride?" I'm sure everyone will need to know those things."

Kat stood up and punched her fist into the night sky. "And I'd like to know, where were YOU! While I was taking care of my home and kids, and teaching Bible study, talking about how good You are, where were You?" Preston's gut wrenched as he watched his wife lash out at the God she loved. "Were You out amusing Yourself…watching over my husband while he made out with another woman? What kind of God does that? Why didn't You intervene? Where were You?" Her voice echoed against the church walls.

Preston stood up and grabbed her shoulders. "Kat, stop it." She turned and slapped his face once again. As he reached up to block her, she jabbed her knee into his crotch. Preston doubled over. Kat yelled, "God is not a man that He should lie. But why doesn't He keep men from lying and hurting people? Why doesn't He care enough? Because maybe none of us are good enough or really worth loving?"

Her own words grieved her heart, yet anger, doubt and fear rose inside. She began running down the sidewalk and could faintly hear Preston calling her name. The emotional pain was eating her alive and she had to try to get away from it before it consumed her. Tears flowed again. "Is this how it ends, God? Is this what You're going to allow?" Deep inside of her heart, she heard a small voice, "I won't leave you."

Kat collapsed on the ground, scraping her knees and hands. For all she cared, she could smash her head into the pavement to end the pain. "Kat! Kat!" Preston placed his hands on her back. He began to sob as he laid himself across her back. "Kat, I'm so sorry. I love you."

## Chapter Twelve

Springtime in Holly meant pink, purple, and white crape myrtles in bloom along Main Street, and beautiful roses in pampered yards. Several years ago, the planting of trees and flowering bushes was part of the Mayor's beautification campaign. People from the city took leisurely drives into Holly to take pictures, visit the cafe and browse through the shops. Pottery, jewelry, quilts, secondhand clothing, and the local bakery made for a pleasant outing.

Dylan finished the final touches on his eleventh painting. This particular canvas was destined to sit on the mantle of the fireplace. Dylan wanted it to be the focal point. It displayed the back of a bride with a long, flowing, white train, detailed with diamonds, walking down an aisle of crystal-clear water. The water flowed into an altar. Next to it was the outline of a groom. The picture featured grand pillars in the background, lit by shafts of light that emerged through clouds in a blue sky. Written at the top was, *The Spirit and the Bride say Come.*

Mary Elliott was very impressed with Dylan's ability to paint. "Are you sure you've never done this before?" she had asked. Dylan felt great pleasure in his newly discovered ability.

As he stood on a stool to place the nail in the wall above the fireplace, he heard a man's voice, "I will reveal Myself to you." Dylan jerked in shock. "What?" No one was there. The words rang in his spirit with a tangible power that flooded his heart with life. Hope. It was something he hadn't felt in a long time. Dylan stared wide-eyed into the air, "Thank You, Lord. I know it's You." He climbed down from the stool and knelt on his knees, bowing his head. "Thank You, God. Thank You for not abandoning me. Thank You for watching over Lynette and directing her path toward You." His soul was refreshed.

After a few minutes, Dylan retrieved the letter he was writing to Lynette. Since she left, he committed himself to write her letters everyday, hoping she would someday read them and hear all the things he longed to tell her. Every night, he made his way to the front porch. He walked down the steps and turned to his right, and ducked underneath the crape myrtle tree that grew against the edge of the porch. He knelt on the ground and prayed, "Father, please bring Lynette to our Dream Door. Let her find these letters."

Dylan reached behind their special yellow rose bush and opened the small, antique, bronze door that opened underneath the front porch. When they purchased the house several years before, they found a note behind the door, dated in 1934, that told of a love story that took place in the home. *Dreams do Come True* was carved into the bronze door. Dylan and Lynette decided to place sentimental pieces of their lives and notes about their future dreams inside their "Dream Door." The last item Lynette placed behind it was a pair of baby booties.

Dylan wondered what Lynette was doing at that moment. He hoped she might be thinking of him. His mind was suddenly pierced with an image of Lynette and Owen in each other's arms. His gut wrenched. Dylan found his ability to function depended on him reigning in the negative thoughts that would bombard his mind at the most unexpected moments. Sometimes, he could have sworn the devil was pouring a bucket of wicked visions into his head. His imagination was often his greatest enemy.

After Lynette left him, he found himself nearly destroyed by triggers that released an avalanche of traumatic thoughts and memories, reliving the moment of discovery, and replaying the words that were exchanged between them. A counselor instructed him to allow those negative thoughts to lead him to something positive that had come out of the situation. It was difficult at first, but he was becoming a master at redirecting his thoughts. At least, some of the time.

"Take every thought captive." Dylan spoke it out loud to himself as a reminder. He refused to be held captive by his imagination. In his weaker moments, he could only muster up the strength to tell his thoughts to go to hell where they belonged. When that didn't work, he would cry out, "I'm taking you captive! I'm turning you over to God. Submit to Him." In the last few months, out of desperation, he read multitudes of books about forgiveness and recovery from the trauma of infidelity. His heart would rise with hope and freedom, only to plummet once again into the hell that his life had become. At times, he wasn't sure he'd ever be whole again.

As Dylan entered his house, there was a knock on the door. He turned to open it. "Oh, hey Preston. How are you?"

"I'm sorry to bother you." Preston sighed. "Kat and I are having a really bad night. I needed to take a drive…get out and think, and you came to mind."

Dylan was happy to have company. Jackson would visit occasionally, but most of his time was being spent with Lucy, which thrilled Dylan. It was refreshing to see young love blooming, even though it made him long to go back in time and start all over with Lynette. He often thought how unfair it was that people had to do life without the 20/20 hindsight that presented itself at the most inopportune time. That was the tricky thing about hindsight. It came after it was too late and the damage was already done.

"Come on in, Preston. Would you like some tea or juice? I've got several juices. Pineapple, orange, apple. Springtime gets me in the mood for fruit, I guess."

Preston smiled. "Sure. I'd love some iced tea, actually. Thanks for giving me a few minutes. I don't want to take up much of your time."

Dylan laughed. "Time? I've got all the time in the world. It's the weekend. I'm in Holly, and I have nothing to do but paint."

Preston sat on the edge of the sofa and twirled his thumbs. "I texted Kat to tell her I'm in Holly to see you. After what I did, it's hard for her to trust me. Would you mind doing me a huge favor?"

"What's that?" Dylan asked.

"Could you call or text her to let her know I'm at your house? I don't want her worrying that I might be somewhere else."

"No problem. I'd be glad to. I think a phone call would be best." Dylan handed a glass of tea to Preston. He picked up his phone and dialed Kat's number. "Hi, Kat. This is Dylan. I wanted to let you know that Preston is at my house. We're going to visit for a little while and then he'll be back home. Okay. No problem. I'm praying for you two." Dylan hung up the phone.

"So what's going on tonight, buddy?"

Preston shook his head. "Sometimes I'm afraid we're not going to make it. We make progress but then Kat gets hit with doubt and she starts pulling away. She gets like this every now and then, but usually after a couple of days, she feels hopeful again. She's really pulled away from church. She says it's all too familiar...and she feels like a fool when she's there. I guess because I was...you know...while she was at church. So, she says she feels like church brings back bad memories. As for me, I want to go. I need it."

Dylan nodded. "It's only been a little over a month, you know? It's normal for her to feel those things. I think you guys are doing pretty good considering the situation. Your home is intact. You're there for your kids. Are you treating Kat well?"

"I'm doing my best. I don't want to lose her. Everyday, it's like I'm waking up a little more. I can see more clearly, and honestly, I don't know where the heck my head was before. I feel like that person wasn't even me. I still can't believe Kat let me stay. I hope she won't change her mind, but I couldn't blame her if she did."

"Just give it more time. You guys have a lot of healing to do, but I know it's possible. Stay the course. You're one lucky man to still have your wife and kids. I wish I was lucky enough to have Lynette here with me."

"I'm sorry, Dylan. I really don't want to stir things up for you." Preston looked a bit ashamed.

"No, no. Not at all, man. I'm glad to be here for you. I mean, I'm kind of screwed up, too, so I don't know how much help I am." He chuckled. "I'm glad you came to me. And you, know, I probably never said this before…but I want to apologize for my self-righteous attitude back when I approached you in the cafe. I just didn't want to see a marriage destroyed."

"Dylan, you have nothing to apologize for. If I had listened to you that day, I wouldn't be in this mess. You're a good man." The two men exchanged smiles.

"Preston, you're a good man, too." Preston dropped his head, looking at the floor. His lip began to quiver.

Dylan continued. "I know you don't see yourself as a good man, but you are. You chose your wife and kids. You stopped the affair. When it comes down to it, there's goodness in your heart. That's who you really are."

"Thank you, Dylan. I just hope I didn't learn too late."

"As long as there's grace, it's never too late. Grace changes everything. It empowers people to be who they really are. We were made for righteousness. I think it's because God wants us to have true joy. Have you ever heard the scripture that says it's the kindness of God that leads us to repentance?"

Preston looked inquisitive. "No. That sounds opposite of what I've heard and seen most of my life. That's actually why I hated church for so long. All the judgment, rules and restrictions. It wasn't the rules and restrictions that bothered me. I don't have a problem with doing what pleases God. It was the self-righteous, condemning attitudes of people. You know, like those people that stand on street corners, holding signs telling people God hates them? How could that possibly make people want to know God? It only made me want to run from Him. And some of those marriage conferences Kat and I went to…there was so much pressure to be the perfect husband. I couldn't take the pressure anymore, and started to implode. I can't believe I was so stupid."

"You're not stupid. And speaking of self-righteous people, I was more self-righteous than I thought I was. This whole experience is changing me. A lot. I often feel like a pompous butt when I think back over my time in ministry."

Preston smiled and chuckled at Dylan. "Pastor Pompous Butt. That name has a nice ring to it." The two laughed.

"Honestly, I don't think I'll ever wear the title 'pastor' again."

"Oh, Dylan. Man, I know you feel that way right now, but I think it's what you were born to do. Don't throw that possibility out the window. You're a great pastor."

Dylan nodded his head. "Pastor. I haven't been called that in awhile, and I'm glad. It's actually refreshing not to be a pastor. I get nauseated when I think of the weight that comes with that title. I definitely needed a break. Just wish it wasn't under these circumstances."

"I know you don't want to be in 'pastor mode,' but I'd like some advice. What do I need to do right now to repair my relationship with Kat?"

"Seriously, Preston. I think the best thing you can do is honesty, honesty, honesty. I've heard it said that a person is only as sick as their secrets. And I think it's true. Lay it all out on the table. Repairing the damage is going to take a lot of time, I'm sure. Don't be in such a hurry. Just flow with it. I wish Lynette had been honest with me, no matter how much it might have hurt."

Preston nodded in agreement. "My secrets definitely kept me sick. It's so weird. I was determined to keep the secret, but once it all came out, even though I felt horrible, I felt like a boulder was lifted off of me. Carrying that load literally took a toll on my body."

"The Bible says that confession is good for the soul. What your soul is experiencing is reflected in your body."

Preston raised his eyebrows. "I guess it turns out that old book might be right. Things that I despised were right all along. You know, I was thinking on the way over here tonight about how our paths crossed. The business brought me to Holly and there you were in the cafe. You met me while I was at my lowest point. When Kat started going to Perry's Gym a month ago, she met you, but had no idea you had been a pastor in Holly. She didn't know that I'd met you. It blows my mind how this whole circle came together. It's like God had already planned my rescue. It just blows my mind." Preston's eyes moistened. "I still think about how kind you were to me when you confronted me." Tears rolled down his cheeks.

"God's pretty good at that mercy thing." Dylan chuckled. "I'm still waiting to see how my story's going to turn out. It's hard...the waiting. I try to distract myself with my job. That's all I do. The gym, and then painting on the weekends. It's my therapy."

"I kinda worry about you coming here on weekends. Do you ever feel like you should just stay in Marshall City to get away from it all?" Preston gulped his iced tea.

"People ask me that all the time. Understandably. But this is home for me. Holly was a new chapter in life for me and Lynette. Our dream house and thoughts of a future, you know? And I'm just not ready to let go of that. The story can't end this way." Dylan looked at the floor. "It just can't."

Preston decided to change the subject. "So, what painting are you working on right now?"

Dylan stood. "Come to the bedroom. My painting corner is in there. I just started this one."

"Dude, you keep this place meticulously clean. I'm…kinda scared, but impressed." Preston snickered. "It's almost frightening."

Dylan chuckled. "Frightening, huh? Well, I wasn't like this before. It's just that I have nothing else to do. No one else to focus on."

As they entered the bedroom, Preston gasped when he noticed the beautiful paintings. One stood on the easel and there were eight hanging on the walls. "Did you do all of these?"

"Sure did. I can't believe it myself." Dylan smiled as he looked at his own work. "I never painted in my life, or even drawn a stick figure. I had no idea I was able to do this."

Preston shook his head in disbelief. "That's insane. What inspired you to start?"

"A couple of things. Lynette asked me several times to take an art class with her. I was always too busy. I regret that now. The other thing that inspired me…I know it sounds weird, but it was a series of dreams I've been having. I see canvasses a lot. I get what you might call 'visions.' I felt like God was trying to tell me something. Either that, or I'm going insane," he laughed.

"You're not insane. This is amazing." Preston studied each one.

One painting featured a brilliant blue, glass bottle of red wine being poured into a silver basin. The red wine splashed into the basin and it shimmered with silver and gold. The basin sat on top of a square, wooden table in a vineyard setting. Along the stream of wine, words were painted in silver: *Your love is better than wine*.

The second painting was a beautifully dark, wintry forest that was conjoined with a colorful, spring-like scene. The contrast between dead, scraggly trees that stood in the snow, and the crystal river that divided it from bright, sunlit gardens and sparkling waters was captivating. Written in the river, the words: *Arise, my darling, for the winter is past.*

"Oh, my God. These are incredible, Dylan." Preston continued studying each scene.

The third was a basic outline of a woman's face whose lips were partially opened. The face was black and white, yet the lips were painted a soft red. Golden honey dripped from her lips, mingled with a white, milky substance. "Wow. This one is, uh…slightly erotic, maybe? Beautifully done. But a bit edgy for a pastor." Preston chuckled.

Dylan grinned. "See the words across the bottom? It's actually from the Song of Solomon in the Bible." Dylan pointed to the small lettering along the bottom of the canvas. He read it out loud: "Your lips, my bride, drip honey. Honey and milk are under your tongue."

Preston stood with his mouth open. "No way! I didn't know the Bible was so sensual."

"Well, who do you think created sex, Preston?"

"I never thought of it that way. Wow. I suppose He did!" Preston blinked his eyes at the sudden revelation. He grew up thinking of sex as something slightly dirty and only carnal. He'd never given thought to its origins or the spiritual aspects of physical intimacy. "My mind is being blown again." *Did they ever teach this in those marriage seminars?*

He moved to the fourth painting. A simple painting of a heart against a gray background. Dylan used red wax to create a seal, noble in appearance, and pressed it into the center of the heart. On the seal, he had carved into the wax a sleek letter 'D.' Leaning against the heart, he painted a ladder. "Dylan, what's the meaning of this one?" Preston was intrigued.

"It's another Song of Solomon verse that inspired me. The verse says, 'Set me as a seal upon your heart.' I inscribed my initial on the wax seal. The ladder represents Jacob's ladder where angels ascend and descend. I liked the idea of angels tending to Lynette's heart."

"Dude, I had no idea you were so deep."

"Honestly, I didn't know I was, either." Dylan grinned. "I can't explain it, but it's almost like I was shaken awake by everything that happened, and suddenly there are parts of myself that I never knew existed. I guess tragedy and trial has a way of bringing stuff out of us, both good and bad."

Dylan pointed to the paintings on the other side of the room. "These are the ones I started out with. Those are mainly nature scenes that Mrs. Elliott helped me practice with. They're actually a mess because I painted over those canvasses a couple of times. Did you see the one in the living room that I was about to hang?"

"No."

"Come check it out." Dylan led him back to the living room. "This one will go over the fireplace. It's my favorite so far."

Preston read the inscription out loud: "The Spirit and the Bride say come."

Dylan explained, "It's from the book of Revelation, but it carries a couple of meanings for me. Maybe I can tell you about it another time. I'm still pondering the whole thought."

Preston touched the sparkling diamonds on the bride's train. "Are these rhinestones?"

"Nope. The real deal. My grandmother used to be in the diamond business. She was a jeweler. These diamonds were divided among her grandkids in her will. I wanted to use them for the bride's train in this painting. And see, here? I put a few on the veil as well."

"Real diamonds? You'd better insure this painting. This is a valuable piece of work. That's wildly gorgeous. How you achieved that almost translucent look on the veil…it's incredible."

"Thanks, man. That means a lot."

"Thank you for your time tonight." Preston glanced at his watch. "I think I'd better get back to Kat. I don't want to be gone too long. Thank you for everything. This did my heart good." Preston hugged Dylan.

"Mine, too. I'm glad you came by. And, hey…my advice? You should join Perry's Gym and start coming with Kat."

"I thought about it, but I wanted to give her some space. It's kind of her alone time."

"Yeah, but she's probably felt alone for far too long. Maybe it's time to start going with her. You two have to learn to be a team again."

"Good point. Thanks, man."

## Chapter Thirteen

Old lady Emma Gray prided herself in her speculations and knowledge of the lives of Holly's people. "That man comes scootin' into town every weekend and does the same song and dance. I see him pull up in his driveway on Fridays, usually around seven o'clock in the evening. He gets out of his car, goes around to the side of the house and hunkers down beside the crape myrtle there. I can never quite tell what he's doing. Then he goes inside. Odd character. But I guess when your wife dumps you and you lose your church, you're bound to be odd."

Emma Gray enjoyed keeping tabs on her neighbors. She'd sit on her front porch in her rocking chair with a notebook and pen. She took great pleasure in recording the events that occurred on her street. It gave her something to talk about with her kids when they came to visit.

"And that Jackson Sawyer. What a handsome young man. He writes for the Holly Herald, you know? He lives next door to me."

Beverly answered, "I know, Miss Emma. He's a good writer, too. I sure loved his article he wrote about Pastor Vanberg. I'll never forget that. It was like a turning point for our community. Something special happened."

Beverly Watkins looked forward to her weekly visit to the cafe with Emma. Much of the community knew Miss Emma as 'Eeyore.' Her rough upbringing left a bitter taste in her mouth, and when adult life greeted her with more trials, she lost sight of goodness. Then entered Beverly, like the sunshine.

Emma sighed. "I suppose. Don't know what was so special about the article, other than him singing the praises of Dylan. I'll tell you, I saw that Lynette woman in here awhile back and I knew when I saw her…I knew she was trouble. Unfortunately, men have never been very smart when it comes to picking a woman. They're too enamored with the body. Boobs and butts. How someone can be obsessed with mounds of fat…"

"Miss Emma!" Beverly laughed. "Oh my gosh! Maybe for some, but I know lots of men who are **not** like that."

"Well, you haven't lived as long as I have, so you just haven't seen it yet."

Beverly made it her personal mission to pull the gold to the surface in Emma Gray. She was determined to find some redemptive quality in the old woman.

"So, tell me about some of your good memories. Do you have some memories that really stand out to you? Any highlights of life?" Beverly picked up her coffee mug as she leaned her elbows on the table.

Emma took another bite of soup and then laid down her spoon. Leaning back into her seat, she thought for a moment. "I suppose I have highlights. But they were always taken away."

Beverly leaned in. "Do you think it's possible to not allow them to be erased?"

Emma rolled her eyes. "Perhaps. But how to accomplish that is beyond me."

"Emma, what if the ability to accomplish that is within you?"

"Beverly, that's the thing with some of you younger generation. You're all into that hoodoo voodoo, New Age stuff. I don't have the time or energy to mess with that."

Beverly laughed. "Firstly, I am fifty-five years old. I wouldn't exactly call that the younger generation, but thanks for that. Secondly, I'm not into hoodoo voodoo and whatever you call it. I'm into God's thoughts. The mind of Christ. And I believe He gave us the ability to think as He does. And I believe that no one, no enemy has the power to take away the good that happened in your life."

"That's enough of that talk, Beverly. I'm still thinking about my handsome neighbor. That young Jackson Sawyer. He came out in the front yard yesterday to get his paper, and he was shirtless! I haven't seen muscles like that in ages. Now, that's what I want to talk about."

Beverly nearly spit out her coffee. "Emma Gray! I don't know what I'm going to do with you! But I can't say I blame you." She laughed.

The door chime rang, and as everyone always did at Annie's Café, they turned to see who entered. Jackson Sawyer.

"Well, there's your man, now." Beverly giggled.

Lucy ran toward him and threw her arms in the air. "Jackson! I'm so glad you're here." They hugged. Lucy curtsied before him and with an English accent, asked, "How may I serve you, my lord?"

Jackson shook his head. "That's one of the things I love about you."

She tilted her head to the side. "That I call you 'lord?'"

"No!" He laughed. "I love that you're so stinkin' funny."

"Funny, huh? You ain't seen nothin' yet." Lucy threw her hands over her mouth. "Oh, shoot. I shouldn't have said that. I don't want to scare you away."

Jackson smiled. "Lucinda Flowers, there's no possible way you could scare me away. I quite adore you."

She grinned. "Upon hearing such great news, sir, we must celebrate. Please have a seat at this table and I'll bring you something to feast on."

Old lady Emma rolled her eyes. "Good grief! It's sickening, isn't it? Those two giddy goofballs."

Beverly smiled. "On the contrary, I find it to be delightful. And a happy newspaper reporter makes a better reporter than a depressed one. He has the power to set the tone of this town."

"There you go again, Beverly...'he has the power' thing. You're really into humanity having the power to change communities, aren't you?" Emma smiled at her. "You and your optimistic self."

"Yes, I am. Our words have the power of life and death in them. I always try to be conscious of how I'm affecting the people around me. You should try it sometime, Miss Emma."

"Don't get sassy with me, Bev. I'm surprised you hang around me. It's my nature to spew death." Emma laughed at herself.

Beverly grinned and shook her head. "One of these days, Emma. You're going to find yourself so overcome with joy. You just wait." Beverly winked.

Lucy sat down across from Jackson. "Arnold said I can take a fifteen-minute break so we can chat."

Jackson reached for her hand. "That's the best news I've heard all day."

Lucy squeezed his hand. "That's sayin' a lot, being a news reporter and all. I hope you've heard some other good news today."

"I wish I could say that." Sadness washed over Jackson's face.

"What's wrong, Jackson?"

"I was at the print shop and Mr. Sanders mentioned that he was working on Lynette's wedding invitations. She's marrying Owen. I know Dylan hasn't heard yet, because he would have called me if he had."

"Oh, my gosh! That's so sad." Lucy sat back in her chair. "Poor Dylan. He's still hoping she'll come back home. That's just awful."

"I don't understand why the guy can't catch a break between losing his wife and the church. He keeps coming home on weekends, hoping to find Lynette there. I know he does. I see it on his face. Every time he arrives and she's not there, I see the devastation on his face. I worry about how long he'll be able to endure that disappointment. I kinda thought she might come back, but she isn't."

Lucy wondered, "So, who are they inviting? I mean, it's not like church members are going to attend their wedding." She grimaced.

"Mr. Sanders said it appears to be a small, family event. They're getting married on Owen's ranch, where they've been living. It's about 10 miles outside of town."

"Oh, Dylan. God help Dylan." Lucy shook her head.

Jackson sighed. "I'm afraid I'll end up being the one to tell him. Do you think I should go to Marshall City and tell him, or wait until he comes to Holly this weekend? I can't bear the thought of him finding out when he's all alone. I'd like to be there for him."

"Wow, Jackson. I don't know. Let's think about it for awhile."

"On another note, can we go out again tonight?" He took her hand.

"I would be delighted. Absolutely." Jackson took note of the sunlight hitting her eyes.

"I know this sounds cheesy, but I'm swimming in your eyes, Lucy. The deepest, brilliant blue pools…they pull me in and it feels amazing."

She smiled.

"It's like pools of grace. I can't believe I get to be with you."
Jackson smiled.

"I'm the one who's lucky," she said. "Growing up in this
town, I never felt drawn to anyone. I didn't think I'd find love
here, but sure enough. Funny thing is that I got to serve you
many times before I really got to know you. I think that's a good
way to start. Servanthood."

Jackson laughed. "That could sound bad if taken the wrong
way. You're the one that deserves to be served and taken care
of."

Emma looked over at the two and blurted out, "All right, you
guys. Cut it out. If I wanted to watch all that sappy love stuff, I'd
be at home watching the Hallmark Channel. You'd better give an
old, lonely lady a break!"

Jackson was used to Emma poking her nose in his business.
"Now, now, Miss Emma. Calm down."

The door chime announced another arrival. Elder David
stormed in, his eyes searched the room and landed on Jackson.
He quickly headed straight to his table. "Jackson, I need to speak
with you right away."

"Sure, pull up a chair." Jackson tried to be cordial. He was
still offended by David's treatment of Dylan.

David seemed unaware of Lucy's presence. Frantically, he
spilled his news to Jackson. "You must do something. I need you
to write an article for the next paper. I don't know if you heard
or not, but Lynette and Owen are getting married next month.

This looks horrible for the church. How she could go from co-leading our congregation to acting like a whore...and now this! It only stirs up more gossip and opens up the wounds that we've been trying to heal at Hope Fellowship. Jackson, we need to make sure this is handled with care before some news reporter butts in and destroys everything!"

"Don't worry, David. I'll see what I can do. I'll help, but first, I want to know something." Jackson made sure he locked eyes with David. "I'm still not happy with the way Pastor Dylan was treated. He was dumped like a piece of trash. He deserves some honor and respect. The man was faithful to Hope Fellowship...and to his wife. I'd like to see the church restore him, the way they should. Will you and the board do something to make it right?"

With a contrite look on his face, David nodded. Desperate for Jackson's help, he said, "Yes. I can agree to that. I'll talk to the board. But I want to make sure the church isn't impacted negatively by what's written."

"David, what if we don't have to say anything at all? I doubt that Owen and Lynette will be announcing this publicly, so why can't we just leave it alone?"

"Because someone is bound to publish something about it eventually. And I want us to be the first to say something so it's done correctly."

Jackson thought for a moment. "Let's think about this and see what happens as far as public announcements go. I guarantee you I can stay on top of what's being reported. I'll personally speak to the senior editor and make sure that nothing goes in without my knowledge. Agreed?"

David tried to calm himself down. "I suppose you're right. But I know people will start talking and it'll trickle down to the congregation."

"People are always going to talk, whether it's truth or mere rumor. There's nothing you can do about that. In this case, I think being reactionary will only escalate the gossip and rumors."

David looked at the floor. "What you said about Pastor Dylan…I know, and I'm sorry for the way it was handled. Marcy has been onto me about that and she's helped me to see some things differently. I just haven't taken any action to set things right. But I will." He looked up at Jackson.

"Thank you, David. I truly appreciate that."

David stood to leave. "I'd better be going. I have work to tend to."

Lucy sighed. "Well, that was quite interesting."

"Yeah, that's for sure. The news of this wedding is about to explode like wildfire. I think I'd better head to Marshall City tonight and meet with Dylan."

Lucy agreed. "I think you're right. I'll be praying for you guys. I'm so sorry you have to deal with this." They sat silent for a moment. "Isn't it crazy how one person's decision can affect so many people?"

"Yeah. We're all more connected than we know." Jackson stood to leave, and bent over, kissing Lucy on the forehead. "I love you, Lucy."

"I love you, too, Jackson."

As Jackson made his way to the door, Lucy called to him. "Hey, wait."

He turned around. "Yeah?"

Lucy stared at him with deep admiration. "You're a really good friend."

He smiled and winked as he headed out the door.

## Chapter Fourteen

Jackson walked into Perry's Gym, approached the front desk, and rang the bell. He turned his eyes toward the ceiling, casting a hopeful prayer into the atmosphere. *God, help me.*

Dylan came rushing around the corner, barely looking up while wiping his hands on a towel. "How can I help…oh, Jackson! What are you doing here?"

"Hey man. I just thought we could grab some dinner together when you get off work. I wanted to talk with you."

Dylan looked concerned. "Is everything okay?"

Jackson shrugged. "I just need to talk with you."

Dylan nodded. "Give me about fifteen minutes and I can wrap things up here."

"Sure thing." Jackson breathed in deeply as Dylan walked away. *Oh, God. I need you here right now. This won't be easy.* Jackson stepped outside to get some fresh air. As he stood on the sidewalk with his hands in his pockets, he clearly heard a voice inside his head, *I've been here all along.* Jackson's eyes widened and a grin crossed his face. He whispered, "I hear You." *Why do I forget that?*

Peace settled over Jackson's heart. He pondered how most of his life, he worked hard to get to God, to appease Him, and earn His presence. He felt that anytime he made a mistake, God vanished and left him to suffer alone. Going to church only served as a reminder to him that he would never be good enough and would always fail, so he stopped attending except for special occasions and moments when he felt compelled to go. Out of sight. Out of mind. But there was something about hanging out with Dylan Vanberg that drew Jackson to God. And it drew him away from his fear of failure.

"Hey, man. I'm done." Dylan came out, carrying his gym bag. "Where would you like to eat?"

"You know this town better than I do. Is there a quiet place that's somewhat private? I figured we wouldn't have much privacy at your parent's house."

Dylan thought for a moment. "There's a steakhouse about ten minutes away that has semi-private booths. I'm sure they could set us up."

"Sounds good. Give me the address and I'll meet you there."

"Jackson, why don't you just ride with me and I can bring you to your car later?"

"Okay. It's a plan."

The two men hopped into "Old Blue" and headed down the street. Dylan seemed slightly uncomfortable. "Needless to say, my stomach is a bit in knots. It's not like you to drive to the city unannounced and want to talk privately. Can you just tell me straight up? Is this news going to be hard to swallow?"

Jackson sighed, looking out the window. "Yes."

"Okay? I suppose I need to decide right now whether or not I should enjoy a steak dinner or just take the news up front, which would be risking my good appetite." Dylan tried to keep the moment light for as long as possible.

Jackson smiled. "Yes, I suppose you have that decision to make."

Dylan patted his stomach. "I'm hungry. It was a long day. It would be sinful to lose this appetite to bad news. Let's eat first."

"I agree."

"You and Lucy doing well?"

Jackson smiled at the thought of her. "Very well. She's incredible."

"Fill me in on you two. Talk to me."

"It's pretty serious. I know she's the one I want to spend my life with."

"Jackson, that's awesome! I'm so happy for you. When are you planning to do something about that?"

"Lucy loves Christmas time. I'm hoping to propose then, but it depends on money. I'd like to marry her before too long. I don't know if I can hold out for two years." He chuckled.

"Have you guys talked about it?"

"Enough to know that she feels the same way. I'd like to be making more money before we get married, though. If I could move up to full-time or a higher position at the paper, that would be perfect. I don't want her to have to wait tables, especially when we decide to have kids."

"Wow. You really have thought about this. You two couldn't be more perfect for each other."

"Thanks." Jackson smiled. "We've both decided we want you to do our wedding."

"I would be absolutely honored. Guess I'd better try to keep my credentials so it'll be legal." They laughed.

"Yeah. That would be another story for the newspaper. I could write my own article about our scandalous union…the illegal marriage ceremony. Wouldn't that be big news in Holly? 'The Marriage of Jackson and Lucy Sawyer Found to be Invalid Due to Vanberg's Expired Credentials.'"

Dylan chuckled. "Well, if the ministers' fellowship doesn't decide to extend me more grace, that article might have to read 'Due to Revoked Credentials of Local Divorced Minister, Sawyer Marriage Illegal.'" The two men laughed.

"I'm sure your credentials will be just fine when the time comes. A lot can happen in the next couple of years."

Dylan dreamed out loud, "If my dream came true, I'd be remarried to Lynette by then. I know it sounds ridiculous, being that our divorce was final a couple of weeks ago, but I still have hope."

Jackson's stomach turned. Dread came over him. The idea of telling Dylan that Lynette was getting married made him ill. *Surely Dylan knew she might marry Owen?* "Well, all things are possible, I suppose."

They sat in silence the rest of the way.

"Here we are. Let's dine on some cow."

Jackson and Dylan stumbled through their steak meals with awkward small talk. Jackson tried to hold back the delivery of bad news as long as possible. Dylan sighed. "All right, Jackson. Give it to me."

Jackson wiped his mouth with his napkin and sat up in his chair. "I drove here tonight because I care about you and because I heard some news today that I didn't want you to hear from anyone else." Dylan nodded. "I was in the print shop today and Mr. Sander's mentioned that he was printing wedding invitations for Lynette and Owen."

Dylan sat back in his chair, hands on the table, staring at his plate. Jackson leaned forward. "Dylan, I'm really sorry. The news is getting around and I didn't want you to hear it from someone else. I couldn't bear the thought of you being alone, having to process the news."

"I appreciate that." He shook his head in disbelief. "I just can't believe it. I just can't…" Dylan bit his lip, trying to control the emotions. "Even after our divorce was finalized, I still believed she would come back. I hated signing those papers. I didn't want the divorce, but she did. I just never dreamed that she would actually marry him. I knew Owen well enough to know she wouldn't stay happy with him. I guess that was a wrong judgment."

Dylan motioned for a waiter. "Excuse me, sir. Would you bring me a margarita, please?"

Jackson looked shocked. "Margarita? I didn't know you drank."

"I don't. Never had one in my life." Dylan laughed.

"Look, Dylan. I know this is hard, but please…I can't let you spiral down. I'm sticking with you through this. You're my best friend."

A tear fell down Dylan's cheek. "You've certainly seen me through the worst. But I'm afraid maybe the worst hasn't happened yet. I didn't know this thing could get any darker." He tried to catch his breath to prevent the gush of emotion that threatened his strength.

"Dylan, there's always hope. You taught me that, and I believe it."

"That's what I've always taught people, but right now, I'm not feeling it." He set his face like a rock. "So, when is this wedding happening?"

"Next month, apparently."

"Where?"

"At Owen's ranch."

Dylan rolled his eyes. "How romantic. There's nothing more romantic than a cow pasture filled with dung. I hope Owen falls face first in a cow pie."

The waiter interrupted, "Your margarita, sir."

Immediately, Dylan picked it up and gulped it down. "Dylan! Slow down. That's not how you're supposed to…" Jackson's objection was ignored. "You're supposed to sip it. Not slam the whole thing down at once."

Dylan licked his lips. "That's pretty good stuff."

Jackson stared at his friend, slightly amused, but more concerned. "I'm definitely driving you home tonight. And I hope I don't have to carry you. That was not cool. You're not used to that stuff. At least the glass is small."

"Tell me, Jackson. What does that overweight, long-chinned, chinchilla-lookin' man have that I don't have?" Jackson giggled at Dylan's choice of words. "It makes no sense. And the house that Lynette and I bought...that was her dream house. She's trading it for an old ranch house with decor from 1983, which Lynette hates, and a pen with some goats and pigs. And a man that's divorced because his wife couldn't handle his porn addiction! Does this make any sense?"

"No. Not at all. She's just blind right now." Jackson feared leaving Dylan alone tonight.

"And all of those dreams I've had...I was sure they meant that Lynette was coming back home. I'm such a fool."

"Dylan, you're not a fool. Listen to me." Jackson leaned forward. "Look at me, Dylan. You are not a fool. Lynette is the one being fooled right now."

Dylan's chin quivered. "How can she do this to me? I know my faults, but do I deserve this?"

"Of course not. No one deserves this kind of pain."

"I think God's forgotten about me…or He's just teasing me, leading me along with false hope. I really thought she would come back home."

"Dylan, those paintings you've been doing…they have meaning and they're powerful. I believe you've been inspired by God. You've got to remember the things that God has spoken to you in your heart. I'm no minister and I don't know much about the Bible, but I do know that God is in those paintings and it's not for nothing."

"But she's getting married, Jackson. How did it get to this point? This was never supposed to happen."

Jackson thought for a moment. "I think there are lots of things that aren't supposed to happen, but they do, even to the best of people. But those things don't have the power to take away your hope, and those things don't have to dictate your life or decide your future."

Dylan nodded, "Good word, there. You sure you're not a preacher?"

Jackson mockingly stuck his finger in his mouth and made a gagging sound, "There's no way I'd ever want that job! That's your calling, not mine."

"Yeah, well. Apparently I'm no good at it. I'm not a pastor anymore, and I don't care if I ever am again."

"Dylan, you were the best pastor I've ever known."

"Jackson, do you realize I'm the **only** pastor you've ever known?" They chuckled.

"I'm glad to see you still have a sense of humor." Jackson smiled at him as he pushed a glass of water his way. "You'd better drink this, and it would help if you'd eat something. You're not looking too sober. It's hitting you fast."

"I'm really dizzy. I don't even know if this is real. Surely none of this is real." Dylan grinned. "Why do I feel so warm inside? Is this real, Jackson?"

"I wish it wasn't." Jackson's heart was heavy for his friend. He thought for a moment. "I have an idea. I'm not sure if the gym would allow it or not, but I think you should request a week off next month when this wedding is happening. You need to get away. Go somewhere, maybe as far as Europe. You've been stuck inside this nightmare for months and I think it'd be good to get outside of it as much as possible."

Dylan nodded. "I would love to, but I don't have the finances to pull it off. I'd be doing good to afford a bus ticket across town at this point. I'm barely making my mortgage on the house. The utilities and all the gasoline I burn up going to Holly every weekend, it takes every penny I make."

"Maybe you can reconsider leaving Holly? I hate to even suggest that, because I would miss seeing you there."

Dylan's eyes filled with tears. "No. It's my home. Being in Marshall City, working this job…it all feels foreign to me. I have no purpose here. It's so dumb. I feel purpose when I'm at home in Holly, yet the truth is, I have no purpose there, either. I'm just lost."

"I'm sorry, Dylan. One thing I do know for sure is this will pass. And I know you'll be all right."

Dylan scoffed with a puff of air. "Hmph. I used to tell people that all the time. 'It's going to be all right.' I appreciate you saying that, but I don't see how anything can be okay."

"I know," Jackson replied with defeat.

A familiar voice called out, "Hey, Dylan!"

He looked up with his watery, slightly inebriated eyes and saw Preston and Kat. He tried to muster up a smile. "Preston. Kat. How good to see you."

Preston immediately noticed the slight slur in his speech and the sadness in his eyes. "Hey Dylan. I'm sorry to interrupt. I was just glad to see you."

Jackson interjected, hoping to diffuse an awkward situation. "Hi Preston. I'm Jackson, a friend of Dylan's from Holly." He reached his hand out to greet him.

"Hi. It's nice to meet you. I think I've seen you in the cafe in Holly before. And maybe your picture in the paper?"

"Yes. Jackson Sawyer. Your local newspaper reporter." Jackson grinned, slightly embarrassed at his corny response. "I recall seeing you in Annie's Café."

Preston's stomach lurched. *Oh, God. He saw me with Fay.* "Oh, yeah. The Holly Herald. Of course. Well, I'm glad to meet you. I don't come around Holly much anymore, but I will be soon. I have some business deals in the works."

"Cool. When you're in town, stop by the newspaper office and say hello. I'd be glad to show you around our booming metropolis."

Preston pointed at a table nearby where Kat was sitting, thumbing through the menu. "And that's my beautiful wife, Kat, over there."

Jackson remembered witnessing Preston's dates with Fay in the café. He had heard about the fall out that followed. It made him happy to see that Preston was with his wife.

"You're a lucky man, Preston. She's gorgeous."

"Thanks. I **am** lucky."

Preston leaned towards Dylan. "Hey, man. Are you okay?"

Dylan shook his head. "Not really."

"You have my number. If you need someone to talk to, please let me know. You've been a huge help to me. I'd love to return the favor."

Dylan nodded. "Thank you." He swallowed some water. "Lynette is getting married."

Preston looked surprised. "Oh, man. I'm so sorry. I'm…I don't know what to say."

Dylan took Preston by the hand and looked up at him. "We're all going to survive, right?"

"Of course we will."

Dylan patted Preston's hand for a moment. "Okay, then. If you say so."

Preston was unsure how to respond. "I'm gonna let you guys get back to your dinner. Call me later, Dylan."

"Will do."

Preston returned to his table. Jackson leaned forward and whispered, "I'm sure glad to see he's with his wife. He seems different than he was at the cafe with Fay. He looks more alive. Like he woke up from the dead. There's hope sitting right there, Dylan. Lynette can wake up, too."

"I suppose."

"Now, finish your food and let's get you home. And no more margaritas for you, sir!" Jackson wagged his finger at Dylan.

"If you say so."

## Chapter Fifteen

"Hello, David. This is Jackson Sawyer. Would you have a few minutes to meet this afternoon around three o'clock? At the cafe?" Jackson sat with his feet propped on his desk. "Excellent. I'll see you there."

David hung up the phone. "Who was that?" Marcy asked.

"That newspaper reporter, Jackson Sawyer."

"What did he want?"

"He asked me to meet him this afternoon at three. I'm not sure for what." David walked over to the large bay window in the living room. He peered across the street at Miss Lilly's Floral Shop. As usual, she was outside watering the flowers that seemed to overtake her building. Her philosophy about flowers was painted on her window, *You can never have too many.* From the looks of her shop, it was obvious that she believed it.

David sighed. "I really care about this town. I suppose I haven't shown that in the best way. It's just that...I don't know. I guess I just want everything to be perfect. When we moved here from the city, Holly was like a refuge to me. After the drama with my brother and his drug addiction, and the hell that he put our parents through, all I wanted was to live a peaceful life, free from trouble. Is that too much to ask for?"

Marcy patted him on the back. "I know, honey."

David continued. "I was so happy when we found Hope Fellowship. It was the name that drew me to it. Hope. Twenty years of being in that church…I feel like it's my own child." He turned and looked at Marcy. "And no one wants anything bad to happen to their child." His eyes teared up.

"I know, David. I know." Her eyes moistened. "It's so sad."

"I'm trying hard not to be angry at Lynette and Owen for destroying everything. I understand Owen doing something like this. But, Lynette? I do feel somewhat responsible."

Marcy looked surprised. "Don't be silly. How would you be responsible for her actions?"

"I pushed Dylan really hard. My desire to see the church grow and thrive became a noose around his neck. I felt like he needed more drive and ambition. I took it upon myself to create ideas for programs and ministries within the church and then I'd press it on him." He looked into his wife's eyes. "You know me, Marcy. I tend to get crabby when I don't get my way. I can admit that. For some reason, that young man listened to me. I suppose he was trying to prove himself. He poured every ounce of himself into that congregation." A tear fell down David's cheek and his chin began to shake. "And I didn't realize it until now, but I think I might have destroyed that man."

Marcy reached to hold David's face in her hands. "Oh, David. It's not your fault."

His eyes closed tightly as his shoulders began to shake. "But, Marcy, it is. I've been so cruel to him through the whole process. Part of me blamed him for this happening to the church. And all the while, he was serving the best he knew how."

Marcy wrapped her arms around him. "Sweetheart, I think it's time you meet with Dylan." She lovingly rubbed his back.

He wiped his eyes. "Why can't life just be simple? Here we are in a small town, and the drama still follows."

"Well, David. That's because this town contains what we call 'humans,' and where humans are, there's confusion, misunderstanding, and decisions that cause pain. I wish it wasn't that way, but it is. And that's why grace is necessary." Marcy's gentleness melted his heart. The way she said 'grace' was like a waterfall of goodness to a barren desert. "Don't you blame yourself, honey."

David pulled her tightly to himself.

### At the Print Shop

Lynette stepped into Mr. Sander's print shop dressed in a long, blue and white sundress with white high-heeled sandals and white sunglasses. Mr. Sanders glanced up and caught himself staring for a second. Finally, words surfaced. "Hi, Mrs. Vanberg. Don't you look all dolled up today?"

She removed her sunglasses. "Thank you. I came to pick up the invitations."

"Yes, yes. Let me get those out of the back for you."

Old lady Emma was taking her weekly walk on Main Street in which she would systematically stop in each shop along the way, gathering the latest news of the town. Mr. Sanders always proved to be a great source of information since he did all of the printing for the town of Holly. Emma hobbled as she pulled the door open.

Lynette fought the urge to turn around to see who had arrived. She still felt uncomfortable showing her face in town. Most people were friendly enough toward her, but she definitely had enemies who made it clear that they highly disapproved of her.

Being nosy, Emma stepped to Lynette's side and peered over to identify the mystery guest. "Why, Lynette Vanberg. What brings you in here today?"

The way that Emma said 'Vanberg' made Lynette shudder. She tried to force a smile. "Oh, hello, Miss Emma. How are you doing?"

Emma always had a creative answer: "I'm hanging in there like a peel hangs off a half-eaten banana."

Lynette giggled. "You always have a way with words."

"And I want to know what brings you in here today," Emma pressed.

"I'm picking up some cards." Lynette hoped she wouldn't ask more questions.

"Oh? What kind of cards?

"Invitations." Lynette's jaw tightened.

"Are you having a party?"

"I guess you could say so. Just a small family thing."

Emma nodded, looking suspicious.

Mr. Sanders returned from the back room. "Here you go...your wedding invitations."

"Wedding invitations!" Emma raised her voice. "You didn't wait long after divorcing your heartbroken husband. Hmph." Disgust was written all over Emma's face. "That poor man."

Lynette and Mr. Sanders stood speechless. She began to fumble with the box, trying to open it to view the invitations. She was disconnected from what her hands were doing while she fought back tears of anger and shame.

"Do you know how many women in this world would give their right arm for a husband like Dylan Vanberg?"

Lynette looked at Emma, fighting back tears. "Miss Emma, I know he's a good man. But there are things that no one understands. Would you please mind your own business?"

Mr. Sanders interjected, "Miss Emma, would you please leave her alone? She's my customer and I'd appreciate it if you don't bother my clients."

Emma rolled her eyes. "That's the way of the world. Close your eyes. Close your mouth. We just let the world fall apart while people hurt each other, and no one's supposed to say a dang thing." Emma turned to walk out the door, mumbling mockingly, "He didn't please me, so I'll go get myself a new boyfriend. See how long that lasts."

Lynette wiped a tear from her eye. Her jaw clenched.

"I'm really sorry about that, Lynette." Mr. Sanders placed his hand on her arm.

"It's not your fault. I guess I deserve it, right?"

He shook his head. "Nah. You don't deserve that. Look, I've made decisions in my life that no one understood. Shoot, I'm on my third marriage. I can't judge you. Relationships are difficult. Now, how about you take a look at those invitations and let me know if everything's correct?"

She took a Kleenex from her purse and wiped her nose. "Yes. Give me a minute and I'll look them over."

"So, you're getting married at the ranch? I attended Owen's college graduation party out there years ago. It sure is nice."

She nodded. "Yes. It's lovely. His parents bought it several years ago and passed it on to Owen after they moved into Heartland Senior Living. They enjoy it over there. The ranch was a lot of work for them."

"You said the wedding is a small family event?"

"Some family and a couple of friends. Some family members refuse to come. Too scandalous, I guess." She shrugged.

Mr. Sanders tilted his head, inquisitively. "How are people in town treating you?"

"I avoid coming to town as much as possible. Obviously, you can see why. I go to Marshall City to do most of my business. I don't feel comfortable around Holly anymore." Lynette found herself rambling, flustered by the encounter with Emma. "Most of the businesses here are owned by people we know. I understand that it's difficult for everyone, but I wish they could be more kind. I suppose Owen and I pretty much turned things upside down. Dylan is a good guy, but we grew apart. I couldn't live like that."

"That happens."

She picked up the invitations and began reading over them. "These look great. What's my total?"

"You know what? They're free. I want to do this for you. Consider it a wedding gift."

Lynette was shocked. Her eyes filled with tears again. "I don't know what to say, Mr. Sanders. I can't let you do that."

He smiled. "Oh, yes you can. I insist. I wish you the best of luck."

### At Annie's Cafe

"Hi, Jackson."

"Hey, there. Have a seat." Jackson motioned for David to sit across from him. "Thank you for meeting me today. I wanted to discuss a proposal of sorts."

"Okay. First, I have something I'd like to tell you, and then we can get into that."

"All right. I'm listening." Jackson sat back in his chair and placed his hands on the table. He braced himself for the possibility that David might say something rude or disrespectful about Dylan. If that happened, he wasn't sure he would be able to control himself.

David folded his hands in his lap and looked down at the table. "I've been wrong. Very wrong. I want to apologize to you for the way I've treated Dylan. I recently realized how I've added to his pain and how I might have played a part in keeping him too busy to tend to his marriage. I owe him a huge apology. I'm so sorry for the way I've acted, Jackson. I intend to do everything I can to make this right."

Jackson leaned forward, appearing deeply moved. "David, I'm dumbfounded. I honestly wouldn't have expected this. Wow." Jackson stood up and walked over to David with his arms open. "Can I give you a hug?"

David smiled as he stood. As they embraced, David shed a tear. "You're such a good friend to Dylan. I'm thankful that God sent you to him." Jackson beamed.

"So, what is this proposal of sorts?" David asked.

"I drove to Marshall City to be with Dylan last night, to tell him about Lynette's upcoming wedding. I realized the news was getting around quickly and I didn't want him to hear it from someone else."

Sadness washed over David's face. "How did he take it?"

"Really hard. He's deeply hurt. Dylan fully believed that she would come back home, so he's pretty shocked. I'm worried about him. He knows the wedding is next month, so I suggested that he try to get off work and take a trip during that time. The problem is he has no money. He works that job at the gym just to pay his mortgage and utilities. By the time he spends money on gas to come to Holly every weekend, there's nothing left."

David shook his head. "I'm surprised he holds on to his house here."

"Yeah. He says he won't leave. It's his home. Apparently it was Lynette's dream house."

David's heart had never felt so heavy for Dylan. "I'm going to make this right. The way I handled his departure from the church was so unChrist-like. I want to do everything I can to repair the damage I've caused. I'll go to the board and talk to them. I'll make sure we get the money to send Dylan somewhere and I'll see if we can drum up some extra support to help him with his mortgage."

Jackson's face glowed. "Oh, my gosh! Thank you so much! Thank you. I know this will mean the world to him."

David smiled. A million pounds lifted off his chest. Something about acting kindly brought him unexpected joy. "Is there any chance you might attend Hope Fellowship anytime soon? We'd love to see you there. I feel like your insight would be helpful in selecting a new pastor. We're having some candidates come in soon to preach and be interviewed."

"I'd be glad to visit sometimes, David, but I'm just not ready to commit to the church. I don't know how that would be for Dylan, you know? He still misses it. I feel that might cause him more pain."

David looked surprised. "I hadn't considered that. I guess that could be awkward."

"Thanks for asking, though. I'd be glad to help in anyway I can."

David patted him on the shoulder. "Jackson, you're a fine young man. You've been a tremendous help to this community and to Dylan. The way you've handled situations when it comes to your articles amazes me. The way you've matured and been such a picture of grace to all of us...I can't thank you enough."

"Thank you, sir."

## Chapter Sixteen

Dylan placed his carry-on in the overhead compartment of the plane. He took his seat and fumbled with the seatbelt, feeling like a kid going to camp for the first time. He was excited about seeing Rome, but he hadn't flown on an airplane since he was a kid. He and Lynette often talked about flying to an exotic location together, but they became consumed with ministry at home instead.

The thought of a ten-and-a-half hour flight made his gut clench, but he figured he had nothing to lose. He comforted himself with the idea that whether or not the plane crashed, he'd be arriving at a really cool destination. He hoped if that destination was Italy, it would somehow, magically erase his pain. He knew that if he ended up dying in a crash instead, he'd be free from all torment. *It's a win-win*, he thought to himself.

Dylan closed his eyes and quietly began a monologue with God in his head. *Well, here we go. You're with me, right? I know You are, but I thought I'd ask anyway. I hope this trip is a good one. You'll have to help me because I have no idea what I'm doing. I hear You're pretty involved over there in Italy. I mean, Vatican City is there, so I'm guessing You've been busy speaking to the Pope? Now that I think about it, the Pope doesn't marry, so I think You should probably be speaking more to the married people because a lot of us are pretty screwed up.* He grinned at the silent speech he was giving God.

*Forgive me, Lord, for my sarcastic attitude. I know You understand that I'm going through a hard time.*

A voice echoed in his core. "My grace is sufficient."

*Okay. Help me to understand what exactly that means.*

"My love is enough."

*Then why do I hurt so deeply? It's like death to my soul.*

"Nothing can separate you from My love. As long as you and I are one, there is plenty for you. All you ever need is found in Me."

*Then please give me the eyes to see this. I've always loved You. I've always felt like You were there with me, but this rejection from Lynette…the fact that she chose someone else makes me feel like trash. I can't value myself when the one I love throws me away.*

"I know, My son. I was rejected, too. But your value is not found in another."

*But You're God. Nothing can take away Your ability to love. And, Lord, I wish I could forgive the way You do. That forgive and forget thing… 'I will remember your sins no more…I've cast your sins as far as the east is from the west.' How do You do that, God? I need that. If I can't get that, I just might die.*

"You will live."

*But I don't want to live without her.* A tear pushed its way between the slit in his eye.

"You are still one."

*What? You've got to be kidding. She divorced me and is marrying another man. She broke our oneness.*

"All of My children are one. They just don't know it yet."

*Oh, great. So, I'm one with Owen, too? That's disgusting. I can't accept that. Oh, I forgot, he's not Your child.*

Silence.

The sound of the plane's engines lulled him into another realm. Dylan fell into a deep, deep sleep.

A massive canvas stood in the middle of a forest clearing. Shafts of light pressed their way through the tall pines and doused the forest floor. A majestic lion paced slowly, toward the canvas. His mane swished back and forth with each step. He stopped and stood still, staring at the canvas. The wind tussled his mane. His eyes caught a glint of the sun's rays and flashed golden. The lion stepped forward, eyeing the canvass.

Suddenly, a gust of wind swept through the forest, stirring up the leaves, throwing them into the air like rockets charging into the sky. The lion opened his mouth as if to devour the canvas, but he let out a powerful roar instead, blasting the canvas with his breath. The lion shouted, "Awaken!"

Dylan squinted his eyes, attempting to see what was on the canvas. His view was hazy but it appeared to be hearts that were randomly scattered across the canvas. Interspersed between the hearts, he saw hands, legs, arms and many faces of men, women and children. At the bottom of the painting was a river of blood. *This is morbid*, he thought to himself.

The lion stepped away from the painting and disappeared into the forest. Dylan stepped forward, making his way toward the piece of art. Written in the river of blood was a saying.

*You were called to freedom, brethren; only do not turn your freedom into an opportunity for the flesh, but through love serve one another. For the whole Law is fulfilled in one word, in the statement, YOU SHALL LOVE YOUR NEIGHBOR AS YOURSELF. But if you bite and devour one another, take care that you are not consumed by one another.*

Dylan spoke out loud to himself. "I know this. I think it's from the book of Galatians." He turned his eyes to the forest, seeking the lion, but instead, he saw that he was surrounded by various creatures. Panthers, beavers, birds, bears, leopards, foxes, cougars, rabbits and more. Dylan was overwhelmed by the variety of creatures. Every one of them stood still, watching him. The forest was completely silent.

A gentle whisper of wind swept past his ear. "They long for the revealing of the sons of God." Another voice whisked past his ears. "John seventeen."

As quickly as the dream came, it was sucked away in an instant. Dylan jerked awake. The sound of the plane engines reminded him where he was. He stretched and yawned. He bent over to grab his Bible from his backpack, repeating to himself, "John 17...John 17." As he turned to the book of John, he happened to open to the seventeenth chapter and immediately, his eyes fell upon verses 22-23.

*The glory which You have given Me I have given to them, that they may be one, just as We are one; I in them and You in Me, that they may be perfected in unity, so that the world may know that You sent Me, and loved them, even as You have loved Me.*

Dylan mouthed the words as he read, "…so that the world may know that You sent Me, and loved them…" He read the verses several times. *So without being perfected in unity, the world won't know…*

He remembered what God said. "All of My children are one." Dylan recalled his response to those words. *So, I'm one with Owen? I cannot accept that.* Every cell in his body was vibrating as he considered the fact that he was connected in spirit with the man who seduced his wife. *No. How can that be?* He wanted to scream in protest, yet he knew it was true. He had no right to say who was or wasn't God's child. How could he be connected to someone so vile and lost?

Owen professed to be a Christian. Though he struggled with his own issues and darkness, deep down, he held a belief in God. Owen's life had been a constant struggle of trying to measure up, trying to get close to God. When he fell, he fell hard and he'd come to Dylan for help. Dylan empowered Owen with every tool and prayer that he knew to give. Owen always saw himself as smart, but inferior. Sometimes he relished in his own filth, but there were moments when his spirit and soul would collapse in surrender to God and he would beg to be clean. Dylan watched Owen cry several times as he shook under the weight of his failure. "Dylan, I love Jesus so much. Why do I keep slipping up?" Surely, Owen had a purity in him somewhere.

Owen's father was never affectionate, and his mother often rejected him because of her personality disorder. As a teenager, he found camaraderie among his peers who proved their manhood through drinking beer and drooling over porn magazines. It was the place he came to feel most accepted, loved and comforted. Gatherings with the guys became a refuge.

His addiction to porn continued to be his escape from stress-filled days, even though his first wife of three-and-a-half years met most of his needs. Cybil was a loving, Christian woman who adored Owen, yet after the discovery of his addiction, and over two years of counseling and therapy, he failed to conquer his demon. Despite his wife's best attempts, Owen could never believe he was worth loving. Cybil felt betrayed multiple times and she finally called it quits. Dylan remembered how devastated and heartbroken Owen was when she left. And now Owen was the cause of Dylan's divorce. The thought caused his blood to boil.

How emotions could range so widely within mere minutes evoked fear in Dylan that perhaps he was going crazy. It seemed the lies and betrayal of a friend and his spouse opened a deep darkness inside his soul. And it scared him. In silence, he began the internal talk with God again. *God, why is my heart so divided? What's happening to me? I feel like an evil person. I forgive, yet I don't. I love, yet I hate. Please, help me before my heart completely caves in to wickedness. I know what bitterness and anger does. I've seen it eat people alive and consume their bodies with disease. Please, God, create in me a clean heart and renew a right spirit within me. I'm drowning here.*

He took himself on a tour of life's disappointments, piloting his soul into a nose dive. *I'm an absolute failure. A broke, lonely, divorced pastor, booted out of his church for being a blind, naive, ignorant fool. It's no wonder people mock ministers. They all know the truth. We're just blind fools.*

As Dylan led himself on a path of self-destruction, a voice in his head interrupted. "And was My life on earth considered successful, Dylan?" He acknowledged the voice of Jesus. Images of the life of Christ that Dylan had read about in the scriptures began playing through his mind like a movie. At the end of it, he knew what Jesus wanted him to see. *Okay. Okay, I get it. You were born in shame. You lacked worldly wealth. You weren't attractive to the eye. You were chased down by the religious who wanted to kill you. You were accused of speaking by the power of the devil. You had a handful of disciples, most of which betrayed you or failed to believe you at one point or another. I get it. But You still accomplished the defeat of death. But this is different.*

He sat quietly for a moment. He began to see himself mirrored in Christ. He was betrayed, shamed, rejected by the religious, and even some of his friends. "We are one, Dylan, and you've been raised with Me." He pondered the possibility that perhaps he was as Christ is now. Victorious. If they were truly one, then he was sure he could forgive and show mercy as Christ had shown to those who hurt Him, and to those who sinned. Dylan shook his head. *You're going to have to help me understand this oneness thing. Part of me hates Owen. It sickens me.*

He focused on the hum of the airplane and became aware of the constant vibration. He thought about the power that propelled the massive piece of metal thousands of miles across the ocean. He closed his eyes and began humming with the engine. *Hmmmm.* As Dylan hummed, he saw himself as a tiny speck in the sky, and he contemplated his size in the universe. How could something so microscopic contain so much power? Man-made power combined with Divine power.

As he envisioned himself hovering in the universe, his imagination morphed him into a tiny cell, and he realized that he was a cell inside of God. They shared blood. They shared breath. He pushed his breath out, purposefully, and inhaled. And soon he was in a deep sleep, far away from torment.

## Chapter Seventeen

At the Blakey-Smith Ranch

Lynette examined herself in the full-length mirror. Being that it was her second wedding, her Christian beliefs and guilty conscience surfaced just enough to convince her not to wear white. A southern wedding in the month of May called for something cheery, so she chose a strapless, pale green wedding dress with a beautiful, white overlay from the waist down, that swept to the sides, leaving an opening in the front that revealed the pearly green skirt.

She stepped closer to the mirror to check for blemishes on her skin. She felt beautiful, yet her excitement was tainted with a touch of grief. She brushed it aside as she considered the joy that Owen brought to her. These last few months of living with him and being the focus of his attention had given her what she was longing for.

She looked into her own eyes, fighting the thoughts of what others might be saying about her. Lynette convinced herself months ago that she didn't care what anyone thought about her decisions. It wasn't their business anyway. Only she and Owen could understand and that was all that mattered. Them against the world. They would marry and have children, and share a love that would last.

"Lynette, are you ready?" Her sister stuck her head in the doorway. "It's about time." She smiled.

"Jamie, I can't thank you enough for being here for me. I wish mom and dad could understand. It'd be nice if they were part of this."

"I know, Chickadee. It's their loss. But try not to blame them too much. It's the way they were raised. Besides, when grandkids come along, they'll get over it."

Lynette smiled. "True."

"All right. That's enough talk about the parents. Let it go. You've found your man and you need to pour your attention onto him, and you. Not anyone else. I just want you to be happy, sis." Jamie adjusted Lynette's veil and brushed a couple of hairs out of her face. "So, did he tell you where you're going on your honeymoon?"

"Yeah, he finally did. He was trying to plan something exotic but he decided to save money for the addition we want to build onto the house, you know, for when we have kids?" She smiled. "We're keeping it low key. We'll be staying in his uncle's lake house in Lake Benton, Minnesota for the week."

Jamie clapped her hands like a giddy, little girl. "I can't wait to be an auntie! I'm so happy you found someone that wants to have kids right away. This ranch, this kind of life suits you so much better."

Lynette tried not to think of the highlights of her former life. "I suppose. It's definitely more peaceful than living in a glass bubble where everyone judges every move you make."

Owen's brother, Jesse, came down the hall. The rough, rugged cowboy cleaned up well. Tall and tan. A rancher man. "Hey, lady. Can I give you away yet?"

"Yes. I'm coming!"

Lynette stepped into the hallway, taking note of the old, stained, mauve carpet. *That's gotta go.* Jesse held his elbow out for her to take hold.

"You're sure beautiful, lady." Jesse smiled at her.

"Thanks, brother. I hope Owen likes my dress."

"Oh, let me be honest with you. He won't be paying much attention to your dress, if you know what I mean."

Lynette popped him on the arm. "You're bad, Jesse."

Lynette stood next to Jesse in the screened-in patio, waiting for their cue. She took a deep breath as she looked out over the twenty guests who sat in the white, rented chairs in front of the gazebo. Her mind flashed to her wedding to Dylan. She didn't mean to think about it. *Memories just have a way of presenting themselves when you least expect it.* She and Dylan had almost 400 guests. They spent $45,000 on their wedding. It was the wedding she always dreamed of having. This time around was so different. So small. So insignificant, but she was happy with it. With the connection and love that she and Owen had for each other, Lynette felt simplicity was perfect for the occasion.

The music began. As Owen stepped into the gazebo to wait for his bride, Lynette's heart skipped a beat. "Well, here we go," she said.

"No turnin' back now," Jesse chuckled.

## In Rome

Dylan reached for his cell phone to shut off the alarm clock. It was his first morning in Rome. It was dark when he arrived. Between the taxi ride to The Colors Hotel and the crazy feeling of being in a dream world, he wasn't sure what to expect from the daylight. He sat up in bed and looked around his small room, admiring the simplistic green walls and modern art. *Am I actually here?*

He walked toward the window and pulled open the wooden shutters. "Oh. My. God." He squinted from the brightness of the morning sun and peered across the street at the apartment balconies that held flowers and bicycles of its residents. He opened the window and listened to passersby, speaking Italian. "My, Lord." He smiled like a little boy on Christmas morning.

Dylan made his way to the shower, full of excitement, ready to explore. As he watched the soap run down his legs, he thought of Lynette. He determined to push memories of her aside during the trip so he could enjoy his time there instead of suffering through it, but he was already finding that to be nearly impossible. He knew Lynette was probably married by now, and that fact shot like a sword through his heart.

Lacing up his good walking shoes, he headed downstairs to the breakfast room, anxious to get outside and begin his journey. A young couple sat in the corner next to him, enjoying their morning tea and handholding. They were obviously on their honeymoon. Dylan fought the urge to stare. His mind was torn between thoughts of happiness for the couple, and sarcastic, bitter thoughts that mocked their naivety. He redirected his attention to his breakfast. *Dear God, help me. Suck the poison from my heart.*

He opened up his notes on his cell phone and quickly reviewed the list of places that Jackson named as definite must-sees. The Colosseum, Capitoline Hill, Trevi Fountain, Pantheon, Mamertine Prison, the Spanish Steps and all that Vatican City had to offer. Not having a clue where to go first, he began ripping apart a paper napkin and writing the locations on each piece. He mumbled a little prayer to himself. "Let mercy lead me." Dylan picked up the pieces and walked toward the young couple in love. *God, I'm expecting You to show up here. Please speak to me. Open my eyes to see. Lead me.* He figured it was appropriate to allow young love to be part of his decision.

Dylan approached the couple. "Excuse me. I know this is a strange request, but I'm trying to figure out where to go today and I've written several locations on these pieces of napkin. Would you do me a favor and choose one without looking?"

The young lady appeared amused. "I'm always up for a game. So, you want me to pick one?"

Dylan nodded. "If you don't mind." *What am I doing? Dylan, you dork.*

"All right then." She reached into his hand and pulled a piece of napkin out of the mix. "Here you go."

Dylan looked at it. "Mamertine Prison. Cool. Thanks for helping me out."

The girl grinned, "You're welcome."

Dylan considered how strange he must seem to the couple, but he didn't care. *That'll give them something to remember,* he thought.

He stepped out onto Via Boezio and began his walk.

### At Annie's Cafe

"The sorry whore got hitched. Any decent person would've waited longer. Poor Dylan. It's a good thing he's not around here right now." Curt held onto his beer tightly, shaking his head in disgust.

Mike chimed in. "Owen ain't even a good-lookin' fellow, really. He's okay, but kinda odd lookin' like a…I don't know…some kind of creature from somewhere, yet with endearin' eyes." The men laughed. "Must have been those eyes that lured her in like a fish to the bait."

"Nah. I'd put my money on the ranch being what lured Lynette in. The Blakely-Smith Ranch has been the envy of every person in town, for over a century! It's got the best view around this area."

Lucy overheard as she walked by. "Are you serious? You guys really think that Lynette wanted the ranch? You need to stop your ridiculous gossiping."

"Well, well. Suddenly you're on the whore's side?" Mike dropped his fist on the table.

Lucy sighed. "Mike, I'm not on any side. I'm just saying that sometimes people make decisions in their own blindness. I'm not saying that what she did was right, but for you to suggest that she was trying to get the ranch is ridiculous. And I don't appreciate you referring to her as a whore."

"Since when do you have a soft heart for the tramp?"

Lucy felt the sting of grief. She sat her serving tray down and peered into Mike's eyes. "Dylan and Lynette Vanberg helped me through the most difficult time of my life. They have loved people in this town deeply and laid down their lives, sacrificing for people who needed help. Have you ever stopped to consider that they were so focused on serving others, like you, that they forgot about themselves? Can't you see how someone might lose sight after years of doing that? And, Mike, how can you scoff at either one of them? Don't you remember how good they were to you?"

Mike's smirk turned to a somber frown. "Little lady. You're a good one. I guess I needed that reminder." He patted her hand.

Curt piped up, "Who's the softie now?" His bearded mouth parted, revealing his haggard grin.

Mike held his hand up with a warning. "Shut it, Curt, or I'll smack you right outta that chair."

Lucy made her way to David and Marcy's table. "How's it going over here? Can I get anything for you?"

"We're good, thank you." David smiled at her.

"If you don't mind me asking, is everything okay? I sense some sadness happening here." Lucy's eyes were filled with compassion.

"Well. You know. The wedding…" David's eyes carried a deep grief. "I think we all hoped she would come back home. Dylan believed for that. We're really worried about him."

Marcy patted David's hand as she nodded in agreement.

Lucy shook her head. "I know. It's so tragic. Jackson and I were talking about how to encourage him. And, of course, there's the awkward things to deal with, like running into Owen and Lynette in public. How do we handle that the right way? What *is* the right way? When someone has caused so much pain, how do you continue being a community with them in it?"

Marcy shrugged. "I don't exactly know the answer to that, but I do know that Owen and Lynette are going to need help along the way. They've made a choice that they believe is right, so what can we do? They've definitely made some enemies. That's for sure."

Lucy thought for a moment. "That's probably one of the toughest things Jesus ever told us to do. 'Love your enemies and pray for those who persecute you.' I'd say that Lynette's choices have persecuted a lot of hearts around here. I've been thinking about how unnatural it seems to love those who cause you pain. Granted, some cause pain unknowingly. They're too caught up in their own confusion to think about others." Lucy set her water pitcher on the table so she could use both hands to express herself. "Do you know what really boggles my mind?" She grabbed the sides of her head. "The part where Jesus said, 'You are to be perfect as your Heavenly Father is perfect.' Why would He tell us to do something so impossible?"

David raised his eyebrows. "My goodness. I never really paid attention to that verse before. Hmmm. Maybe it's about becoming perfect? He does say that nothing is impossible with God, so I guess it's possible that we can be perfect like Him."

Marcy chimed in. "But not on our own. It has to be through Him. 'I can do all things through Christ who strengthens me.' No man can make himself perfect. It's through Christ and what He's done. If we work to become perfect, we'll become prideful in our self-righteousness and think more highly of ourselves than others."

Lucy responded. "Well, this conversation got deep, real fast." They all chuckled. "I'd better get back to work."

"Thanks, Lucy. I think we're ready for the check."

"Sure thing," she smiled.

The door chimed. Several people walked in, dressed nicely. Lucy approached them. "Welcome. How many are in your party?"

"Thirteen," answered a gruff, bearded, heavy-set man.

Setting up a table for them, she wondered who they might be and why they were in Holly. *They're most likely here for Owen and Lynette's wedding.* She fought waves of nausea that began to roll over her.

"Your table is ready. You all look so nice. Special occasion?" She inquired.

The blunt man responded. "Brother-in-law's wedding."

"I see." She bit her lip.

Lucy took drink orders and returned to the table with their beverages. The men and women around the table were spouting off their impressions of the wedding ceremony.

"That ranch sure is nice. I've heard the family talk about it for years, but I'd never been out there before.

"Yeah. Owen's pretty lucky. Inheriting a ranch…that'd be my dream come true. I'm sure it makes his parents feel good knowing there's someone to take care of it. I know they always wanted to keep it in the family."

A grumpy-faced man spoke up. "Didn't Owen want to live in Wyoming and be a park ranger, or something like that? Before he married Cybil, I thought he was making plans to move there."

"Park ranger? Nah. He wanted to be a wildlife specialist, but he married instead and decided he'd settle down in Holly."

"Hmph. That didn't last very long. I thought after the divorce, he'd move to Wyoming," the grumpy face declared.

A less considerate family member butted in. "Instead, he stuck around and laid the pastor's wife. Talk about managing wildlife. Apparently, the pastor couldn't keep his pretty little lioness tamed." The hairy man laughed.

"I guess he got a bit more than he bargained for from the church. Went for a little encouragement, paid some tithes and got himself the lady. I'd call that a win-win." A couple of them laughed.

A thirty-something woman spoke up. "All right, guys. That's enough."

"Well, come on, Maurine. You've gotta admit it's kinda funny."

Lucy couldn't take anymore. With tears in her eyes, trying to remain calm, she looked at the uncouth man. "Sir." She paused as she considered her words.

"Yeah?"

"Please. I would appreciate it if you didn't make fun of the situation." A tear rolled down her cheek.

Half grinning at his self-supposed humor, he tried to correct his mistake. "Sorry, Miss."

Lucy walked into the kitchen and removed her apron. "Burt, would you ask Elsie to take my table? I'm not feeling well." She spun around and quickly left through the back door.

## Chapter Eighteen

Dylan lay in bed thinking over the significance of each place he visited. The smell of the Mamertine Prison still sat in his nose, beckoning him not to forget the texture and thousands of years worth of memories within the stones and rock that he touched. It was believed that the Apostle Paul and Saint Peter were imprisoned there before they were executed.

"For which I am an ambassador in chains…" Dylan quoted portions of Paul's writing to himself. "Remember my imprisonment. Grace be with you." He thought about Paul being lowered into the hole in the ground and how he had written several books of the Bible while a prisoner. Paul's focus on being one with Christ, united with Him, and his talk of grace boggled Dylan's mind. He considered his own lack of ability to impart grace to others while he was locked in his own mental prison.

"Consider yourselves dead to sin." Dylan's habit of speaking out loud was growing as he attempted to fill air space in his lonely little bubble. "Ha. Dead to sin, are we? Well, Lord, as You can see, apparently no one on planet earth is aware of that. We're all a bunch of screw ups." His mind fluttered through the scriptures that stuck in his brain.

Since the breakdown of his marriage, Dylan often used sarcasm to soothe his soul. He raised his hand into the air, pretending to hold a wine goblet and spoke with the accent of a noble, British aristocrat. "For sin shall not be master over you, for you are not under law, but under grace. Then why are people always caught in sin? I don't get it. What's missing here?"

Dylan stared at the ceiling, feeling delirious, listening to the leaky sink in the bathroom. He sat up, opening his suitcase to retrieve his Bible. *Romans 5...Romans 5. Why is it stuck in my brain?* His eyes fell on the verses.

*Very rarely will anyone die for a righteous person, though for a good person someone might possibly dare to die. But God demonstrates his own love for us in this: While we were still sinners, Christ died for us.*

Suddenly, his focus was silenced with an invasive thought that shot through his mind and heart, shattering his soul into pieces. Lynette was with Owen, as his wife. Dylan picked up the Bible and threw it across the room. He smashed his fists into the mattress and buried his face in the blanket, trying not to scream and get himself kicked out of the hotel. His face burned like fire as raw pain sought an outlet from his body. His back arched and shook as sobs fell into the thick cloth.

"My wife. She's my wife." Dylan felt his chest ripping open. If death came, he would welcome it. Images of Paul in prison emerged in his mind, face to the dirty floor. He felt one with Paul. He felt one with Joseph when his brothers sold him into slavery. He felt one with Hosea whose wife continually betrayed him. Then he thought of the irony of each one; Paul, Joseph, Hosea and Jesus. They gave grace, love and compassion in the middle of betrayal, mistreatment, and false accusations. He saw the face of Jesus, bloodied and beaten beyond recognition, barely human..."Father, forgive them."

*How, God? How? How do I let go?*

"Release them from your judgments."

*I can't.*

"Release them so they can hear."

*I can't.*

"Release them so they can see. They're only blind."

Dylan felt himself slipping into a vortex of hell as hope diminished from his heart. His hopelessness was in the thought that he could never let it go. He sat up and peered across the room at the Bible, pages bent, on the floor. Like a desperate man about to fall from a crumbling cliff, he leapt across the room and threw himself on top of the book. He pulled it to his chest, pressing it hard into himself. "Put this word inside me, God. Put You inside of me. I can't do this without You. I'm going to die if You don't fix my heart."

"I AM inside of You. And you're in Me."

Dylan wept until he fell asleep on the floor.

He found himself in his bedroom in Holly, surrounded by canvasses of gold and silver. Within each one, colors swirled, spinning quickly. "What are you going to paint, Dylan?" He turned quickly and his eyes met with Lynette's. She was wearing one of Dylan's gray dress shirts. A white, wool blanket was wrapped around her shoulders. "What are you going to paint, Dylan?"

"Lynette?" His heart pounded in his chest as he reached for her, but her body seemed to float away from him. He looked at the floor that became a raging whirlpool, and Lynette stood across from him in a grassy field, hair and shirt blowing in the wind.

"What are you going to paint, Dylan?" Her face began to fade into a hazy gray.

"Don't go, Lynette," he cried. "I'm painting. See?" Dylan turned to face the paintings that continued to swirl with whirlwinds of color. "Here. I'll paint you some flowers." He reached toward one of the canvasses. Red roses, white tulips and pink azaleas began to cover it. He turned to look at her as her face began to reappear. "And here's our dream porch, Lynette." He pointed at a canvas and an unseen hand began to sketch an old, wooden porch with a white swing. The porch railing was like gold. The spindles appeared as sparkling red rubies. Trumpet vines began growing across the ceiling above the porch, wrapping themselves down the silver chains of the swing.

"See? If you had been patient, Lynnie!" His heart darkened at the remembrance of what she had done. "Why didn't you love me? Why couldn't you warn me and tell me you were going to find someone else?" The canvasses behind him turned black and began oozing blood. Lynette's form darkened and she hunched over in pain.

She winced. "I didn't plan on it happening, Dylan. It just did. But I still love you."

"No. That's impossible! You can't love someone and do something so wicked!"

Lynette cried out in anguish, wrapping her arms around herself. "It is possible. Did Peter not love Jesus when he denied Him?"

Dylan stomped his foot and punched his fist into the air. "That's a poor analogy! We're talking willful, continued sin versus a moment of weakness."

At that, an ear-piercing, crackling sound filled the room. A hole opened in the floor and the entire scene was sucked into it. Dylan was left standing, alone.

Still in a deep sleep, another dream emerged. A lush, translucent mountain stood in the sunshine. Peace and quiet tugged at his heart, drawing him to climb to the top. There was no striving in the walk. No weight. He felt he was floating to the top. An easel and canvass awaited. Dylan heard music coming from the canvass. He tried to see the picture before him, but it was full of blinding light. Laughter spilled out from the light, capturing Dylan's soul and filling it with a joy unlike anything he had experienced on earth. The tune morphed into one he recognized. Words filled his ears. "Giver of immortal gladness, fill us with the light of day."

His attention was drawn below, to the bottom of the mountain. Lynette danced gleefully in a field of brilliant flowers, grabbing the hem of her white dress like a little child. She tilted her face upward, into the light, and laughed from the depths of her being.

"What will you paint, Dylan?" A voice from above vibrated through his body. "Surrender yourself to the painter and you'll be free." Dylan squinted into the brightness, searching for the face of the speaker. He couldn't make out a form, but his face was embraced in a joyful warmth he'd never known.

"Yes," he wept. "I will. I will." His soul was immersed in a fatherly embrace from another world. The infusion of love drenched every facet of his being. Light invaded every fragment, pulling him together into wholeness, into one with the Source of all. "No matter what happens, we are one. Remain in Me. And we will paint as one."

A river appeared at Dylan's feet. Unlike any river on earth, it was absolutely pure with waters that were nearly invisible. It was fully alive, like trillions of perfect cells flowing in one direction. "Stepping into Me. Remember, Dylan. Stepping into Me." He dipped his foot into the waters and he was overcome with ecstasy. Letting go, he jumped in.

"Oh, excuse me, sir!" Dylan startled awake at the sound of the woman's voice. She peered down at him, holding her hand over her heart. "Are you okay? Did you fall?" The woman was alarmed.

"Oh, no. No. I fell asleep on the floor last night." Dylan was embarrassed. "A little too much to drink, I guess." He hadn't had anything to drink, but he thought it sounded like a good excuse.

"I apologize, sir. I came in to do housekeeping. I knocked but no one answered. I had no idea anyone was in here."

"No problem. I'll be outta here in about 30 minutes."

"Okay. I'll be back. Again, I'm sorry for the intrusion."

Dylan took a quick shower. His mind was filled with images from his dreams and he wondered what it all meant. "Stepping into Me." He repeated the words to himself.

### Honeymoon

"Oh, Owen. This is beautiful! I had no idea Minnesota was so charming."

As the honeymooners descended into Lake Benton's valley via Highway 14, Lynette marveled over the tall trees and sloping hills that displayed historic homes. "So much charm! Oh, look at the cross on top of the hill!"

Owen smiled. "That's why I wanted to bring you into town from this direction. It's my favorite vantage point."

"I'm still fascinated by these giant wind turbines. They're so majestic." She gawked out the window.

"Lake Benton is known as the 'Original Wind Power Capital of the Midwest.' I'll have to take you to the local museum while we're here. That is, if you get too bored with honey-moonin.'"

He nudged her arm and they chuckled. "Let's go have a look at

Hole-in-the-Mountain park. I spent a lot of time there as a kid. Our family used to camp there every summer."

They turned into the parking lot and stopped near a tree. "I wish we had trees like this in Holly. They're beautiful." Owen smiled at her childlikeness.

"You should see it in the winter when this hillside is covered in snow. This hill makes for awesome sledding. I've got a scar to prove it. Most triumphant day of my childhood." He smiled at the memory. "I was the talk of the town. It was one of those wipeouts that every boy hopes to survive. Makes you feel like a conqueror. I flew right across this road." He pointed. "Popped right out of my sled and went airborne."

"Sounds pretty exciting." She admired him with her eyes.

"Let's take a walk to the top of the hill." Owen took her by the hand.

"So, why do they call this 'Hole-in-the-Mountain?'"

"It has something to do with being a passage way. I think it's a valley where Native Americans passed through. I always loved those creative Indian names. 'Hole-in-the-Mountain.' They simply described what they saw." Owen breathed a sigh of relief. "I can't believe we're here together."

"Yeah." Lynette took in a deep breath. "I have to admit, I wasn't thrilled with the idea of coming here at first. I had my heart set on Paris or Italy…something more exotic. But this is rather refreshing. So far, I like it." She squeezed his hand.

Owen looked at his new wife. "There may not be an Eiffel Tower or romantic Italian alleyways to explore, but there's something about this town that I've always loved. The lake is peaceful. The hills are gentle. The air is pure."

Lynette stepped back and looked at Owen with surprise. "I've never known you to be poetic."

"Poetic?" He laughed. "What was poetic about that?"

"Oh, come on. 'Gentle hills. Peaceful lake.' I've only ever seen your tough-man, football stud side." Lynette was intrigued.

"Maybe not poetic, but I'm romantic sometimes. How do you think I won your heart?" Owen grinned.

"By being you. That's how you won my heart." Lynette kissed him on the lips.

Owen patted her backside. "What do you say we head on to the cabin?"

"I say 'yes, please.'" She smiled flirtatiously.

Upon arrival at the cabin, Lynette was slightly appalled by the 1970's furniture and linoleum. The dust was thick. "Obviously, no one has been here since…the 70's? Don't any of your family members take care of this place?"

"I'm sorry. I know it's not a palace. I'll dust things up a bit. The sheets and blankets are kept in the hall closet in air-tight plastic, so no worries. They're clean. If you can put them on the bed, I'll get things cleaned up."

Lynette headed down the hallway, trying to maintain a positive attitude. *Well, this will definitely be memorable.* As she pulled the sheets out of the closet, Lynette couldn't help but compare this honeymoon with her first. Dylan had taken her to a four-star resort in Crested Butte, Colorado. She sighed, trying to shake the thought from her head. "Guess this is what I deserve. Putting sheets on the bed of our ugly love shack."

She thought for a moment about talking to God, but she stopped herself. What was there to say anyway? She wanted to ask Him to bless her and Owen. On one hand, she felt she had the right to demand His blessing. After all, she served her time for the Lord, for many years, and at the expense of her dreams and desires. On the other hand, she felt eternally separated from the love of God. *Who am I to ask for anything? He didn't answer my prayers before, so why would He start now?*

Owen hollered, "Who you talking to in there?"

"No one. Just myself."

"What were you saying to yourself?" Owen peeked his head around the corner.

"Nothing, really."

He shrugged. "Hmph. Well, all righty then. Enjoy the conversation."

As she struggled to stretch the sheets onto the mattress, tears filled her eyes. She tried to control her emotions with a silent pep talk. *Dang it, Lynette. Get a hold of yourself. What's wrong with you? I didn't want it to start off this way. But this sacrifice is for our future, Lynette. We chose a cheap, low-key honeymoon so we can afford our future dreams. But I want to be a princess, I guess…but I don't deserve to be one. What am I thinking? What if this place is a picture of our future? Oh, God, no!*

She failed at encouraging herself. Deep down inside, she truly wanted the princess treatment. An expensive wedding and a fancy honeymoon would have been perfect. *Why did I agree to this?*

Owen walked into the bedroom, feeling amorous. He leapt over to Lynette and swung her around to face him. His smile faded. "What's wrong?"

Tears began to flow from her eyes. "Nothing. I'm fine."

"Listen, Lynette. We have to be honest with each other if we're going to make this marriage work. We've talked about this before. After our experiences, we know what it's going to take to make this work. You need to tell me the truth. What's wrong?"

She wiped her eyes with her blouse. "It's just, I know we agreed to do this trip in place of spending too much money, but I guess I…maybe I was wrong. I wish we were someplace really nice. Really romantic."

"Look. I know you deserve more. And you're going to get more. The ranch house will be updated before too long and we'll add on for the future. I thought we agreed that sacrificing now was what we needed to do."

"I know. I know. I think I'm just overly emotional right now. It's been a crazy year, and, here we are, finally. I think it's all hitting me. And you know women. I think we all have this unspoken wish to be a princess. I know life isn't a fairy tale, but it'd be nice, you know?"

Owen appeared both concerned and disturbed. "Hasn't it been a good year for you, since we first got together?"

"Of course."

Owen placed his hands on her shoulders. "Weren't you happy when we got together a year ago?"

"Yes, I was. You made me feel alive."

"And you were sure you wanted to leave Dylan?"

She stepped back angrily. "Why do you have to speak his name right now? It's our honeymoon!" Lynette turned to face the window.

Owen threw his hands in the air. "I'm sorry. I'm just trying to make sure you're good with this. Are you having doubts now?"

"No, Owen! I'm not having doubts. I told you I'm just emotional. I'm tired. All of the planning and waiting. I'm just tired right now. And this place isn't what I envisioned for a honeymoon. Give me time to adjust."

"Lynette, we've been living together for months. I'd call that our 'adjustment time.' I thought we adjusted just fine. Are you telling me it's different now?"

"Well, this *is* different. We're married now."

"Then tell me, why the heck did we just get married? You and I were fine before. Now that we've signed a document and made it official, you're suddenly a basket case?" Owen sat on the end of the bed as Lynette continued peering out the window.

"Look, woman. Let's finish getting this bed put together and get some rest. Things will be better tomorrow."

She turned to face him. "So, we're not going to have sex tonight?"

He sighed. "Look at yourself. Am I supposed to want to make love to that?"

Lynette's mouth dropped open. "Oh my God!" She began to cry. "I can't believe you just said that."

Owen tried to explain. "You're misunderstanding me. I mean, how do you expect me to make love to someone who's unhappy to be here with me? You look sad and angry. Why would I think you want to be intimate?"

She wiped her eyes. "Well, it **is** our honeymoon."

"Yes, it is, but look at you. You're a wreck. You're really confusing me with these mixed signals. I don't know if I should touch you or not."

Lynette put her palms to her face and began to sob. "I'm sorry. I'm sorry. I don't want it to be like this. I want to start over. Can we just wipe the slate clean and start over?"

Owen wrapped his arms around her. "Sure. Slate's clean. You just tell me what you want, and when. You're gonna have to be clear with me because I'm not very good at reading women. You're an interesting breed."

She leaned her head into his chest. "Thank you. I think."

## Chapter Nineteen
ONE YEAR LATER

Jackson and Lucy took a Friday night drive to Marshall City for a long-awaited date. Lucy noticed his cologne as soon as she stepped into the car. "Wow! Don't you smell good? And you're looking good, too." She leaned over and kissed his cheek.

"Thank you. Is it too strong?"

"Not at all. It's delightful." She smiled.

"You look amazing, Lucinda Flowers." He smiled and reached for her hand, intertwining his fingers with hers. "I hope you're hungry."

"I am. Nearly starved."

When Jackson turned into the parking lot of Perry's Steakhouse, Lucy hollered, "Oh, my gosh! No way! Really?"

"Yep. You've talked about Perry's all year. I thought you deserved the experience." He was extremely pleased with himself.

They pushed through the revolving glass door and into a world unlike anything that Holly had to offer. A huge, ornate chandelier hung in the foyer above the glass-topped hostess desk. Blue, green and silver mosaics swirled along the entry walls. "Hello. Welcome to Perry's. How may I help you?" A cheery, long-legged, blonde woman in black heels and mini-skirt stood to the side of the countertop wearing a huge smile.

"I have reservations for Sawyer, for two."

"Jackson, I can't believe this place! The pictures on their website don't do it justice. It's incredible." As they followed the hostess up the winding, wooden staircase with a swanky, red runner, Lucy gasped at the sight of the wine wall to her left. "That's impressive."

Jackson grinned. "You like?"

Jaw-dropped, she nodded. "This is beautiful. These are the things I drool over in my interior design magazines. Do you remember my book of palaces? This is the closest thing I've seen to that."

"Well, my lady. You will see more, I'm sure. I know you'll get your trip to Europe someday."

The loft was dimly lit with delicate, dangling lights shaped like bubbles floating in bunches against the dark wood ceiling. Groups of red roses tied in sparkly ribbons sat upon every table. Flickering candles reflected in the glass vases. The aroma of gourmet foods lingered in the air, causing them to salivate.

"And here's your private booth, sir. Your waiter will be right with you. Enjoy."

The red, velvety seats formed a half-circle. Walls extended upward from the top of the booth, creating a private space for the two lovers. "Jackson, thank you so much."

"For what?"

"For bringing me here. I don't know what to say."

"You don't have to say anything. Just enjoy yourself and take it all in. It makes me happy to make you happy." Jackson touched her hand, tracing her fingers.

Lucy smiled.

The waiter came and explained the exquisite options that the chef offered for the evening. Most of the menu sounded foreign to Jackson and Lucy, but they were game for trying something new. "Surprise us," Jackson said. "Are you brave, Lucy?"

"Sure thing."

"As you wish, sir." The waiter nodded as he left to converse with the chef.

Jackson reached both arms across the table and enclosed her hands in his. "Lucy? What are your dreams?"

She grinned. "You know. I think I've sufficiently bored you with those details, but I'm flattered that you ask."

"Bored me? Are you kidding? Your dreams are beautiful. I find them to be wildly fascinating." He squeezed her hands. "I'd really like to hear them again. I want to know which dreams you're most passionate about."

"Well, then. As I've told you before, other than my interest in archaeology and travel, the thing I'm most passionate about," she tilted her head and grinned, slightly embarrassed. "...I know this sounds insignificant, but I'd place being a wife and mother at the top of my list. I'm not sure why, but that's what's on my mind the most."

He smiled. "I love that. And it's very significant."

Lucy was delighted. "I'm glad you think so. You know how many college applications I started filling out over the last year. And every single time, I get that feeling in my gut that I'm making a wrong move. It's just not me. It's not who I am. Everyone wants me to go to college, and, it's not that I don't want to learn, but I feel like it would be a waste of money for me. I've asked God many times why this married-woman-with-kids thing feels right. I've lamented over it, trying to figure out what's wrong with me. I mean, people expect me to have a career in mind, but as hard as I try, it's just not there."

"Lucy, I've told you before that you shouldn't feel pressured by other people's expectations of you. Besides, it's not their life. And not everyone has the same calling. If you stop and think about it, raising a happy, healthy family is one of the most powerful and noble things a person can do with their life. Someone's got to raise up the future generation. Think of the impact you can make on this planet by raising some of its future citizens. Honestly, I think being a mother should be a highly regarded position. And as awesome as you are, you definitely need to reproduce." Jackson smiled at her.

Lucy giggled. "It's too bad moms don't get paid to be moms."

"True."

Lucy looked down at the table for a minute, her expression becoming serious.

"You okay?" Jackson asked.

"I'm okay. I can't help but think about Dylan and Lynette. He still laments over the fact that she wanted children and he wasn't ready to start a family. I don't want you to think that I'd be like her. I mean, if I got married and never had kids, that would be fine with me as long as I have a husband that loves me. I think couples should stick it out through thick and thin. Right? That's what I want. Someone who's not afraid to walk with me through the valley of the shadow of death, if that's where I happen to walk. I don't mean to sound morbid, but you know what I mean?"

Jackson nodded. "I know what you mean."

Lucy continued her thought. "I get tired of seeing couples throw in the towel when they hit the valley. Does it make sense to separate when you're in that place…in the dark? Shouldn't that be the time when you stick together? One goes this way, and one goes that way, and somebody dies in the process. I stumble over the dead all the time. They sit in the cafe, drinking away their depression, dabbling in drugs or criticizing everyone in town who's happy. People left in the valley alone…it's tragic."

Jackson stared at her in awe. He always loved hearing her thoughts.

"Lucinda Flowers. I love you."

Her face instantly beamed. "And I love you, too, Jackson Sawyer."

After they enjoyed an evening of fine dining, they left for a joyful stroll through Britton Park. A few minutes before sunset, the lake was calm and peaceful. The brilliant light of the sun danced on the waters. Jackson and Lucy sat together in the old, wooden tree swing, facing the lake. Gentle summer winds tussled their hair. Lucy leaned her head over on his shoulder. "I think I have an addiction problem."

Jackson raised his eyebrows. "Oh? What kind?"

"When I'm with you, everything feels right and I'm at peace. When I'm not with you, I have terrible withdrawals. You'd think the longer we've been together, we'd need time apart, but I can't seem to get enough."

Jackson chuckled. "That's very interesting, because I have an addiction issue, too. What you described is right on. I guess we're in this thing together."

"Seriously?" She smiled. "Wouldn't people say this is unhealthy? Like we're co-dependent or something?"

"If this is what co-dependency is, I'm perfectly content with it." He grinned. "I don't think there's anything wrong with two people enjoying each other's company so much that they prefer to be together. Besides, we're both very independent spirits, so I don't see a problem with our hunger for each other."

She looked at him and made a funny face. "Hunger, huh? That sounds pretty intense."

Jackson kissed her cheek. "I can't think of a better way to describe it. Your presence fills my soul."

"Aw, Jackson, what a beautiful thing to say." She snuggled up to him and let her eyes fill with happy tears. "I'm one incredibly lucky girl. I used to lay in bed at night, thinking about what my husband would be like, and he wasn't even as amazing as you are. I don't know how it ended up that I have a boyfriend that surpasses my dreams." She pressed her cheek into his chest.

"Wow. I've never received such a compliment in my life. I hope I don't let you down. I'm not perfect and I've been known to annoy people from time to time."

Lucy quickly chimed in, "I've been around you enough to know your habits, and I find them to be endearing. I'm not annoyed yet." They laughed.

The couple lingered in satisfied silence for a minute.

"Lucy?" Jackson stood from the swing and turned to face her.

"Yes?" Her bright eyes filled with utter joy as Jackson knelt down in the dirt. She threw her hands over her mouth.

"Lucinda, would you do me the honor of allowing me to be by your side, everyday, for the rest of my life? And stand with me despite my annoying habits?" He smiled. He pulled a white gold, diamond ring from his pant's pocket and slid it onto her finger.

Lucy began to cry as she nodded her head 'yes.' Her eyes squinted as the tears flowed. Her smile was as wide as her face. "Yes! Yes." She threw her arms around his neck and wept. "Oh, Jackson. I love you so much. So very much. I'd be honored to spend my life with you."

"I love you, too, Lucy." He held onto her tightly. "I can't believe you're going to be my wife. I want you to know…I promise to love you and protect your heart. I'll walk with you through anything. I **will** be faithful to you."

She continued squeezing him tightly. "Jackson, I promise to be faithful to you. I'll always love you, and I'll do my best to protect your heart. For the rest of my life."

He pulled back to look into her eyes. He caressed her face in his hands and traced the edge of her lips with his thumbs. "You've captured my heart, young lady." He gently kissed her lips.

He wrapped his arms around her, pulling her close to himself. "You know, after seeing the issues that my parents had, and watching marriages crash around me...especially after the Lynette and Dylan thing...I told myself I'd never get married. It scared me. But you've done something to my heart and I know I'd regret it if I lived my life without you in it. I want to be your husband and the father of your children. I want to support you in seeing your dreams fulfilled."

She brushed her fingers through his hair. "You're a beautiful soul. I love your heart." She paused for a moment. "And I guess this marriage thing will help my addiction problem." They laughed.

"Yeah, well, I don't want to completely break you of your habit, but I can help ease it a bit."

She leaned back, catching his eyes. "So, shall we talk dates yet? Are you thinking a long engagement...or?" Her eyes were hopeful.

"How long do you need for planning the wedding?"

"Oh, Jackson, when it comes to marrying you, I could do it tomorrow. We need to discuss what kind of wedding we want. Big. Small. Simple or extravagant. What do you think?"

"Honestly, I would love to have a big celebration."

She smiled. "Me, too. The town of Holly can use some excitement for sure. My guest list would be relatively small. Mainly family and a few friends, but with your town connections, your list will be the long one. Have you thought about where you'd like to get married?"

Jackson nodded. "What do you think about Hope Fellowship? It's the closest thing to a home church that we have. Not that I've gone much," he chuckled.

Lucy agreed. "I like the idea. And what do you think about Dylan doing the wedding?"

"Yes! I was hoping you'd say that." Jackson was pleased at the thought of his best friend doing his wedding.

Lucy piped up. "I'd say I could have everything planned in three months. Is that too soon for you?" She looked concerned.

"Too soon? Absolutely not. I hope I can hold out that long, though." He raised his eyebrows with an enticing smile. "Three months is actually perfect. It gives me time to prepare the house. Since I worked that lease-to-own thing with the landlord, we can do whatever we want. I'd like to paint and put in some new floors. Do you like wood floors?"

Lucy's face shined with delight. "I love wood floors. You can put in whatever you want, though. It's your house."

"No, Lucy. It's *our* house. I want your input. It's time to start transforming my groovy bachelor pad into a grown up, responsible, married man's home."

Lucy tilted her head to the side. "Responsible, yes. But grown up? Not so much." She giggled.

The sun had fully set. The two embraced each other in the nighttime breeze, dreaming of their future.

## Chapter Twenty

Old Emma Gray met up with Beverly at Annie's Cafe for breakfast. She waddled in, wearing a long, purple muumuu that she purchased in Hawaii twenty years earlier. The employees knew the donning of her muumuu meant she was in a cheery mood. Emma's typical dreariness was sometimes interrupted by moments of hilarity and clownish behavior. The dress was known well by those in town as an indicator of possible happiness.

She looked around the cafe, searching for Beverly. Spotting her, she shuffled her feet quickly to the table. "Beverly, you won't believe what I saw this week. Unbelievable! People these days..." Emma reached into her tote bag and pulled out her notebook.

"Why don't you have a seat first?" asked Beverly. "You come trampling in here like a happy, purple hippo, out of control."

"Hippo?" Emma opened her mouth, aghast. "Well, I..."

Beverly laughed. "Well, c'mon. The purple muumuu, Emma. You can't blame me for thinking of a hungry hippo."

Emma glared. "You can think it, but you shouldn't speak it, you ole crow." Emma and Beverly had grown fond of each other's verbal jabs. "Now shut your mouth and listen to what I have to say." Emma plopped her notebook open on the table. With a cheery disposition, she delivered her news. "So last

Friday night, I was sittin' on my front porch having my midnight snack."

Beverly sat up straight, embellishing a look of shock. "Midnight snack? That explains the hippo part of the equation. You should've been in bed!"

"Just listen! You know the newspaper reporter, Jackson? He lives on my street. He pulled up in his driveway and went inside with that waitress, Lucy."

"Well, that's no surprise. Everyone knows they've been dating. So what?"

Emma wagged her finger as she spoke. "She went inside and stayed inside. All night!"

"How do you know she stayed all night, Emma?"

"Because I stayed up for two hours waiting for that girl to come out. Finally, I set my alarm for 5:00am and went to sleep. Sure enough, at 5:00am, her car was still there! Young people these days, fornicating. They can't seem to keep their pants on. I swear. No shame. No shame."

Beverly stared at Emma as if she'd fallen on her head. "You walk in here all excited and happy, like you've won the lottery. I was expecting some good news, and that's all you've got? You confuse me, Emma Gray. You're happy because someone might've had sex?"

"No, Beverly!"

"So you're happy because you might've caught someone in sin, and that makes you feel good?"

"How appalling, Beverly! I'm merely trying to tell you what's going on. The goody-goody-two-shoes waitress who speaks of virtue and morals spent the night with newspaper man. Now, don't you find that news to be revealing?"

Beverly sighed. "Honestly, I don't give a rat's rear end about what they were up to. You don't know what was going on in that house. Turn your attention to other things. And, for the love of God, go to bed! No old woman should be sitting on her front porch at midnight, not even in Holly."

"It's safe in Holly." Emma huffed. "Well, just forget what I told you, then. But I'm keeping an eye out. You know what happens. One little compromise starts an avalanche of sin that'll take over the whole town! Lynette Vanberg already set that in motion."

Beverly laughed. "Seriously? Is God that weak? Are you saying that someone's bad choice is more powerful than He is? What do you really put your faith in, Emma? Focus on the good things and maybe you'll see that the good stuff is far more powerful. If you make sin your focus, that's all you'll ever see. Your attention to it only empowers darkness. You're making a mountain out of an insignificant mole hill, I tell you! If you want to see people walking in the light, then focus on the light so they can walk into it. Your perspective can be a deathtrap or a pathway to life for others."

Emma was agitated. "Bev, so people should just get away with doing wrong?"

Beverly picked up her reading glasses and stared through them at Emma. "Oh, hello, Holy Spirit! Oh, wait…oh, it's Emma Gray." She pulled her glasses off. "Emma, if you'd get your big, purple muumuu out of the way and trust the Holy Spirit to do His thing, you'd be surprised by what you see. Correct me if I'm wrong, but the last time I checked, keeping a record of wrongs never helped anyone to see the light."

The door chimed. Lucy entered. Emma shook her head, clicking her tongue against her teeth. "That naughty little girl."

Beverly tossed a sugar packet at Emma. "Emma. All you ever do is gossip. You and your notebook. Doesn't it make you feel sick to be digging up everyone's garbage?" Beverly picked up the notebook. "It's like your little book of sins. And you know what? I'd bet half of it isn't even true. It doesn't take a genius to dig for dirt. Why don't you try digging for gold? It's all around you, but you're missing it."

"If it wasn't for me, no one would've known about Mr. Becker killing his wife sixteen years ago! If I wasn't watching, it would still be a mystery today, and he'd be on the loose. And if I hadn't heard the Vanberg's argument and watched as Lynette ran away from Dylan in fear when he lost his temper that morning…"

Beverly interrupted. "Stop it right there!" She pointed her finger in Emma's face. "Lost his temper? That's not what Jackson Sawyer, your 'newspaper man' told me. He and I had a conversation about that day. Dylan was on his knees, begging his wife not to leave, and there's not an ounce of bad temper in that man. Emma, you should be ashamed of yourself for making such accusations."

Lucy approached the table. "Can I get anything for you ladies?"

Beverly spoke up. "Hi Lucy. I think you should know that Miss Emma here, is accusing you of spending the night with your boyfriend, as if it's her business. I thought maybe you could clear things up for her. If you are, you are. But if you're not, this woman needs to know because I don't want her gossiping about anyone, especially if it's not true."

Emma sat with her mouth hanging open. "Beverly!" She glared.

Lucy spoke matter-of-factly. "Miss Emma, yes, I spent the night at Jackson's house because I was too tired to drive home after our date in Marshall City. He's such a kind man. He let me have his bed and he took the couch." Emma sat speechless, not knowing what to say. Lucy continued, "You know, I see you on your front porch often. You must spend hours out there." Emma nodded. "You know what? I have a wedding to plan. Jackson and I are getting married in September. Weren't you a wedding planner several years ago?"

Emma finally spoke. "Getting married? Well, congratulations, young lady. And, yes. I used to plan weddings. I must have done several dozen over the years."

Lucy smiled. "I could use some advice. Can I bring some bridal magazines over sometime this week?"

A nervous, but delighted little smile came over Emma's face. "Why, yes. That'd be just fine."

"How about Tuesday afternoon? One o'clock?"

"Yes. Perfect."

Lucy headed to the kitchen. Beverly smirked at Emma. "Well, well. Your 'naughty little girl' doesn't seem so bad, after all, does she? Sounds like you have a wedding to plan."

Emma looked down at her notebook. "Oh, hush your mouth."

### Telling Dylan

Jackson parked his car in front of Perry's Gym. He couldn't wait to tell Dylan the news, face-to-face. "Jackson! What are you doing here?" Dylan made his way around the front desk to hug his friend. "What a sight for sore eyes."

Jackson beamed from ear-to-ear. "Tell me about it. I wish you'd come to Holly on the weekends like you used to. We all miss you, man."

"I know. I miss everyone, too. But, it's hard, you know?"

Jackson nodded. "I know. But you'll have to come out soon. A couple of your shutters got wrenched in that storm a few weeks ago."

Dylan nodded. "Yeah. I might come out this weekend, actually. I need to tend to the house and yard."

"Dude! I've wanted to call you all weekend to tell you some news, but I wanted to tell you in person." Jackson's face beamed.

Dylan's face lit up. "Well, it's nice to see you driving all the way here with good news for a change. I think I have an idea what it might be. Do tell."

"Lucy and I are getting married! In September!"

"Jackson, congratulations, man! That's great. I knew you were rolling the idea around. You and Lucy are perfect for each other."

Jackson nodded. "I figured 'why wait?' Time goes by so quickly and I want to be with her as long as I can. I don't want to wait until I'm an old codger to have children." He chuckled.

Dylan hugged him. "I'm happy for you. I assume you two will stay in Holly?"

"Yes. As far as we can see. I should be getting promoted at the Herald soon. Since they moved me to full-time and gave me the pay raise last year, I'm doing well. The next promotion will provide more than enough for us. If Holly will keep growing, I'm sure the paper will, too."

"That's awesome, man."

"So, Lucy and I want to know if you'd be able to marry us. Is that a possibility?"

Dylan smiled. "I would be absolutely honored."

"Cool. So you can still perform weddings legally, right?"

"Yep. I've still got my license. You'll be legal. No worries." He slapped Jackson on the back.

"So, I have a question for you." Jackson wrinkled his forehead. "We'd like to have the wedding at Hope Fellowship. Will that be too uncomfortable for you? We could always change the venue."

"Nah. I can handle it. Especially for you." Dylan smiled warmly.

"Thanks, Dylan. You're the best friend a guy could ever have."

### At Hope Fellowship

Elder David sat at the conference table across from Pastor Dean and the rest of the board. "Pastor, I have one more item for discussion on the agenda. Do you remember Jackson Sawyer, the newspaper reporter from the Holly Herald?"

The forty-something pastor had been at Hope Fellowship for nine months now. The town grew to love the man and his family. His five children brought new life and fresh hope to the congregation. Other than losing a few disgruntled people who were poisoned by bitterness over Dylan and Lynette's "failure," the church was recovering well and being refreshed. "Yes, I know who Jackson is."

David continued, "Well, he and his fiance have requested to be married at Hope Fellowship in September. Dylan Vanberg played a large role in their lives, and they would like him to perform the wedding ceremony. Do you have any objection to that?"

"No, not at all. Have them talk with the secretary about dates and we can arrange for that."

One of the board members spoke up. "Being that Jackson is well-known in our town, I'm pretty sure most of the community will be there. Do you think that having Dylan perform the ceremony here, being that he used to pastor this church, do you think it could cause any upheaval? You know how sensitive some people are."

Pastor Dean responded. "I have no problem with it and neither should anyone else. Dylan served in this house and community faithfully. He has the right to be on that platform, performing the ceremony. Honestly, if anyone has an issue with it, it's their own problem and I'm not going to coddle childish behavior from grown adults. This community can afford to show some grace."

David smiled. "I'm so glad we hired you."

The board member chimed in again. "You're not afraid of reigniting the hopes of people who wanted Dylan to come back?"

"Charles! That's rude," David exclaimed.

Pastor Dean leaned forward in his chair. "No. It's all right, David. Charles, I suppose that's a possibility, but I'm not afraid of losing my position in this church. It's only natural that people have a heart for Dylan, and I'm not threatened by that. He was an important part of their lives for a number of years. They have a right to love him. I'm actually excited about this wedding. It's an opportunity for us to honor Dylan in this house. And I highly suggest that we all treat him with respect and make him feel at home."

David nodded. "Yes, we will. You all know that I was a thorn in his side for awhile. I'd like to change that, and I sure hope you'll join me. Dylan was deeply moved by your kindness in sending him to Italy. Let's not cause him any feelings of regret for accepting that gesture. Agreed?"

The board replied in unison, "Agreed."

"David, will you let Jackson know it's a go?" Pastor Dean asked.

"Will do."

The meeting was dismissed.

## Chapter Twenty-One

Jackson saw Dylan's car in the driveway across the street. He picked up the phone and called Lucy. "Hey pretty lady."

Lucy answered, "Hello, Love."

"I noticed Dylan is home. Maybe this is a good time for us to talk with him about the invitation issue?"

"Sure thing. I'm glad he came this weekend. I wanted to chat with him about it face-to-face, you know? I'm kinda nervous about asking, but I feel like we don't have a choice."

Jackson sighed. "I know. Me, too. Come on over and let's get this part behind us."

Lucy encouraged him, "It'll be all right. I'm on my way."

Jackson went into the kitchen and poured himself a glass of tea. He sat in his rocking chair on the front porch, waiting for his future bride to arrive. He stared across the street, noticing the crooked shutters that Dylan continued neglecting. The yard was shaggy and mostly dead. A deep sadness came over his heart as he remembered the Christmas House in its former glory. He thought about how the future might have been if things were different for Dylan and Lynette. *I hate that they're not together anymore.*

Jackson recalled one particular evening shortly before Christmas. He took his dream girl on a date. Kristin, the sweetheart of their high school. She was the girl that every guy wanted. She was the most beautiful and talented, and to his surprise, the most rude and disrespectful. He remembered sitting across from her at a restaurant in Marshall City where they shared a wonderful candlelight dinner. After she spent thirty minutes telling him all about her life and her ambitious dreams, she finally thought to ask him about his desires.

He told Kristin about his desire to be a writer. The more he talked about his plans to start with the local newspaper and work his way up, possibly going as far as New York or Paris, Kristin laughed. "Jackson, you've got to be kidding? That's the most ridiculous thing I've ever heard. I've seen some of your essays from Mrs. Meller's class. I was her assistant," she giggled. "I helped her grade papers, and I definitely remember yours." She grabbed her stomach and laughed. "Oh my gosh. I can't even imagine you being a newspaper reporter. It would be entertaining for sure."

His heart sank that night and he felt like the biggest fool. He was happy to drop Kristin off at home and get as far away from her as he could. He would've rather dumped her on the side of the road, but he was a gentlemen. When he went home that night, he sat in his room and cried. After a few minutes, he peeked out of his window and found a calm in his soul as he focused on the scene across the street.

The Christmas House was lined with colored lights that glowed along the edges of the rooftop and wrapped around the posts of the front porch. The lights were intertwined with decorative garlands. The two little trees in the front yard were wrapped in white lights and the tree branches displayed beautifully lit ornaments. The Vanbergs had installed a small speaker on their front porch and they piped Christmas music outside to enhance the atmosphere. The wide window behind the porch swing framed a scene that looked like something out of a Christmas movie. The fabulous tree sparkled inside. Several people sat on the sofa sipping coffee and hot chocolate.

Jackson pushed past his sadness and made his way to the porch that night and listened to the music, capturing the words. *Long lay the world in sin and error pining, til He appeared and the soul felt its worth.* Those words rang in Jackson's heart. He wondered about this One who revealed the worth of peoples' souls. He found himself pulled like a magnet to the Vanberg's front door. He knocked. Dylan answered and invited him to come inside. That evening, he experienced family, love and value in a way he'd never known. Dylan and Lynette made the Christmas House a place of healing and belonging for many in the community. It was in their home that he believed in his dreams once again.

Tonight, as he waited for Lucy's arrival, he found himself in tears as he stared at the neglected house. He rocked back and forth in his chair, lulled into nostalgia and regret by the rhythmic creaking of the old, wooden porch. Finally, Lucy drove up. He composed himself and came back to the moment. Lucy's arrival reminded him of how lucky he was. He thought for a moment of the possibility that he and Lucy might also be a lighthouse for others.

"Hey, babe!" Lucy threw her arms around his neck. "I missed you."

"I missed you, too, Beautiful. I'm glad you're here." He kissed her forehead. "Would you like some tea?"

"That sounds great, but how about after we talk to Dylan?"

Jackson nodded in agreement. "Yeah. Let's get this part over with."

They headed across the street, hand in hand. "Oh, Jackson. This is nerve-wracking. I'm trying to psyche myself up for this."

He thought for a second. "Should we pray, or something like that?"

"That's a good idea. Go for it."

Jackson gripped Lucy's hands and began to pray. "Father. Thank you so much for bringing Lucy into my life. Thank You that we get to be together forever. Tonight, we ask that You be with Dylan. Help him with what we're about to ask. Let his heart be ready, and give him strength." Jackson sighed. "Oh, God…we don't want him to hurt anymore. And I know this could cause him pain, so please be here with us and just heal his heart. Thank You, Jesus."

Lucy looked up at him. "Wow. That felt good. We should do that more often."

"Yeah."

Jackson reached up and clacked the antique, brass door knocker that Dylan installed the week that Lynette left. He went nuts during that time looking for projects to distract him from his pain. The door opened. "Hey guys. Come on in." Dylan motioned for them to step inside. "How are you doing?"

"We're great," Jackson replied.

Dylan motioned for them to sit on the sofa. "Would you like some sweet tea? I just made some."

Lucy dramatically clasped her hands together and bounced up and down. "Oh, yes. The drink of Heaven. Please."

Dylan smiled. "That's one of the things I like about you, Lucy. You're like a real-life Tigger. I hope you'll consider doing that bouncing thing down the aisle at your wedding." They laughed. "Have a seat. I'll bring the tea."

Jackson and Lucy sat side-by-side on the sofa. He reached over and wrapped his hand around hers. They looked at each other anxiously. Lucy took in a deep breath. "Well, here we go," she whispered.

Jackson mouthed to her, "Divorce sucks."

She nodded in agreement.

"Lucy, let's never do that." He looked deeply into her eyes, as if to plead with her.

"Never," she said.

Dylan came back in the room. As he placed their drinks on the coffee table, Lucy admired his paintings. "Dylan, I've never seen all of your paintings. They're incredible!"

"Thank you. I haven't painted in quite awhile. Not motivated, I guess," Dylan muttered.

"The one above the fireplace is my favorite," Lucy said.

Dylan looked at the painting. He hadn't paid much attention to his work over the last year. "Those are actually real diamonds in her train and veil."

"Oh my gosh! Dylan Vanberg. You know, your name even sounds like a famous artist's name." Lucy smiled. "You really should keep painting. You could easily sell your work."

"Thanks, Lucy. Maybe. So, what brings you guys here tonight? Wedding details?"

Jackson responded, nervously. "I guess you could say that. There are some details we didn't think about before."

"Honeymoon sex, huh? You have questions?" Dylan grinned. They all burst out laughing.

"Well, I might have questions about that later," Jackson winked. "I wish that's what we were here for, but we need to discuss a dilemma regarding wedding invitations. I really hate to bother you with it."

Dylan nodded. "Yeah. I think I already know what it is. I thought about this while driving to Holly today. You need to invite Lynette, right?"

Jackson sighed. "You and Lynette have impacted both of our lives on a deep level. Lucy and I didn't see how we could not invite her. We want to be sensitive about it. We agreed that if we didn't invite her, that could cause her a lot of pain, and we don't want to hurt anyone. At the same time, we don't want to cause you pain, either."

"I understand. Divorce sucks for everyone involved. I was thinking about this detail earlier and I got worked up for a bit, but I had a long talk…," Dylan grinned, "or more like a fight, of sorts, with God, and I think I got it resolved. I've found there's something almost magical about pressing into the pain. I get through it faster than if I resist it. Anyway, I don't want to cause Lynette any pain, either, so please feel free to invite her. I thought about how awkward it would be, doing a wedding with her there, but then I thought about you guys. This is your day. And I'm going to focus on you two…not on myself or anyone else. And honestly, this gives me an opportunity to press into the pain more, and hopefully heal more."

Jackson breathed a sigh of relief. "Dylan, I don't even know how to thank you enough. I know it's extremely difficult. You're absolutely the most amazing friend I've ever had." Jackson stood to hug him.

"Anything for you, friend. When my entire life was falling apart, you were the one who came to my door." Dylan's eyes filled with tears. "I was dying that day. You have no idea how much it means to me that you knocked on my door at that moment. You're a gift from God, Jackson." He placed his hand on Jackson's shoulder.

Lucy sat on the sofa, wiping tears from her eyes. "Dylan. I'll be praying really hard for you on our wedding day. I hope somehow, something really beautiful will happen for you. You certainly deserve it."

He smiled. "Thank you, sweet Lucy."

Dylan thought for a moment. "I should probably contact Lynette. Maybe break the ice, and let her know I'll be doing the ceremony and that you guys would like her to be there. I can tell her I'm okay with it, and then leave it up to her. I'd feel better clearing the air now instead of going through the awkwardness on your wedding day."

"I think that's a good idea," Lucy agreed. "Do you have her phone number?"

"If she still has the same cell number, I do."

Lucy replied, "She doesn't. I ran into her at the store a few months ago. We chatted and she gave me her new number. She was getting prank calls and a couple of threats from people after she moved to the ranch, so she had to change her number. I'll give it to you. I'm sure she wouldn't care."

Dylan sighed. "Okay. I'll do it soon."


### The Call

Dylan half-dialed Lynette's phone number at least a dozen times. It took him a whole week to work himself up to following through. He was in Holly for the weekend and he had just opened the little "Dream Door" on the side of the porch to make sure his letters remained inside. Before Lynette remarried, he painted a small 11x14 canvas for her. It was wrapped in multiple layers of plastic and then placed inside of a special box to protect it. He wondered why he kept it all there, but he promised himself he would. He was determined to keep his promise. On that awful day when Lynette left, he told her not to forget their "special place." Deep down inside, he hoped she would return for it. Now he knew she would never come back, but he kept their special place filled with treasure anyway.

Dylan went inside the house and plopped himself on their bed, still fully decorated with the throw pillows that used to annoy him. He watched the ceiling fan circulate on low, just enough to stir the stale air. *C'mon, Dylan. You've got to do this.* He held his phone in his hand, staring at the numbers. Finally, he dialed.

As he listened to the ringing, he muttered, "God, help me."

"Hello?" A woman's voice answered. It was really her, but he wondered if it was a dream.

"Hello, Lynette?"

"Yes?"

"It's me. Dylan. I hope you don't mind me calling, but I need to let you know about something. I hope that's okay."

She hesitated. "That's fine," she replied. She sounded somewhat glad to hear his voice. "So, what is it?"

"Jackson and Lucy are getting married in September."

"Oh, my goodness. That's great! I figured they would before too long."

Dylan paused before continuing. "They want me to do their wedding. At Hope Fellowship."

"Wow. That's...something. Should be interesting for you." She didn't know what to say.

He hesitated. "They would really like for you to be there to celebrate with them. You really impacted their lives. They're hoping you and I can work it out, you know...for both of us to be there? I know it's awkward, but I wanted to let you know before you receive the invitation. I didn't want you to reply to it, not knowing who was doing the ceremony."

She half-smiled at his consideration. "That was thoughtful. Thanks for letting me know. I'll think about it. I suppose it can work."

They sat in silence for a few seconds. Dylan's chin began to quiver. He fought hard to stay in control of his emotions. He wished he could tell her that he still loved her, but she was married to another man. "So, how are you?"

She sighed. "I'm doing all right. It's been a tough time, actually..." Her voice cracked slightly. "I've had two miscarriages." She bit her lip, trying to contain her sorrow. "It's hard."

"Lynette. I'm so sorry." Dylan's voice shook. Inside his head, he was screaming, 'She should be having my baby!' But he remained calm. "I'm really sorry you're going through that. I know how much having a baby means to you."

She spoke softly. "Thank you. I'd better go. I'll probably see you at the wedding."

"Okay. Lynette?"

"Yeah?"

"I'll be praying for you."

"Thanks, Dylan. Goodbye."

Dylan laid the phone on his chest and a tear fell down the side of his head. "Oh, Jesus."

Lynette hung up the phone and pressed it to her heart. She couldn't understand the longing that had never gone away since she left home. As hard as she tried to settle in at the ranch, it wasn't home. She and Owen had some good times, but life was growing mundane and she had trouble connecting with him. She wondered what was missing.

Owen was becoming impatient with her. He was bothered by her obsession with trying to have a baby, which she couldn't understand since they both agreed they wanted to have children right away. He complained about her ovulation charts and spending money on the nursery that she painted and decorated. After losing the two babies, she would often cry beside the empty crib. Owen would simply shut the door and leave. She never felt so utterly alone.

Their relationship swung on a pendulum, from one extreme to another. Owen would romance her and speak of their future together, and other days she wondered if he was ready to call it quits. Lynette was determined to make the marriage work. All of the turmoil and upheaval for their family, friends and community…it couldn't have been for nothing. She reminded herself of this often.

During the times when she felt alone, she'd lie in bed, thinking about the time she and Owen first made a connection in art class. He understood her like no other. He had listened carefully. The words he spoke to her always came at the right moment and awakened her heart to something she hadn't felt in a long time. He seemed to know her thoughts. She remembered longing for Owen, thinking of him every time she returned home to Dylan. She felt a sense of truly being free, independent, and valued for who she was when she was with Owen. Eventually, Dylan faded away from her vision, like an insignificant detail. She'd wake up in the mornings, seeing Owen in her mind before turning to see the face of Dylan who lay next to her in bed.

Now, she sat, staring into the air, wondering when and how things had shifted, because Dylan was beginning to consume her thoughts.

## Chapter Twenty-Two

### The Wedding

It was a mild and sunny September afternoon. The arched doorway of Hope Fellowship was framed with garlands of green ivy and white bows. Inside the sanctuary, the first few rows were marked with ornate, antique brass candelabras. A snowy white aisle runner made its way to the altar where communion and the unity candle awaited the two lovers who would become one. Lucy's dreams of combining decor from the Victorian era and the Roaring Twenties was evident in the room which was now filled with classical music. The harpist and cellist swayed with the sounds that flowed from their instruments. Lucy seemed to have a knack for doing gaudy tastefully. Not too overdone. Excessive, yet simple. It reflected her spirit, which Jackson loved deeply, and he found the decor to be quite fitting.

Jackson, Dylan and the groomsmen gathered in a Sunday School room, chatting and laughing as they prepared for the ceremony. The guys babbled on with the typical jokes and jabs that most bachelors hear right before they get married. As one of the groomsmen lifted up a bottle of water, he commented, "Jackson, here's to you, for being brave enough to forfeit your freedom forever." The guys chuckled.

Jackson raised his water, grinning, "And here's to you, my friends, who will remember me when you're wishing you had an amazing, attractive woman in your bed every night."

"Aw, man! Not fair!"

"You're under new management, now, Jackson. Just wait and see."

Tony piped up. "Jackson, didn't you do the news report about the original Holly courthouse being torn down a couple of years ago?"

"Yeah. Why?" Jackson thought that was an odd question in the middle of everyone's jesting.

"Don't you remember the wrecking ball, dude? I'm just sayin'…your life is about to change in a big way." Tony smashed his fist into his own palm. "Bam!"

"And for that, I'm thankful." Jackson smiled.

Dylan was getting annoyed with the negative jokes and remarks about marriage. He began pacing back and forth, considering an exit. *Why am I so sensitive about this stuff? They're just having fun.* He couldn't bite his tongue, however.

Dylan cleared his throat. "Hey guys. Can I have your attention for a minute?" The groomsmen quieted down and turned their attention to Dylan. "I know this is the typical stuff that men say before a wedding, and I know you feel an obligation to bring the same old, snarky comments that have been passed down through the years. You know, the 'old ball and chain' comments? But personally, I'm sick of it. You guys know about the hell I went through awhile back, but you know what? I don't regret getting married at all. Sure, our marriage ended but I learned more about love than I ever knew before. My heart has come alive in ways that I didn't know was possible. I see people differently. I see life differently. What Jackson is doing today is the most noble thing a man can do, besides laying down his life for someone."

One of the men butted in. "Isn't that what he's doing? Laying down his life for someone?"

Dylan thought for a moment. "You know, you're actually right. And I wish I had laid down my life for my wife the way I should have. We'd probably still be together today. I'd appreciate it if we shift things here and start speaking some positive stuff into Jackson's life. You never know what life might bring, and this is your day, as his friends, to fill him with good things to encourage him and give him strength through the hard days. Is that too much to ask?"

"Sounds good to me," said Mark. The rest of the guys nodded.

Jackson shook Dylan's hand and threw his arm around his neck. "Thanks, man. I really appreciate that."

In the women's lounge, the ladies calmly helped Lucy get into her dress. The room smelled of hair spray and perfume. Bobby pins, hair clips and cosmetics were strewn across the floor and countertops. Large mirrors covered two walls. Bras were being strapped and zippers were being zipped. "It's time for your veil, Lucy!" The women squealed with excitement.

"Oh, my gosh. You look gorgeous!"

"Ugh…I'm already starting to cry. Stop it, stop it," one girl said as she waved her hand in front of her eyes. "I'm going to be a mess! It's a good thing this mascara is waterproof."

Lucy smiled. "I made sure to wear the waterproof stuff. I hope it works."

Lucy's dark hair was pulled back into a small, Victorian-style bun and curly fringes framed her face. Her hair was dotted with white pearl pins. Her side-swept bangs complimented her face, and her red lipstick enhanced her silky, fair skin. As her mother positioned the veil, Lucy looked at herself in the mirror. Her blue eyes glowed with immense light.

Guests whispered amongst themselves as they waited for the ceremony to begin. Dylan excused himself from the guy's room. "I'll be right back." Jackson's excitement took a momentary plummet as he considered what Dylan was facing. He checked the time. Fifteen minutes to go-time!

Jackson interrupted, "Hey, guys. I'm gonna step out for a minute. I'll be right back." Jackson wanted to check on Dylan before it all began.

"Uh-oh. You thinking about runnin'? Gettin' cold feet?" One of the guys poked at him.

"No way! I'd be a fool." Jackson winked.

"Preacher man just left, and now you. I hope y'all make it back in time. But no worries. If you don't show up, I'll step in for you. I wouldn't mind having Lucy."

"In your dreams, Tony." Jackson stepped out.

He checked the men's restroom, but there was no sign of Dylan. He hurried through the hallways, peering into each classroom and office. Nothing. *God, please help Dylan. Please let him be okay.* He opened the exit to the small playground.

"Thank God!" He spotted Dylan sitting on a swing.

Dylan looked up at him. "Hey, man. Are you ready?"

"I am. Are you?" Jackson put his hand on his shoulder.

Dylan dropped his head and shuffled the gravel with his shoe. He sighed heavily. "I'm ready. It's going to be weird to see Lynette. I'm dreading the sight of seeing her with Owen."

"I doubt Owen will be here. But if he is, just remember that you're the better man." Jackson felt terrible for putting his friend in a difficult situation. "Man, I'm sorry to put you in an awkward position."

"Don't even think of it, Jackson. I'm honored to marry you and Lucy. Honestly, this is a highlight for me. You and Lucy getting together is the best thing that's happened to me in quite awhile. I'm glad to get you two hitched." Dylan stood from the swing and patted Jackson's back. "It's time. Let's do this!" The two embraced.

As they pulled apart, Jackson shook Dylan's hand, smiling. "You are the best friend I've ever had. Ever."

Dylan nodded. "I can say the same thing of you."

As the wedding began and the men took their places on the platform, Lynette's body surged with adrenaline at the sight of Dylan. The mixture of emotions took her breath away. The resentment she once had for him was no longer there. The anger she carried toward him was a vapor. All that remained was a gentle compassion, and something that caused her to shift in her seat. *Oh, my God. I think I still love him.* It was hard to remember exactly why she had resented him so deeply. Waves of guilt and shame threatened to sweep her heart away. Though no one was paying attention to her, she felt as if the entire room was caving in on her with accusation.

Lynette reminded herself that what's done is done. *It is what it is*, she would often tell herself. She thought about her love for her new husband, Owen, and how his kindness and attention had given her life when she was drowning under the weight of being a neglected pastor's wife. She thought about the way he regarded her dreams for the future. Dylan was once oblivious to them.

Now she sat, staring at the man on the platform who used to be her husband. There he was in real life, yet he was like the ghost of someone she thought she once knew. She was suddenly glad that Owen didn't want to attend. Having him at her side would be too awkward, especially while she was experiencing emotions that she hadn't felt for so long. Deep down inside, she sensed a longing for the man on the platform, remembering a time when their two hearts were knit together. It wasn't until this moment that she became aware of the torment of their separation.

Lynette recalled that day when Dylan wept on his knees in their front yard. At that time, she felt nothing for him. Her heart was numb and cold. Now, she considered the depth of pain that a man would have to feel in order to humiliate himself publicly. She remembered walking into their bedroom to pack her things. She remembered Dylan lying on the floor, crying. She wondered how she could have been so heartless. *My God. I seriously owe him an apology.* Seeing Dylan was doing something inside of her, and she wasn't sure she liked it. Parts of her heart were awakening, and she wondered at what point they even died.

Dylan decided before walking out onto the platform that it would be best not to scan the crowd. He didn't think his heart could handle the sight of Lynette. He longed to see her, but it would hurt too much. He chose to focus on the first rows only, where Jackson and Lucy's families would be seated. He watched each bridesmaid walk down the aisle, and then he set his gaze on the sanctuary doors, waiting to see Lucy in all her glory.

As Lucy approached the doorway, Dylan's face glowed with joy for the young couple. His mind flashed to his own wedding and the overwhelming elation that filled his being at the sight of Lynette as she made her way toward him. He quickly pushed the thought aside. Dylan glanced at Jackson. He hadn't seen a happier man. He was in awe of the beauty and purity of Jackson's tears. He hoped with everything in him that his friend would never know the agony of infidelity. Watching loved ones step into the covenant of marriage was frightening and exciting all at once. *Truly, getting married is the most stupid and most brilliant thing a man can do. It's the ugliest and the most wonderful union.* Dylan was considered the irony.

Lynette glanced to her right and met the glaring eyes of old Emma Gray. Emma positioned herself where she could accomplish her self-righteous mission of firing daggers into Lynette's soul. Lynette quickly looked down, trying to shield herself from the flames. She tried hard to listen to the ceremony, but her focus was distracted by the voice of the accuser that rang through her head.

She pressed into Dylan's words to the congregation. "Love is patient. Love is kind and is not jealous. Love does not brag and is not arrogant, does not act unbecomingly. It does not seek its own, is not provoked, does not take into account a wrong suffered. Love does not rejoice in unrighteousness, but rejoices with the truth; love bears all things, believes all things, hopes all things, endures all things. Love never fails." The words of the famous love chapter from First Corinthians evoked guilt in Lynette as she considered how she failed at love.

Dylan continued. "As a minister, I've read this chapter numerous times. I memorized it. I could say it in my sleep, but I really didn't comprehend it. How often do we tell someone, 'I love you?' We say it, but perhaps the better question to ask is, 'Do you feel loved by me?' We may think we're loving someone, but it's possible that we could be lacking in the art of loving. Throughout your marriage, Jackson and Lucy, I encourage you to frequently ask each other, 'Do you feel loved by me?' This question isn't for the purpose of manipulating one another, but for making sure that our spouse is comprehending the love that we believe we're giving. It's for the purpose of learning to speak each other's love language. When we become vulnerable with our spouse and provide them with a safe place for honesty, our connection is strengthened. In that place, we can empower each other."

Dylan laid his Bible on the altar. "When Jackson and Lucy first came to me to talk about their desire to get married, I asked them the question, 'Are you willing to walk with him…are you willing to walk with her, through the valley of the shadow of death?' Now, I know that sounds dark and I don't mean to suppress the joy of this occasion, but I want to point out the incredible maturity and willingness that these two carry. Neither one is afraid of the shadow. They are willing to walk with each other."

The young couple smiled. Dylan continued, "There's something about knowing that when the shadows and doubts come in life, you have someone by your side who's willing to walk with you through your dark night. This is why it's important to ask, 'Do you feel loved by me?' Because it's easy to lose sight and become oblivious to the feelings of your spouse, especially when challenges arise."

Lynette shifted in her seat, uncomfortable with hearing her ex-husband give marriage advice, but she appreciated his words. She supposed that everyone could learn from their mistakes. Her discomfort, however, came from her awareness of her blindness that led her to walk away from Dylan in his blindness.

Dylan's words grabbed her attention. "…and know if your spouse is falling into that valley alone. Stay aware and be the protector of their soul. You never know what someone might be facing, and your spouse should never face the darkness alone. Love regards the other above self. Love is willing to lay down everything for the other. And love is patient while the other walks their own journey. Love does not judge, but only gives grace. And grace…grace heals."

Several minutes later, the ceremony was complete. The jubilant couple beamed as they walked the aisle as 'Mr. and Mrs. Sawyer.' At the reception, Lynette chose a corner table, hoping to hide herself away from the crowd. She didn't want to be rude to Jackson and Lucy by skipping out.

"Hi, Lynette!" Sweet Marcy wrapped her arms around her. Lynette noticed the perfume that Marcy always wore. Tresor. The fragrance evoked warm memories of many wonderful conversations with Elder David's wife. Marcy was the one woman that she felt safe with.

"Marcy!" Lynette threw her arms around her. "How are you doing?"

"Very well. Oh, I'm so happy to see you here today. I know it means a lot to Jackson and Lucy. They love you so much." Marcy's eyes poured love and compassion into her soul.

"Well, I wouldn't miss it. They're a special couple."

"How are you doing, Lynnie?" *Lynnie*. That's what Dylan often called her. She hadn't heard that nickname in ages, and it reminded her of who she used to be…the woman that no longer existed, yet it felt wonderful to be reminded of her.

"I'm doing all right. Things are good for the most part. I'm just having a hard time working through two miscarriages." Her eyes filled with tears. Lynette wouldn't have shared the news with anyone else at Hope Fellowship, but she knew that Marcy would have compassion for her despite her lousy decisions in the past.

"Oh, no. I'm so sorry, sweetie. I can identify with you. Forty-three years ago, I lost a little boy one month before his due date. His name was John. It's something you never forget."

Lynette looked surprised. "I had no idea you'd been through that. I'm so sorry, Marcy."

"Well, I don't tell many people, especially after all these years. It's one of those things we don't understand. It just seems senseless. But life goes on and we adjust, I suppose. What gives me peace is knowing that John is fully alive and someday I'll get to meet him." Marcy smiled.

Emma Gray approached the table. "Well, well. I never thought I'd see you here. What'd you think about that ceremony your old hubby pulled off?"

Marcy winced and prepared herself to shield Lynette from Emma's bitterness.

"It was lovely," Lynette smiled.

"Sounds like he's learned quite a bit about love and marriage. It's interesting what we learn from our mistakes, eh?"

Marcy glared at Emma.

Lynette remained calm. "Are you saying that I was a mistake, Miss Emma?" She could play this game.

"Why, of course not! I'm just saying we can all learn from our mess-ups. Oh, never mind." Emma flicked her hand as if to wipe away the whole encounter. She walked away from the table.

Marcy raised her eyebrows. "You know ole' Emma Gray. Bitter old woman has no shame."

The two ladies giggled. "Well, it's good seeing you. I'm going to check with the servers and see if they need an extra hand."

Lynette looked intently at her old friend. "Marcy? It's refreshing to see your face." The ladies exchanged smiles.

"And yours, too, dear." Marcy embraced her before walking away.

As Lynette exited the building, she found herself face-to-face with Dylan. She was stunned.

"Dylan!" She fumbled for words.

"Hey. I'm glad you came. So, did I do okay?" Dylan always cared about what Lynette thought of his public speaking skills. Her opinion mattered the most, at least in the beginning.

Lynette nodded. "It was lovely. Just perfect for Jackson and Lucy. You did a great job."

"Thanks. Are you doing all right? I've been praying for you."

Dylan's kindness touched her deeply. How could he pray for someone who had hurt him so terribly? She nodded her head 'yes,' and dropped her gaze to the ground. "It's crazy how you can grieve over someone you never got to meet. Carrying a life inside of you…it's pretty intense."

"I can only imagine."

She wasn't sure she should ask him, but she managed, "And you? How are you doing?"

Dylan sighed. "I'm hangin' in there. Pretty much a loser, actually. I live at my parent's place during the week so I can be close to my job. I'm sure you've heard about all of that?"

"Actually, I haven't. No one tells me anything."

"Oh?" He looked surprised. Apparently there wasn't as much gossip going around as he'd imagined. "I work at a gym in Marshall City, pretty much working the front desk, cleaning and maintaining the place. I'm looking for other jobs, but there are few to come by."

"Are you going to get a place there?"

Dylan shook his head. "I love it here in Holly. I don't want to give up the house. This is home. Since I've got the mortgage, it's pretty impossible for me to afford another place. I keep hoping a job will open up here so I can move back."

Lynette felt awful for him. *Once an influential minister, adored and admired by a whole community, now a gym boy, living at his parent's home? How horrible.*

"Dylan?" Her face appeared heavy.

"Yeah?"

She clenched her eyes shut. "I owe you a major apology, and honestly, I know that 'I'm sorry' isn't enough." She opened her eyes and looked at him. "I didn't even see it until recently, how badly I treated you. It was unfair and I'm really sorry for what I put you through. I hope you can find happiness with someone you deserve."

Dylan's eyes filled with tender tears of relief. Unspoken burdens lifted from his heart. Without thinking, he wrapped his arms around her tightly. For a moment, she felt herself sinking into him, but she pulled away as Owen crossed her mind. She fought back tears. Her mother's frequent quote rang through her head, *You've made your bed. Now lie in it.*

"I'm sorry, Lynette. I don't mean to make you uncomfortable."

She wiped a tear away, looking down. "No. It's okay."

Dylan thanked God for a moment to say things he wished he could. "Thank you for what you said. I owe you an apology as well. I was selfish. I was feeding my own ego with the praises of people. I really lost sight of what was important. I'm sorry for the suffering you experienced because of me. I'm sorry for every moment when you felt alone. I wish I'd done things differently. And I want you to know that I forgive you."

Her chin trembled at his words. "Thank you. I'd say I forgive you, too, but I really don't have anything to forgive."

Dylan stepped back, knowing he needed to keep his distance. He couldn't afford to let his heart go where it wanted to. He tried to find appropriate words for a final departure, yet he didn't want it to be final. But it had to be. She was married now. "Is he good to you?"

She nodded. "Yeah. He is."

"That's all that matters." They looked at each other for a few seconds. Dylan's eyes shifted to the ground. "I'd better be going."

Lynette nodded again. "Me, too. Good luck, Dylan."

"You, too, Lynnie. And, may all your dreams come true. I really mean it." He turned to walk away.

The way he called her 'Lynnie' stirred up a sense of belonging and security that was now a hazy recollection. Lynette knew he was making a reference to their Dream Door. '*May all your dreams come true.*' It was once their tagline.

In the beginning of their life together in Holly, they spent hours on their porch swing and in their rocking chairs, discussing dreams. Many good memories were now haunting her and she wondered why she threw them away. It seemed she could no longer remember the offenses that peeled her heart from his.

Lynette walked quickly to her car, frantic to remove herself from Hope Fellowship and the longing she was experiencing. As she pulled onto the road, she let out a scream from the pit of her stomach as she pounded the steering wheel. Regret crushed her like a steamroller. She felt her soul ripping apart. She pressed the accelerator hard as she turned onto the county road that led to the ranch. Tears blinded her vision and she wailed so loudly, she swore her throat was being shredded by the tormented soul inside of her.

A truck passed by. Owen's truck. She looked in the rearview mirror and saw him turning around to follow her. "This is all I need!" She slammed her palm down on the steering wheel. "Why?" Owen came up close behind her, honking his horn and motioning for her to pull over. As she slowed down, she tried wiping every tear away, but she knew there was no hiding it. She failed to wear waterproof makeup. She looked at herself in the mirror just to double-check. "Idiot!" She loathed the person in the mirror.

She came to a stop on the side of the road. Owen slammed his truck door shut and came toward her car, stomping his feet. "Lynette! What the heck are you doing? Do you realize how fast you were going? Are you trying to kill yourself or someone out here?"

She turned her face toward him. His mood shifted. "My God, woman. What's wrong?" She collapsed into a sobbing mess. Owen went to the passenger's side and opened the door, scooting in next to her. "What, baby? What happened?"

All she could do was cry. "The wedding was too much, wasn't it?"

She nodded.

"I was worried about you going to that wedding. I'm sorry. I shouldn't have let you go." He wrapped his arms around her. "Shhh. It's all right. It'll be okay."

She laid her head on his shoulder and groaned. "I'm sorry, Owen."

"For what?"

"For everything. I don't know. Just everything."

Owen caressed her cheek. "You don't have anything to be sorry for. Let's just go home and get some rest."

She was grateful for his gentleness. It had been awhile since she'd experienced this side of Owen.

## Chapter Twenty-Three

Dylan sat in his house, writing a long letter to Lynette, detailing his thoughts and emotions after encountering her at the Sawyer wedding. *Why am I doing this to myself?* He couldn't understand his need to continue writing, but he was compelled to keep filling the space under the porch, and it was strangely therapeutic for Dylan. *Someday, I'll burn everything.*

He placed the letter in a red envelope, sealed it, and proceeded to put it behind the Dream Door. As he reached around the overgrown rose bush, he pricked his hand on a thorn. He stared at the puncture wound, watching as blood came to the surface and slowly trickled out. He was intrigued by the sight. He waited patiently to see what path the blood would take. The red line traveled down his thumb and fell onto the soil below. "Beautiful," he muttered to himself.

Dylan watched the blood and dirt mix into mud, and he thought about Jesus in the garden, awaiting his persecution. Dylan once preached a sermon about the stress that Jesus endured throughout the process of His suffering. He spoke about Luke, who was a physician and disciple of Christ, and how he'd written about Jesus being in such anguish that His sweat was like drops of blood. Dylan did some research and found several articles written by doctors who spoke of a stress that's so intense, it could cause blood vessels to rupture, pouring blood into the sweat glands.

*Wow*. He pondered that level of anxiety and wondered how Jesus lived through it. Dylan was sure that he himself nearly died from a broken heart, and not even he had sweat drops of blood. He reached down and rubbed his finger in the bloodied mud, studying it. He wiped it on the red envelope as he placed it inside. *I'm leaving more than my heart in here. It's odd how morbidity comforts me at times.*

He rounded the corner of his house and noticed Emma Gray sitting alone on her front porch. She was still dressed in her wedding attire. She rocked back and forth, sipping a glass of lemonade. Dylan felt drawn to the old woman, so he made his way down the street to pay her a visit.

"Hey, Emma."

She saw him coming, but she was shocked that he actually stepped foot on her porch. "Well, hello, Dylan. It's not everyday that I get a visit from a handsome, young man. Come have a seat." She pointed at the rocking chair. "Did I win the lottery today?"

Dylan chuckled. "How are you doing?

"Oh, I'm doing fair for an old woman, I suppose. That was sure a nice wedding you did today."

"Thanks. I'm happy for Jackson and Lucy. They're some of the finest people I know."

"Yes, I believe they are. That Lucy turned out to be quite a jewel. I couldn't believe she asked me to help with her wedding plans. Sweet gal."

"Oh, yeah! I forgot you helped her. Everything was beautiful! You two did a fantastic job."

"Thank you." Emma beamed.

Silence lingered for a minute. "So, Dylan. If you don't mind me asking, how was it seeing Lynette again?"

He knew the question would arise, so it didn't catch him off guard. This would be good practice for formulating an answer for the other hundred people that would ask the same question.

"Well. I'd be lying if I said it was easy."

They rocked in unison. "Do you still love her?"

Now, that was a question he didn't expect. It hit him like a bullet, grazing his heart. He took a deep breath.

Emma explained. "I don't mean to be nosy. It's just that I think she still loves you."

He was shocked. "Really? Why would you think that?"

"I've lived long enough to notice a woman with regrets. And I can recognize a woman who's still in love with someone. I should know."

The observation was like a breath of fresh air to Dylan's heart, yet it pained him because there was nothing he could do about it.

"She's married, though. I guess it's pointless to think about. But, yes...I still love Lynette."

"I knew that." She grinned.

A black, Mercedes SUV slowly rolled in front of Emma's house and came to a stop by the curb. "I've never seen that car before. Who on earth could that be?"

A well-dressed, middle-aged woman approached them. Emma piped up, "I paid my taxes, so it sure can't be the I.R.S."

The woman stepped onto the porch. "Hello. I'm looking for Emma Gray."

Nervously, Emma answered. "I'm Emma. How can I help you?"

The woman gawked at her, and put her hand over her mouth. "Oh, wow."

Emma was puzzled. "May I ask who you are?"

"My name is Kathleen Vinsant. I'm from Nashville, Tennessee."

Emma questioned her. "So what brings you here? You're causing me alarm, Miss."

The woman approached, gently touching Emma's hand, "Oh, no, please don't be alarmed. I'm sorry. I just came because..." The woman's eyes moistened. "Well, did you happen to give birth to a baby girl in Phoenix in 1960?" The woman was oblivious to Dylan's presence. He sat watching inquisitively.

Emma gasped and placed her hand over her heart. "Oh, dear." Emma hesitated. "Yes, I did."

The woman shed a tear. "I'm your daughter."

Emma stood from her chair and looked into her daughter's eyes compassionately. She reached to touch her cheek. "Oh, baby." Emma gasped. "It's you."

"Can I hug you?" her daughter asked.

"Why, of course!" Emma embraced her little girl for the first time. The two wept. Dylan wiped tears from his eyes.

"I've wanted to meet you for years, but I didn't think you wanted me. I started doing more research and, long story short, I found out that you gave me up reluctantly. I knew I had to find you."

Emma held her daughter's face in her hands. "I've always wanted you. It was a tough situation. I was forced to give you up. Circumstances were bad and I was convinced I wouldn't be able to give you a good life. Oh, look at you! You're more beautiful than I ever imagined."

Emma turned to Dylan. "Look at my daughter, Emily. Isn't she beautiful?"

Kathleen was taken aback. "Emily?"

"Yes, dear. That's the name I gave you. Emily Rose."

The woman sobbed as she held her chest. "You named me? Oh, my gosh."

A young man and woman stepped out of the SUV and approached them. Kathleen motioned for them to come. "Mom, I want you to meet your grandson and granddaughter. This is Maximilian and Mandy."

Emma was overcome with emotion. She held both hands over her mouth, overwhelmed with excitement and joy.

Beverly Watkins was taking her dog for its evening walk. She wondered what the commotion was on Emma's front porch. "If there's a party going on, she had better invite me!" She climbed the steps. "Hey! I'm here! Now the party can start!"

Emma turned to her. "Oh, Beverly! Come meet my daughter and grandkids."

Beverly stood, blinking her eyes. "Uh. Your daughter?" Beverly looked at the woman. "Can someone explain?"

Emma patted her on the back. "Oh, Bev. It's a long story that I'll tell you about later. But this is my girl, Emily Rose. Well, her adopted name is Kathleen."

### The Richland's

Kat lay with her back to Preston. He held her while she verbally processed her thoughts. "That was kind of Jackson to invite us to his wedding. He doesn't know us that well. I'm glad we went. The stuff Dylan talked about…about walking through the darkness with someone…it's so true. I've never heard anyone talk like that at a wedding before. It's usually all light and fluffy. It's like, why don't people talk about these things in the beginning? It reminds me of when I had Larson. Nine months of carrying a baby…you read books and have baby showers, but no one bothers to warn you about the first time you look down at your stomach after giving birth, and it's like a deflated balloon.

No one tells you about the possibility of cracked nipples, the necessity of lanolin lotion, dealing with episiotomy stitches, or just how many times you'll get pooped on."

Preston chuckled. "I guess you've got a point there."

"Life is messy. Even those women's meetings I led. I didn't count on how much snot I'd have to wipe off my shirt. I thought women's ministry was all about fun, little ladies groups, studying the Bible. I had no idea what I'd be dealing with. I've been thinking about the pretty pictures we paint for others, and how we've made unbelievers feel like if they'd just come to church, their lives will be without problems. At least, that's what I thought. If you just do A,B,C, and D, then everything will be under control. I'm beginning to think God really isn't in control. It's like, He allows people to make their mistakes, and He doesn't control them…but He has authority to make everything work out for good."

"Man, Kat. I've never heard you talk like this.

"I think this way all the time, lately. I feel like my eyes are wide open. I don't always like what I see, though."

Preston caressed her cheek. Kat continued thinking out loud. "I wonder if suffering is necessary. Like, can't we know what we need to know and see what we need to see without suffering?"

"I don't know. I just feel like a fool for being the source of your suffering. I regret it everyday."

She took a deep breath. "Well, I'm glad you're here now. I'm glad you're who you are." She patted his hand.

He kissed her head. "You're the most amazing woman I know."

Kat stared at the ceiling, thinking. "I was so angry at you for breaking our covenant. And all along, I was sinning, too, for being unforgiving. We're commanded to forgive. If I can't forgive, then I'm doing something against God's heart, and I'm just as guilty. I had this thought. 'Was your sin strong enough to break our covenant?' I had a dream that made me think perhaps the covenant is more powerful than anything that tries to break it. The strength of the covenant lies in this: that God Himself keeps covenant even when we fail, and He's faithful to restore what we've tried to break. It just blows my mind. It's all so hard to comprehend."

Preston raised his eyebrows. "That's an amazing thought."

She continued her thought process. "I heard a preacher say that God can win with any hand He's dealt. At first, I didn't understand that because I don't know how Poker works, but someone explained it to me. I'm beginning to believe it's true. I hate the hand that was dealt to me...to us...but with Him, we're winning. Some days, I feel like I'm losing, but then there's some good days."

Preston closed his eyes. "Every now and then, it'll hit me, how close I came to losing you. And the kids. And I feel like a man that escaped death. I'm beyond thankful."

Kat rolled over to face him. "I can't even bear the thought." They embraced and began kissing. As they shared breath, they both became aware of their union and connection in spirit. Preston imagined her kisses as cleansing him. He thought he heard a whisper, "Stepping into me. I in you and you in me."

He opened his eyes and looked around the room.

"What's wrong?"

"Nothing. I just thought I heard something."

### At the Ranch

"So, are you ready to talk about what happened today?" Owen sat on the bed next to Lynette.

"There's really nothing to talk about. It was just an emotional day."

"Hmm. Let's see if I remember this correctly. A wild woman, speeding dangerously down the road, bawling her eyes out. And you say there's nothing to talk about?"

"I'd just rather not. I want to forget it and move on."

"Lynette, are you talking about the church, or about…him?"

"Just everything."

Owen's jaw tightened and he bit his lip. "If I understand what 'everything' means, then it includes Dylan."

She didn't answer.

"You said you were sure about this marriage, Lynette. You promised me you had no desire to be with him." He tried to remain calm. "Look, I had my doubts, too, but I committed and went for it. I laid all my cards on the table."

"I don't want to be with Dylan. It's not that. We grew apart."

Owen watched her inquisitively. "But you wonder if you could've grown back together, don't you?"

Lynette hesitated. "No. Look. It was just hard being there and seeing familiar faces. Some of them scowled at me, but for the most part, people were considerate."

"So, that's all?"

"That's all." She sat up and kissed him on the lips. He grabbed the back of her head to pull her close. The smell of his cologne reminded her of their first encounters and her body responded to the memories.

Owen's cell phone rang. It was his best buddy, Will. "Hang on a sec. Will doesn't usually call me in the evenings. Let me see what's up." Owen answered and left the bedroom.

Lynette stepped into the bathroom to freshen up. She gargled mouthwash and brushed her hair. She gazed at the woman in the mirror, trying to connect with her. She felt like two different people. Many years ago, she was confident and sure about who she was, but now she could barely remember the woman that used to be. Her identity was once wrapped up in being Dylan's wife. Now, she needed to be Owen's wife. She wasn't sure who she was outside of that. She wasn't even sure she really knew Owen.

Lynette slipped her bathrobe on and as she tied the belt around her waist, she thought of the babies she lost. She placed her hands on her belly. Thinking about the two who lived a short life inside of her, she longed for the destiny that was stolen from her. *Maybe I deserve it.*

In the mirror, she saw Owen step into the doorway, face red, and glaring at her. She turned around. "What's wrong?"

"Apparently, you left out some details about your outing."

"What are you talking about?"

"It's real nice finding out from a friend that your wife was in the arms of her ex-husband."

"Oh, my gosh, Owen. I had a brief conversation with Dylan on my way out and he hugged me. That was it! 'In the arms' of my ex-husband? How ridiculous."

"Well, I find it interesting that you neglected to mention talking with Dylan! That's kind of a big deal. From what I was told, you appeared to be pretty emotional, and the hug wasn't just an ordinary hug."

"I was apologizing to him! Nothing happened."

"So after all this time, you decide an apology is necessary?"

"Owen, it was the first time I've talked to him in ages. And I never said I was sorry for what I put him through. What's so wrong with that? It's common decency. Did it ever dawn on you that maybe you should apologize, too?"

Owen slapped her face. "I never intended to betray a friend. You led me on and I gave into it!"

Lynette held her cheek, breathing heavily and holding back tears. "My God, Owen! What are you doing?"

He stood in the doorway, breathing hard. Fear crept over his face. He stepped backwards into the bedroom and collapsed on the floor. "My God. Oh, my God. What have I done?"

Lynette wept as she watched him process his actions.

"I didn't mean to do that. I've never hit a woman in my life. Lynette, I am so sorry. I'll never do that again." Owen began to weep.

Lynette got on her knees next to him. She wrapped her arms around him as he sobbed. "It's okay. I know you didn't mean to. I'm sorry I didn't tell you about Dylan. I'm sorry."

## Chapter Twenty-Four
### At Annie's Cafe

Beverly noticed that Emma arrived empty-handed. "Well, I'll be. Emma Gray, where's your little notebook?"

Emma rolled her eyes. "Give me a break, Beverly. I've got enough to tell you about without my notebook. It's all about me this time."

Beverly smiled. "So fill me in. Suddenly, out of nowhere, a daughter pops up? Why didn't you ever mention you'd given up a child for adoption? We've been friends for quite some time."

Emma shrugged. "I know. I never told anyone. I was nineteen and new to college. I fell in love with a man, and you know...stuff happened."

"Who was the man?"

Emma looked out the window, her vision peering into the past. Beverly realized she had missed an entire part of who Emma Gray was, and she'd never seen her eyes look so soft...and distant.

"It was bad, Beverly. I was young and vulnerable. I fell in love with someone that I probably shouldn't have. But to this day, I still have feelings for him."

"Who was he?"

Emma looked at Beverly straight in the eye. I only tell you this because I know you to be a woman of grace. You've taught me things about loving people that I refused to accept. Probably because I couldn't forgive myself." Emma sighed. "His name was August Tatley. He was my music teacher."

"Oh, my." Beverly listened intently.

"We were madly in love. He was only three years older than me. We talked about getting married when I finished school, but I got pregnant. We tried talking with our families, but that didn't go well. My dad went to the college board and raked August over the coals." Emma looked down, shaking her head. "August was fired, and because of the scandal, he couldn't stay in the area. No one would hire him. Our parents forbid us marrying and mine convinced me that I had no choice but to give the baby up for adoption. The only way my dad would keep funding my education was if I gave her up." Emma's eyes filled with tears.

Beverly reached across the table and patted her hand. "I'm sorry, Em. Did you stay in touch with August?"

"We tried for awhile, but it was complicated. We had no support. He was broke. I had nothing. We eventually decided we had to part ways, for good. It was the hardest thing I've ever done in my life."

"Didn't he want the baby?"

"Yes, but his entire family pressured him, as well. The Tatleys were highly regarded in the community and quite the snobs. They'd never accept me. Or a child born out of wedlock."

Beverly inquired, "Your husband, Harry…he knew about this, right?"

Emma shook her head. "No. I should have told him, but I was afraid. I thought he might leave me."

Beverly gasped. "Oh, my. I can't even imagine how hard it must have been to hide such a secret."

"Yeah. When he was diagnosed with cancer, I thought about telling him, you know? I didn't want to live our entire lives carrying a secret. But I couldn't bring myself to burden him, especially after he got sick. I hoped he'd get better. But he didn't. Stubborn ole' coot. Sometimes I despised him, but really, I just despised myself. And I guess I didn't tell him because of my false pride, and fear of rejection."

"My goodness. Well, I understand so much more about you now."

Emma smirked. "Explains a lot, doesn't it?" She giggled. "I know I've been a big pain in the butt."

"But how wonderful that your daughter found you! Isn't that miraculous?"

Emma's face lit up. "Yes. I'd say it is."

"Emma? Can't you see the grace and mercy of God in your life? This reunion is a kiss from Heaven!" Beverly proclaimed.

She nodded. "Yep. Interesting that it all happened right in front of the preacher man. Dylan was sitting right there. He had a front row seat for the whole unveiling. Emily, I mean… Kathleen couldn't contain herself."

Beverly smiled. "I'd say God planned it that way. Dylan's been through a lot. He can use some happy news in his life. I'm glad he was there."

"That's for sure."

Beverly stared at Emma for a minute, grinning with delight at the transformation she was witnessing. "Emma? I just have to ask you, what are you going to do with that little notebook of yours?"

"Oh. Chunk it in the trash bin, I suppose."

"Wow! I'm delighted to hear that, because if you didn't, I would have!"

"I don't have a need for it. Guess I just need to write about something different."

"That notebook was your security blanket, wasn't it?" Beverly smiled at her.

"Dang it, Beverly! You always have a way of diggin' deep, don't you? I can't hide anything from you and those x-ray-vision eyes of yours."

Beverly made a funny face and rounded her fingers over her eyes, as if looking through binoculars. "Oh, what's that I see? Emma! You forgot your bra today!"

Emma shook her finger at Beverly. "Unfortunately, no one needs x-ray-vison to see when I've forgotten my bra. Let me tell you, these ladies have been through a lot. They've been quite trampled and have fully submitted to the earth's gravitational pull. I know there's no hidin' it."

They laughed.

"Em, were you one of those bra-burners back in the 60's?"

"Good Lord, no! My sister was, but not me."

"How about we go burn that notebook today? And if you feel the need, we'll throw a bra in for old time's sake."

"Beverly, you crazy bird."

"Well, seriously! You don't have a need to keep tabs on people's faults anymore. Freedom!" Beverly punched her fist in the air. "Isn't that part of the reason bras were burned? For the sake of freedom?"

Emma laughed.

"And, I'll buy you a new notebook, but you can only write good stuff in it. I'll challenge you. By the end of the year, you have to write good observations about your neighbors. And if you flunk the test, I'll smack you over the head and burn your purple muumuu."

"Deal."

Rugged Mike passed by with his coarse, fuzzy beard. "Did I hear you two broads mention bra-burnin'?"

Beverly and Emma burst into laughter.

Mike continued, "Cuz I was thinkin' it looked like you burned all of yours a real long time ago," he grinned, "and I was hopin' you knew about the invention of the two-ton, boulder holder." He pulled out his wallet. "I'd donate to your anti-droop fund, but I'm all out." Mike belly-laughed at himself.

Beverly shook her head. "You think you're real hilarious, don't you?"

Emma chimed in, "Mike! You need your own anti-droop fund for that big beer belly of yours."

Mike made a sad face. "Ouch." He rubbed his belly. "Lady, go easy on me. I worked hard to get this far." He leaned over and gently patted each lady on the shoulder. "Now, now, I'm just being silly with ya. No offense."

Emma quipped, "No offense taken, as long as you remove yourself from our table now. Thank you kindly, sir."

Mike stepped back, removed his hat and bowed to Emma before turning away.

"Goofy, ole coot." Emma chuckled.

Beverly smiled. "I'm sure that one has quite a life story."

### In Marshall City

Dylan finished his third job interview that week. The first two produced nothing and he was sure he bombed them both, but this last one gave him the phone number of a beautiful woman who was more interested in him than his job skills. Kelsey flirted with him throughout the entire interview. He knew she had issues, but he really didn't care. It was nice having a woman show interest. He hadn't dated anyone since his divorce from Lynette.

He headed to the gym to finish his last two hours of work. Josh was gracious in allowing him time to leave for job interviews. As he went about his duties, he took notice of attractive women working out. Dylan was frequently surrounded by beautiful, young ladies in their workout gear and he wasn't sure why he ignored them for so long. He had certainly been pursued, but his heart wouldn't allow him to see or respond. Lynette still filled his mind.

Today was different. After the encounter with Lynette at the Sawyer's wedding, he knew he had to let go. Dylan forced himself to cut her loose from his heart. No more letters. No more paintings. The Dream Door wouldn't be opened again. That was that. He decided he'd hold onto the house with the hope that it would grow in value. Maybe down the road, he would sell it, but not yet.

As he worked, he thought about Kelsey. "Why not?" He mumbled to himself. After he clocked out, he pulled her phone number from his laptop bag and studied the whimsical card for a moment. The card fit her perfectly. Light-hearted and fun. Dylan dialed her number.

"Hello. This is Dylan Vanberg. I just interviewed with you today."

Kelsey was elated. "Yes, how could I forget?"

"Look. Honestly, I'm not interested in the job. However, I was wondering if you'd like to go out tonight? Or tomorrow. Or whenever works for you?" He felt awkward. *I've totally forgotten how to ask a girl out.*

"Oh my gosh! Yes. I'm free tonight." She bit on her lip as she smiled.

"How's seven o'clock?" *I can't believe I'm going on a date.*
Her voice was squeaky and jolly. "Perfect. Where shall we go? I know this great seafood restaurant. Are you into seafood?"

"Sure."

"Meet me at Bahama Harry's at seven."

"Will do." Dylan hung up the phone, grinning from ear-to-ear.

"What are you so happy about?" asked Josh.

"Got a date tonight."

"Dude! You go get it!" Josh elbowed him in the ribs.

## The Date

"So what's a handsome guy like you doing without a girlfriend?" Kelsey was more forward than Dylan had expected, but the flattery drew him in.

"If you want to know the truth, I'm divorced. I haven't had a girlfriend since."

"Oh, really?" She smiled at him, seductively. "A free man."

He nodded. "I suppose so."

"What do you do for a living?"

"I go to job interviews for a living." He chuckled. "And I work at Perry's Gym."

She reached up and squeezed his biceps. "Nice. A gym man. I like a solid guy."

"Tell me about you." Dylan hoped to get the attention off of himself.

"Well, I'm twenty-eight. I went to law school at University of New Mexico. I returned home to Marshall City to work at the firm. I love my job. Fortunately, everyone in our office is great to work with. I've heard horror stories, but not here. So, what did you do before the gym? Did you go to school?"

"My background's not as prestigious as yours. I've got one whole year of Bible school under my belt. Impressive, I know. I was a minister for several years in Holly."

She was captivated. "I've never been out with a preacher man before." She smiled. "How did you end up here?"

"My wife ran off with one of my friends, and that was that. No more ministry. No more church. Everything was gone within a day."

"Oh, my God. I'm sorry."

"Thanks. So, now I'm here trying to figure things out and get some direction for my life. I guess I'm just floating right now."

"Well, that's not a bad place to be. Why don't you get a job at another church?"

Dylan laughed. "It's not that easy. You haven't been around church much, have you?"

"No. Other than holidays with my family. Methodist church."

"Kelsey, I'm pretty much disqualified. No one's going to want a divorced guy...especially a divorced pastor. They figure if you can't keep your home intact, what good are you for a church? And, honestly, I'm not interested in ministry anymore.

It's harder than people think. Either that, or maybe I was just doing it all wrong. I don't know. It's not for me right now."

"And here you are, interviewing for a desk job at the firm. Wow. I really admire that."

"I'm grasping for straws, really. I'm trying to find something new and different, something to make more money."

"So, where do you live, Dylan?"

Dylan groaned. "Oh, God. The million dollar question." He sighed. "I'm living at my parent's house in Jester Estates. I have a home in Holly, though. I go there a couple times a month."

"There's nothing wrong with that. So, what are you doing with your house in Holly?"

"I don't know. Just hanging on for now. It was our dream house. Sentimental reasons, I guess. I'll probably wait for the value to go up and then sell. Hopefully make millions." He winked, grinning.

Kelsey looked into his eyes with compassion.

"Hey, what would you say about going to my place after dinner to watch a movie?"

Dylan's heart jumped at the thought. "Sure. I'd like that."

They finished their meal and he followed Kelsey to her apartment.

"This is nice." He complimented her neatness and taste in decor. He felt like a giddy high school student, alone with a girl for the first time. It was a foreign feeling that left him wondering who he really was. Dylan and Lynette knew each other since middle school. This experience was completely new. He just met this woman. Since Dylan settled in his heart that Lynette would never come home, he not only threw the idea of her out of his mind, but he cast many of his beliefs to the wind. The answers he once knew were now only questions that raged in his heart. He still loved God. But he didn't fully trust Him. He still believed that Jesus was his salvation and righteousness. But he was disappointed in His lack of ability to save him from the hell that had become his story.

While Kelsey put on a kettle of tea and excused herself to change into something comfortable, Dylan sat on the sofa, pondering this most unusual situation. He considered his efforts to always do the right thing and to avoid the appearance of evil. *Where did those self-righteous acts get me?* He wondered what the point was. Dylan pondered the idea of throwing aside his convictions. *Why was I convicted anyway?* he wondered. He always considered physical intimacy to be sacred. The fact that his wife didn't feel the same way and had given herself to another man created a strange, deep loneliness inside of him. He wondered if the ache would go away if he gave himself to another woman.

Kelsey sat next to him. "So, what kind of movie are you in the mood for?"

"I don't really care except I'd like to avoid love stories and chic flicks."

Kelsey laughed. "That doesn't leave many options, in my book. I suppose I could handle a suspense or mystery film, or…I don't know…just no shoot-em-up movies. I can't sleep after watching those. What's your problem with love stories? Those are my faves."

"I used to enjoy them. Not so much now."

She put her hand on his leg. "I'm sorry, Dylan. I didn't think about that."

"No worries."

Kelsey moved closer to him. "You seem like an amazing person. You're good-looking, intelligent, and funny, too. I can't imagine why a woman would cheat on someone like you."

Her comment was both flattering and painful. He wasn't sure if he should thank her or reprimand her for speaking of it, but the sensation of her hand on his leg erased thoughts of pulling away or despising her forwardness.

"I don't know. Some things can't be explained," he shrugged.

Kelsey moved her hand further up his thigh. "You mentioned you haven't been with anyone since the divorce. So have you thought about it?"

Dylan gulped. "About what exactly?"

"Being with someone."

The words aroused senses that remained numb since the discovery of Lynette's betrayal.

"Honestly, I haven't."

Kelsey leaned over and whispered in his ear, "Well, maybe you should, Dylan." Her breath sent chills down his spine. His heart raced. Physical desire had long been dormant and this stranger was awakening it from its slumber. Dylan sat speechless. His spirit wanted to object but, in his mind, he'd spent years trying to live by the spirit, and it only led to pain, so he thought.

She ran her fingers through his hair and kissed his neck. Dylan's mind was caught in a battle. *Dylan, get a hold of yourself. This is wrong. You'll regret this. So what? Lynette's gone. Everything's gone. Just do it. This could erase the pain. Put yourself on level ground with Lynette. Besides, who's faithful, anyway? There's no one to be faithful to. You're probably the only man on earth that's only slept with one woman. Oh, God...help me. I'm drowning here.* His soul was under siege.

Kelsey laid her lips on his. His heart jumped. His thoughts raced. *Oh, my God. I haven't felt this in so long.* He let himself sink in.

A few minutes went by before she tried to take it further, but something snapped inside of Dylan. He backed away. "Kelsey. Kelsey, stop."

"What's the problem? Did I do something?"

"No. I just can't do this."

"I know it's been a long time for you, but it's okay. I'll be patient." She leaned in to kiss him again.

"No, Kelsey. Please."

She looked perturbed. "What's going on?" she asked.

"This isn't who I am. This just isn't me. I don't even really know you."

"We've been visiting all evening! Of course you know me. I've told you everything you need to know."

He shook his head. "No. This isn't right."

"Oh, I get it." She smirked. "It's because you were a preacher man, right? Look, I won't tell anyone. No one has to know. It can be our secret." She traced her finger along his jawbone.

He pushed her hand away. "I'm sorry, but I'm not interested in having a 'secret' and, no, it's not because I was a preacher. This just isn't who I am. I don't do things like this, and I know I'll regret it if I go there."

She leaned back in the sofa and sighed.

"Look, Kelsey. I'm sorry if I disrespected you in any way…"

"Dude!" She laughed. "Disrespected me? Are you serious? I can't say I'm not feeling rejected, actually."

Dylan looked at the floor.

She patted his shoulder. "Chin up. It's all cool. We can just watch a movie instead."

"I'm sorry, but I've gotta call it a night." Dylan knew if he didn't remove himself from the scene, he would end up in her arms again.

Kelsey looked slightly offended. "Well, can I call you tomorrow?"

He sighed. "I want to say yes, but I'm not ready for a relationship. I thought I was, but it's too soon for me. Can we just say goodbye and leave it at that? You're gorgeous and I had a great time at dinner, but I don't have any business dating right now. Not yet."

"Okay. I can respect that. Can I just have a hug?"

"Sure." They embraced quickly and Dylan headed straight for the door.

"Best of luck to you, preacher man." She winked. "And I just have to say, for a preacher, you're quite a good kisser."

He grinned. "I know the guy that invented kissing. What did you expect?"

With that, he left.

## Chapter Twenty-Five
Several Months Later

Dylan finished sanitizing the hand weights and mats at the gym. As he moved them into their proper places, his cell phone rang in his pocket. He hoped it wasn't Kelsey. She had tried reaching him several times, asking for another date with "the preacher man." He simply responded with text messages, as kindly as possible, to let her know he wasn't interested. Dylan had enough clarity to know that he was being targeted, or rather wanted for the wrong reasons. He knew that for Kelsey, he was something to be conquered, another man to add to her list. It was obvious that his former occupation intrigued her. The voicemails she left him were blatantly flirtatious and tempting.

Dylan sat the weights down and pulled his phone from his pocket. "Awesome," he said as he read Jackson's name on the screen. "Hey man! How are you?" Dylan was thrilled to hear from his friend.

"Hey, I'm great! Lucy and I just finished remodeling the kitchen. You've gotta come see it."

"Nice." Dylan thought about the excitement of his first months at home with Lynette. Buying their dream house and fixing it up. Those were the days he longed for, and he wondered if he'd ever experience that kind of happiness again. Creating an atmosphere in your own space, with the one you love. He missed that.

"So, Dylan. I have a proposal for you. Our senior editor is taking a job in Tennessee and he'll be leaving next month. I mentioned your name in our staff meeting, and I was asked to give you a call. Would you be interested in interviewing for the position?"

Dylan was stunned. The potential of a job in Holly and being back in his home was an idea he'd given up some time ago. The thing that he wanted so badly was the thing that he let go. "Wow. I don't know what to say. This is shocking."

"Dylan, I'm really hoping you'll consider it. Lucy and I miss you around here. You've still got your house."

"True. And I need to get out of my parent's house. It's embarrassing. Every job interview bombs. It seems there are no open doors for me. I'm just not sure about moving back to Holly."

"Dylan! Isn't that what you've wanted?"

Silence. Dylan thought about what life might be like, and how he would handle living in his home without Lynette.

Jackson pressed him. "Please, man. At least come and interview. If they offer you the position, it doesn't mean you have to take it. There's time to decide."

Dylan nodded. "That sounds reasonable. All right. When should I come in?"

Jackson pumped his fist and mouthed a silent 'Yes!'

"Awesome! Can you come in this Friday at three o'clock?"

"Sure."

"And after the interview, just stay in Holly for the weekend. We can hang out."

Dylan smiled as he held the phone. "Okay. Sounds good."

"Man, I'm so stoked about this! I have a good feeling about it."

Dylan smiled. He wanted to say, "Me, too," but he wasn't sure how to feel.

## Coming Home

Dylan drove to the interview. The staff greeted him warmly, like family, and the walls he placed around his heart began melting immediately under the weight of their kindness. He had to admit that Holly was home, no matter how hard he tried to deny it and wipe the memories away. He questioned his abilities to meet all of the requirements of the Senior Editor's position, yet the potential of tackling a new skill and having the ability to be a part of influencing his beloved town made him hopeful.

As Dylan drove from the Holly Herald to his home, he made a conscious effort to pretend he was already living in Holly again; pretending this was his daily journey, pulling into his driveway and entering the house, alone. *Could I handle this*, he asked himself. The neglect that his house suffered was terribly obvious. His awareness of the blindness he'd been walking in since the divorce seemed to shout at him. The Christmas House begged for attention, and Dylan's heart connected with its cry.

The trauma of the past had erased his perception of time. Had it been one year ago since the day of discovery? No, longer than that, yet it seemed like yesterday. Two years? Three years? He couldn't believe how much time had passed. Though the wounds seemed fresh, they were, at the same time, like ghosts from long ago, barely a faint memory. They were gradually losing their power over him.

Dylan thought about how odd it was that even after Jesus was resurrected from the dead, He bore the scars that humanity pounded into His body. He pondered how God could carry the scars of angry men, yet release them from His judgment. *Father, forgive them.* While men ripped the body of God to shreds, He submitted Himself to their sin, yet did not hold their wrongs against them. *What kind of insanity was that,* Dylan wondered. "If only I could do the same," he muttered.

"Stepping into Me." Dylan became aware of the present moment as the voice lingered inside of him. The words took his breath away for a moment and tears filled his eyes. *You haven't forgotten me, have you, God?* Dylan opened the door of his house and stepped in. The sight of his paintings released a compassion in his heart for Lynette and Owen, and for himself. The beauty that the paintings conveyed were merely an expression of what each of them longed for.

Love. How could he blame anyone for searching for love? Dylan thought about the irony, that man's desperation for genuine affection and devotion could actually lead people to do the most unholy things. Blindness. It was all blindness and desperation. He realized the only way to see clearly was through total forgiveness, releasing others from his judgments…to hold them of no account. It was a seemingly impossible task, yet Christ had done it, and He commanded others to do the same.

Dylan thought once more about the scars that Jesus wore. There was no need to despise the scars. They were beautiful reminders of the power of God's grace and His great compassion. For once, Dylan saw the undeniable beauty of his story. He thought of the laughter, songs, and happy conversations these walls held. Certainly they outnumbered the depression and misery that he poured out in their presence.

He opened the curtains and blinds, welcoming the last of the day's light. He carried the couch pillows out onto the porch and knocked them together, emptying them of dust. Certainly this was home. And the vision of home was returning to him. He knew he wanted to be back in Holly.

Jackson drove up. "Hey!" He was beaming from ear-to-ear. "Guess what? They want you! You'll be getting a call with the offer tomorrow morning."

Dylan was stunned by the news. *Someone actually wants me?* "Seriously?"

"Yep. Seriously."

"Oh, my gosh." Dylan stood quietly.

"Dude. Please tell me you're going to take it."

Dylan smiled and threw his arms around Jackson. "Of course!"

"Awesome! I can't wait to tell Lucy! How about coming to dinner in an hour?"

"That sounds wonderful. Jackson…thank you. Thank you for everything."

"I didn't do it." Jackson pointed upward. "I think your Father thinks a lot of you."

Dylan went inside and continued cleaning up. He pulled the old vacuum cleaner out of the hall closet and began moving furniture around. As he moved the sofa, he noticed a Christmas gift. He admired the beautiful gold paper with silver snowflakes, tied with red ribbon. It lay flat underneath the couch. A beautiful tag was attached. *To Dylan, From Lynnie*. The gift was left there since before their break-up.

"Oh. My. God." His hands began to shake. Dylan sat down and slowly began opening the package. He broke the tape on the sturdy cardboard box. As he pushed the decorative plastic paper away, and tugged at the canvas inside, a beautiful scene emerged. He began to cry as he looked at the intricate details of Lynette's painting. Dylan stared at the picture of himself sitting on a rock next to a brook. He wore a white T-shirt and rolled-up blue jeans. His feet were resting in the water. Behind him, a white, crape myrtle tree towered over his head, shading him from the sun.

Dylan wept. He realized that Lynette had listened to him on those nights when he was exhausted from meeting people's needs. He would plop into bed and say, "Sometimes I just wish I could live a simple, quiet life…wear blue jeans and a T-shirt, and sit by the river without demands looming over me." But he would wake up the next day and slip right into Turbo-pastor mode.

Dylan ran his fingers across the painting, admiring the texture and strokes. He was in awe of Lynette's brilliant ability to work with light. The way she made the sun glisten on the water, and the realistic blooms on the tree blew his mind. *I had no idea she was this good.* In that moment, he considered that, perhaps, Lynette was a better person than he thought. Her betrayal made it difficult to see past the lies. He thought of his years as a pastor. How easy it was to regard someone as good when their actions were perfect, but one mistake seemed to have the power to overshadow all that was right. *Why do Christians give so much credit to darkness? Was sin greater than the righteousness of God? Surely not.*

Dylan decided to never again think of Lynette as dirty or cursed, but rather as a child who lost her way, yet the Father was restoring her along the journey. Something shifted. He thought of Elder David's kindness in sending him to Italy. Many years of controlling, manipulative behavior were erased by a simple act. The town gossipers that he grew to despise…they were merely seeking approval and security. His parent's moments of questioning him as to what he did to cause Lynette's departure…he could no longer blame them for their disappointment. Their embarrassment over having a "disgraced pastor" as a son…he could no longer blame them for reacting in accordance with the harsh, judgmental church community they had known all of their lives.

"We are one, Dylan. Step into me, and you will see clearly." The voice of Jesus rang in his spirit. Every cell in his body was becoming alive and aware, awakening from the dead.

He thought about calling Lynette to tell her he just found the painting, yet he didn't know if it would be appropriate. *What would Owen think?* He considered writing a letter, but that would be just as awkward. *What if Owen picks up the mail and finds it? What if he pitches it in the trash?* She would never know what it meant to him. For all he knew, she probably thought he opened it long ago.

Dylan went to the kitchen to make tea while he weighed his options. He knew he had to call her. He picked up the phone and took the leap.

"Hello?"

"Hi, Lynette. It's Dylan."

"Yeah, I saw that on my phone." He was glad to know she kept his contact information in her phone. "What's up?"

He searched for an opening line. "Do you have a…is this a good time for you? I only need a minute."

Lynette peered into the living room to see Owen sitting in his recliner as he watched ESPN. "Yes."

"I was moving furniture around and I found the Christmas gift you left me. The painting. It's amazing." Lynette stood breathless. She had forgotten about the painting. "I just wanted you to know I got it, and I'm really grateful."

"Dylan, I can't believe you just now found it. I figured you opened it years ago. I'm...I'm stunned."

"I didn't know if I should call or not, but I wanted to make sure to thank you. It's beautiful. Blue jeans and T-shirt. You remembered. And your painting skills! I had no idea you were that good."

Lynette smiled, pleased. "Thanks, Dylan."

"I'm going to hang it in my office. By the way, you should probably know. It looks like I've got a job in Holly, so I'll be moving back home."

"Wow. Congratulations. Where's the job?"

"I interviewed with the Herald. Crazy, huh? It's the Senior Editor position. Jackson just told me they'll make an offer tomorrow. It's looking hopeful."

"That's awesome! How exciting. So, you'll be living in the same place?"

"Yep. Back home. I love this house and I'd like to hold onto it for awhile. Anyway, I just wanted to thank you for the gift. I love it. It means a lot to me."

Lynette smiled. "You're welcome."

"You doing okay, Lynette?"

Hearing him say her name brought her joy. "I'm doing well. Living the ranch life. I've gotten pretty good at riding horses and tending to chickens. I just got a donkey last week, although I'm not sure why." She laughed.

"Wow. Well, you have fun with that." He chuckled.

"I guess I'd better go. Thanks for calling, Dylan."

"Goodbye, Lynette."

Owen heard the name from the other room. *Dylan*. He came into the kitchen.

"What did he want?"

"Oh. He was moving furniture and just came across a painting I had done. He wanted me to know he found it."

"That's it?"

"Yep."

"It sounded like you talked for awhile."

"He was just asking how I was, so I told him about the horses and donkey. Nothing exciting."

"Lynette, I don't want him knowing anything about our lives. I'd appreciate it if you keep that to yourself."

"Sure. I didn't see any harm in what I said, but okay."

Owen continued to press. "I heard you say something about living in the same place. What was that about?"

She thought back over the short conversation. "Oh. He might be moving back to Holly.

Owen sighed. "Great. That's just great."

Lynette hated his childish attitude. "Owen, what's your problem? He lived in Holly before, so what's the big deal now?"

"I was glad when he left. Didn't count on him coming back."

She rolled her eyes. "Well, everyone has the right to live where they want. We just have to accept that."

He glared at her. "You seem pleased with the news."

"Owen! Will you just drop it already? Go watch your sports show."

"Don't tell me what to do."

Lynette sighed and left the kitchen, heading to the bedroom. For a moment, she was thankful that she hadn't been able to get pregnant again. Life with Owen had lost its excitement and there was certainly no sense of security.

Owen came into the bedroom. "I got a call from Will earlier today. He and the guys are planning a camping trip to North Carolina next month and they want me to go. Looks like we'll be gone ten days. Are you cool with that?"

"I suppose so. I can hold down the fort."

Owen stared at her.

He was making her uncomfortable. "What? Why are you staring at me?"

"While I'm gone…are you going to stay at the ranch, or will you be going into town?"

"I don't know, Owen. What does it matter?"

"If Dylan's in town, I don't want you there. Not while I'm out of town."

"So, now I'm going to be a prisoner?" She threw her hands in the air. "What kind of life is this? Suddenly, I can't go to the grocery store or run errands in town? What the heck, Owen?"

He put his hands on her shoulders. "Look, babe. I don't want to lose you. I don't want to take any chances."

"Why would you lose me?" She was interested in his thoughts, for sure.

"He neglected you terribly, Lynette. I remember how miserable you were. He didn't pay attention to you, and I think maybe you've forgotten that."

"What's the point of bringing that up? You don't always pay attention to me, either. Sports television and "the guys" often win out over me, Owen."

He tightened his jaw and inhaled. "I treat you far better than he ever did. Don't you forget that. No one will ever love you as much as I do."

Lynette resented his words. "Dylan never hit me." She winced, fearing she had pushed him too far.

"So that's how you really feel. I knew you still had feelings for him."

"I care about him. That's not a crime. Don't you care about your ex-wife?"

Owen's heavy breathing worried Lynette. She hoped he wouldn't drop dead.

"Of course I care about her, but I'm not in love with her. There's a difference."

"So you think I'm in love with Dylan?"

"Why don't you tell me, Lynette?"

She sighed. "If it helps, I don't think about him everyday…if that's what you're trying to say."

Owen's breathing calmed a bit. "I hate divorce. I've been the cause of two of them. I don't want to deal with that crap ever again. Sometimes I'm afraid you're going to leave."

"Why? What makes you think I'd leave?"

"Because, I'm not him."

"I left him, Owen. Why would I want to be with someone that I chose to leave behind?" Secretly, she was intrigued by the fact that Owen sensed her love for Dylan. *Oh, my gosh. It's obvious.*

"People develop regrets over time and they wish they could go back."

"Owen, are you saying that because that's how you feel about Cybil?"

He sat on the bed and dropped his head in his hands. "I was a fool. I lost a really good woman because I couldn't get my act together. She was patient with me, and all I did was hurt her. Now I'm doing the same to you."

Lynette sat next to him. "I can't judge you. Look at what I did."

He looked her in the eyes. "So, basically, we're two losers?"

"Look, Owen. I know that people get second chances. Even third and fourth chances. I've seen that in peoples' lives over the years. When you're in ministry, you witness all kinds of things. Maybe we're not losers, Owen. We're just learning as we go."

He shrugged. "Maybe."

Lynette continued, "I think we just have to see ourselves differently, you know. We've been looking through the lense of what we've done wrong. But I think we can start doing things right."

"Where'd you learn all this stuff?"

"You know this 'stuff,' too. Dylan preached it often. I guess I learned it from him. Do you feel threatened by that?"

Owen sighed. "I guess not."

"I'm sure you can say you learned some things from your ex-wife."

"Yeah." He nodded in agreement. "Cybil was a good woman. I just don't know, Lynette. I don't know if you and I made the right decision, honestly."

She tilted her head, appearing worried. "Owen, what are you trying to say?"

"I'm just saying I'm not sure about marriage in general."

"Owen? Are you trying to tell me you want a divorce?"

He shook his head. "No. I'm just saying that I don't have much faith in the institution of marriage. This stuff is hard. You know the statistics for second marriages? There's a higher rate of divorce. Maybe by getting married, we just shot ourselves in the foot."

She looked at the floor. "I hope not."

They sat in silence for a minute. Lynette stood up. "Look. Go on that trip with Will and the guys. You need a break. I promise I won't be going to see Dylan. All right?"

"Deal."

## Chapter Twenty-Six

The Mountains of North Carolina

"Man, the mountain air makes me feel alive. And this view!" Owen and the guys set up their camp near a clearing that provided a stunning scene. "This right here, this is what I always dreamed of. Being a mountain man, living in the wild and protecting the land." He chuckled at himself.

Will looked at him. "I remember you talking about that years ago, Owen. Why don't you just do it?"

"Life happened, I suppose."

Charlie chimed in. "You've got that great ranch. Why would you want to leave that place?"

Owen nodded in agreement. "I know. But I grew up on the ranch. It's all I've ever known. As a kid, I used to dream about living in the mountains. I was making plans to get into wildlife conservation and forestry. Saw myself growing old in the mountains. It's where I feel at home."

"It's never too late. Why don't you pursue it?"

"Well, I've got Lynette and she wants kids. You know of any woman who wants to raise children in some cabin in the middle of nowhere? That's not her style. And the ranch is basically a free place to live. No mortgage."

"Owen, is this something you'll regret not doing someday?" Will always enjoyed digging deep. Unfortunately, he was all about personal happiness, and he often gave bad advice.

Owen sighed. "Nah. Well, I don't know."

"Why don't you just tell Lynette that's what you wanna do? You might be surprised. Maybe she wants to get off of that ranch, too."

"I'll have to think about it. The problem is, I doubt I could make enough money to support a wife and kids. The job I want is kind of a single-man's job."

"Maybe you should have done it after your divorce. That was your chance. Now you're stuck with a woman you don't know if you can trust." Owen clenched his jaw.

Charlie butted in. "Will! You don't have to be such a jerk!"

"Well, I saw her with her ex-husband, talking and hugging. I'm just sayin'…it looked a bit friendly to me."

Owen glared at him. "Will, are you my friend or not?"

"Of course I am. That's why I'm looking out for you."

Owen's muscles tensed. "Lynette told me about that conversation. It was nothing. Just a little closure for her."

"And you trust her?"

Owen hesitated. "Yes, I do."

"Hmm." Will shook his head.

"What?" Owen's face tightened.

"It's the big dilemma that occurs with every relationship that begins with an affair. In order for her to be with you, she had to cheat on her husband. What assurance do you have that she won't do the same with you?"

Charlie stepped in front of Will, scowling as he gritted his teeth at him. "You dad-gummed, numbskull. What the heck are you tryin' to do? Are you his friend or not? Cuz I sure haven't heard of a friend as rude and uncaring as you are. What good are you doing for Owen? You trying to break up his marriage?"

"No, of course not! I'm not trying to break anyone up. I'm just making a point."

Owen butted in. "Point's taken, Will. Now shut your mouth and mind your own dang business. Besides, I've known of several marriages that have lasted that started under the same circumstances as mine. It's not easy, but it can work, and trust can be built."

"Alrighty then. I don't mean to stir up trouble. I'm just asking the hard questions. It's the dark stuff that needs to be faced and dealt with." Will sipped his beer, wearing an arrogant expression.

"Lynette and I work through things just fine. That's more than I can say about you and your wife."

"Darn it, you guys!" Charlie reached a breaking point. "I paid money to get here and I used up my last few vacation days to be with you. And, if you ruin this trip for me, I'll beat both of you senseless. And I'll tell you what…if Adam had been able to make this trip, you, Will, would already be laid out on the ground with a black eye!"

Will put his hands in the air. "Okay, okay. Truce!"

Owen sighed. "I think I'm gonna turn in early. I'm exhausted."

### The Next Day in Holly

While Owen was away, Lynette kept herself busy dreaming about her future baby. She made a list of hardware items that she wanted to add to the nursery. She carefully measured the windows that looked out over the duck pond. She counted the drawers on the dresser to make sure she bought the proper number of decorative handles and knobs. As she turned to face the crib, she dropped her hands to her belly and sighed. "C'mon, baby. Please." Her eyes filled with tears once again, and she wondered how it was possible that one person could cry so much without dying from dehydration. She longed for a child, and hoped that a baby would lighten the atmosphere for Owen. *Maybe he just needs to be a dad. That'll get his mind off the other stuff.*

Lynette left the room and headed for the car before her emotions had a chance to cave in on her. The drive to Holly was peaceful and gave her time to beg God for what she believed she didn't deserve. Over the last few months, she started believing that death might find her if she continued refusing to converse with God. The fear of punishment and the fear of being rejected kept her locked in a tumultuous prison of her own making. She couldn't remember the last time she heard God speak to her. Self-condemnation convinced her heart that He had nothing to say, only to glance her way from time-to-time with a look of disapproval.

"I'm sorry, God." Her words were true, but she feared He might not believe her. Even she didn't believe herself, though her soul felt the sorrow of the choices she made. "God, I am so sorry." Silence lingered. She began to weep, "Oh, God, I really am sorry."

"I know."

Lynette nearly jumped as the words echoed in her heart. He spoke!

"You are My child and I have always loved you. You stopped loving yourself."

She pulled the car off the road to listen.

"You are forgiven. I've heard your cries."

She breathed in deeply, opening her hands to the sky. "I feel You, Father." Months of longing and aching erupted as her body trembled from the depths of her being. Light filled her completely; body, soul and spirit. "I feel You," she wept.

Owen flashed in her mind. "Oh, God, please help Owen. Please let him feel You, too."

"I'm with him."

"But I know he's walking away. I feel it. He's walking away from me. And You."

"I am with him."

Holy silence settled in the car and Lynette marveled over the presence of God that embraced her. She wept, smiling. "I feel

You! Thank You, God. Thank You for loving me. Thank You for not leaving me." At the thought of His faithfulness, she smiled as she cried. "You're so good! You are so good."

She opened the car door and stepped onto the green grass. *Oh, my God. The color!* Her world of gray became full of color. She lifted her hands to the blue sky and let the sunshine warm her face as she wept. Lynette became fully aware of the dormancy of her heart as the world awakened her senses. She knelt down on the ground and rubbed her fingertips over the soft blades of grass.

"Lynette?" She heard a woman's voice behind her. Turning around, she was shocked to see Marcy's concerned face. "Are you all right, sweetheart?"

"Oh, Marcy! I had no idea anyone was here. I just...I'm having a moment with God." She smiled.

Relief flooded Marcy's face and she dropped to her knees to embrace Lynette. "I'm sorry if I scared you. I just saw your car on the side of the road, and noticed you on your knees. I was worried."

"I'm fine. I'm wonderful. I haven't felt anything like this before. I was praying and it's like, God just showed up. I don't know how to explain it. It's like I can see clearly, and..." She caught her breath. "He said He loves me." Tears poured from her eyes. "I didn't think He loved me anymore."

The women sat on their knees, face-to-face. Marcy beamed. "Lynnie, it's so good to see you like this!" She touched Lynette's cheek. "Of course, you're loved. You are so loved."

Lynette threw her arms around Marcy and sobbed. "I want you to know I'm so sorry for the pain I caused everyone. I really am. And I know Owen is, too."

Marcy patted her back. "It's okay. You're forgiven. We forgive you."

"But I don't know if others can forgive me. I hear people say things, and when I go to town, they glare at me."

"You know what, sweetie? They just don't know any better. They should, but they're blind themselves. People have different ways of dealing with disappointment, but the good Lord will show them as they grow. Even if they can't forgive you just yet, you forgive them. You'll be free. And someday, they'll be free, too."

"Thank you, Marcy. You're an amazing friend."

Marcy stood, pulling Lynette up with her. "So where were you headed today?"

"I was going to the hardware store."

Marcy dusted off her knees. "Would you like to join me at the cafe for an early lunch?"

Lynette smiled. "I would love to."

She drove into Holly, in awe of God's visit with her. For the first time, driving into Holly was a beautiful experience instead of a dreadful one. It was like the first time she and Dylan had come there. The quiet, quaint town greeted her with its charm and simplicity. As she rounded the corner of Avenue A and Main Street, Mr. Edwards waved as he mowed his lawn. She cherished the image of the elderly man pushing a mower and waving warm greetings at the same time. A smile came over her face.

As she drove down Main Street, she passed by her old home. Dylan stood on a ladder, hanging a bright pink bougainvillea . Lynette was happy to see a touch of life being added to the long-neglected house. "God bless him." She began to pray for the man that was once her husband. *Please give him the desires of his heart.*

Pulling into Annie's Cafe, she was overcome with the joy she once knew when going there. Friendship, comfort and relaxation. The exchange of stories from every generation. She pondered how rich the walls were with the echoes of stories of the past. Lynette wondered why she had tried so hard to avoid the place where much goodness happened in her life. As she stepped out of the car, part of her was slightly frightened by the possibility of rejection, yet she felt strengthened and able to accept disappointment. Grace flowed through her veins. She hungered for reconciliation.

As she stepped into the café, Lucy ran to greet her. "Lynette! Oh, my gosh. It's good to see you here."

Lynette squeezed her tightly. "How are you and Jackson doing?"

"We're fantastic! He's the most wonderful man ever." Lucy smiled.

"I'm so happy for you. What's new?"

Lucy shrugged. "Not much. Jackson's enjoying his promotion at the paper, and I'm taking care of home-life and keeping busy at the cafe."

Lynette smiled. "It sounds like you two are settling into marriage well."

Lucy nodded. "Yes, ma'am. Where would you like to sit?"

"Any spot is fine. I'm meeting Marcy here. She should be coming in right behind me."

Lucy's face brightened even more. "I just love Marcy. She's an incredible woman."

Lynette agreed. "Yeah. I've really missed her."

"How's Owen?"

"He's doing well. He should be, anyway. He's camping in the mountains with his buddies. North Carolina."

"Nice. Well, hey, I'd better get busy. How about that table over there?"

"Perfect. We'll have to catch up some more, later." Lynette hugged Lucy tightly.

The door chimed and Miss Emma Gray waddled her way into the cafe. Her eyes performed the typical scan of her surroundings, evaluating the atmosphere. Lynette's stomach knotted up at the sight of her.

"Well, Lynette." Emma approached her table. "Oh, dear. I do owe you an apology. I'm sorry for my rudeness awhile back. You didn't deserve that. I know I have a tendency to be a crotchety old bag of bones sometimes. Can you forgive me?"

Lynette was pleasantly surprised by the look of sincerity in Miss Emma's eyes. "Yes, ma'am. I forgive you. But I suppose I had it coming."

Emma leaned toward her, speaking softly, "Now, I'll tell you, as a woman whose heart was as cold as a well-digger's rear end in a Montana winter for most of her life, I sure had it coming. But instead, God has shown me so much mercy. Lynette, I held a secret all of my life. I gave up a daughter for adoption many years ago. And God just brought her back to me." Emma's eyes filled with tears. "And I have more grandchildren!" She threw her hands in the air.

Lynette stood to hug Emma. "Oh, my gosh. That's incredible. How wonderful to know your daughter and grandkids!"

"Yes, it's the most wonderful thing I could ever imagine."

A look of pain crossed Lynette's face.

"What is it, sweetie?" Emma patted her shoulder.

"Nothing's wrong. I just think it's beautiful. I hope I'll have children someday, too."

"Oh, I have no doubt you will."

"I don't know, Emma. I hope so. What's your daughter's name?"

"I named her Emily Rose, but her adopted name is Kathleen. I have a grandson named Maximilian and a granddaughter, Mandy."

Lynette smiled. "Maybe I can meet them someday?"

"Of course! They'll be coming for Christmas this year."

"Perfect. You let me know when they get here."

The door chimes announced another arrival. Annie's Cafe was filled with conversation and life. Marcy and David entered together, smiling from ear-to-ear. David quickly approached Lynette and held his arms open for a hug. The sight of him melted her heart. The rejection from her parents over her choice to marry Owen left a hole in her heart, and an especially deep longing for her father's acceptance.

"Oh, Lynnie!" David embraced her. Tears flowed down her cheeks. "It's good to see you."

Overwhelmed by the kindness of old friends and foes, Lynette began to weep while David held her. He peered over her shoulder at Marcy who stood with hands clasped together in front of her tearful smile. David's countenance was warm and gentle. "It's all right, dear. We love you. It's all good."

"Lynnie, I hope you didn't mind me inviting David along. He wanted to see you."

"I'm glad you did, Marcy."

Once again, the door chime rang. Dylan entered and instantly caught sight of the huddle in the corner. He immediately recognized Marcy, David and Emma, but he couldn't tell who was being squeezed in the middle. His curiosity drew him to the bunch. As Dylan's eyes fell on Lynette, his heart skipped a beat. Adrenaline surged through his body. Marcy turned to face him, smiling, and she mouthed the words, "It's all good."

Dylan wasn't sure if he should stay, but he couldn't force his feet to leave. Lynette looked up, wiping her tears away as she stared at Dylan. "Hi." She managed that much.

"Hey, Lynette. You doing okay?"

She nodded her head. "Oh, yes. I'm good. I'm just overwhelmed, but in a good way." She smiled.

"I'm glad to hear that." Dylan's feet seemed to be stuck to the floor and his brain lacked vocabulary. The sight of Lynette in Annie's Cafe, huddled together with Elder David and Marcy, and Miss Emma was all mind-boggling. Dylan had accomplished getting through one full week without thinking about his ex-wife, and now here she was, in his territory, interrupting his flow. But he didn't mind.

Everyone sat down as Lucy began taking drink orders. "My, what a reunion today! I wish Jackson could be here."

"It's a glorious day," said Marcy.

Lynette motioned to the empty chair at the table, "Dylan, would you like to join us?"

He shrugged. "I don't see why not."

"Guys, I have to tell you all what happened this morning." Lynette began sharing about her drive to Holly, her prayer to

God and how He showed up in her car. As she described the encounter in detail, everyone at the table mopped their eyes.

She continued her story. "And it all reminds me of a dream I had the other night. In the dream, I saw a light that was like bright, golden sunshine. It was pushing through a thick, dark cloud and one of its rays pierced me in the heart. When it went inside of me, I heard a voice say, 'Stepping into me.'"

Dylan nearly gasped out loud, but he managed to contain himself. He wondered for a moment if he should tell her that he heard the same thing multiple times, but he decided to keep it to himself. He knew that making a connection with Lynette on such a deep level would cause trouble. She was another man's wife now.

Lynette continued, "...and I really believe that was God speaking to me, and I didn't realize it until this morning."

Dylan tried to think of an excuse to leave. "That's so amazing, Lynette. Wow. I'm glad I got to hear this. I hate to cut it short, but I have to head out. I've got a lot of work to do on the house today."

Lynette looked disappointed. "But aren't you hungry?"

"Nah. I actually came in for a glass of tea. Thanks for inviting me to sit with you, though. I'll see you around. Bye, guys." He waved at his friends and turned to leave.

As the door closed behind him, Lynette looked at Marcy across the table. "I suppose it's awkward for him. Honestly, I didn't even think of it. I'm so overwhelmed with what God did today. It's like everything else faded away…like the past was erased."

Marcy smiled. "And that's exactly how it should be."

Dylan arrived home. Closing the front door, he fell to his knees. *God, what are You doing? I don't understand. Why are Lynette and I hearing the same words? I feel like You're teasing me. I've let go of her. I finally let her go, and now You're doing this. She belongs to another man. What's happening?* Dylan's resolve to set her free to the life she chose was weakening as he remembered how connected they were.

## Chapter Twenty-Seven
Several Months Later

Valentine's Day had passed and Lynette hoped that their Valentine get-away would produce a baby. She considered the possibility of naming a boy 'Valentino' but Owen shot the idea down as soon as she spoke it. She giggled at his response. "Let me get this straight. Growing up on a ranch in the south and going to school in a small town…and his name is Valentino? Lynette, did you forget where Holly is? This isn't Tuscany and it sure ain't Rome!" She thought it was funny how his slight southern drawl was more pronounced when he was disgusted by something. And the word 'ain't' was occasionally thrown into the mix to make a point. Owen found it to be much more powerful than 'isn't.'

She had waited four weeks. She knew that a positive pregnancy test could show up by now, but fear of disappointment convinced her not to take one. Owen's mood swings made her determined not to put herself through another 'false' result. When she'd become sad, he'd become mad. "Why are you torturing yourself?" he would ask. The more she focused on a life that didn't yet exist, the more Owen withdrew from her. She found that when she set the topic of "baby" aside, he would become slightly romantic, more gentle and at peace. When she asked if he still wanted a child, he would reassure her that he did.

Several more days passed by and Lynette grew tired. The mornings greeted her with waves of the most awful nausea she'd ever experienced. One morning, as she stood from bed, she was sure her breasts would fall off. *Oh, my. This has to be it.* Lynette went to her medicine cabinet and rustled through random items until she reached the stash of pregnancy tests. Before heading to the toilet, she stopped and closed her eyes, holding the package to her heart. *Father, You know the desires of my heart and You know my longings. I don't want to get my hopes up, but I feel like this is it. Our baby is coming this time. But I'm scared, Lord. Please, please be with me and this baby. I don't think I can handle another loss.*

"Lynette!" Owen hollered outside the bathroom door. "Do you know where my belt went?"

"I saw it on the dresser," she answered.

"Thanks. I've gotta run to town and take care of some business. I'll be back by two o'clock."

"Ok. Would you like to go out for dinner tonight? I'm not feeling up to cooking."

"Sure. Sounds good to me. Love you."

She smiled. It was good to hear him confess his love. "I love you, too."

Lynette took the test. Instead of watching for the line to appear, she laid it down on a napkin and left the bathroom for a few minutes. She poured herself a glass of orange juice and sat in the dining room window seat, staring at the horses. Thoughts about the month's-old conversation she had with Owen about her experience with God rang through her mind.

"So, what do you think, Owen?" she had asked him.

"I don't know what to think. I mean, it sounds cool. But you know how emotional you get sometimes. What if it was your hormones?"

"Seriously, Owen? Hormones?"

"Well, could be. Or maybe it's your body's way of healing some of the turmoil you've been through."

"Don't you believe in God anymore? Don't you believe that He can speak to us?"

He sighed. "Lynette, I'm not sure what I believe anymore. All I know is that He's never spoken to me."

"I'd bet He has, but you just didn't know it. Or you've forgotten. Don't you ever feel Him? Or even think about Him?"

He hesitated. "I used to think I felt Him. That's why I went to church."

"Think really hard, Owen. There's got to be a moment when you knew He was there with you."

He sat silent for a minute. "To be honest, there's one time when I thought I felt Him."

"Yeah? Tell me about it." Lynette could hardly wait to hear what he had to say.

He shifted in his chair. "Well," he sighed. "I hope you understand what I'm about to say, but I think I felt God when

Cybil agreed to marry me. That was the first time I ever felt accepted, and I thought He was there."

Lynette tried not to feel threatened by his statement. "Okay," she nodded. "So, her acceptance of you seemed to reflect God's acceptance of you?"

"I suppose."

"What about when I chose you? When we got married? Did you feel it then?"

Owen dropped his head and let out a long breath. "Gosh, babe. I know this sounds bad. Please understand it's not about you." He looked up at her. "I never had that feeling again. With you, I was happy that you wanted to be with me and I felt your love, but as far as God goes, all I could feel was shame. I knew that what we were doing was wrong, even though in some ways, it felt right."

She dropped her head and nodded in agreement. "I know. I felt the same way."

He continued. "I haven't thought much about God ever since. I'd just rather keep at a distance. I doubt He wants to hear what I have to say. And I'm really not in a place to wanna hear what He has to say, either."

"Owen? What if He's actually been close to you all of this time? Don't you think He's waiting for you?"

He shook his head. "I don't know. I have other things to think about. Business. Dreams. Plans."

"But maybe He's just waiting for you to invite Him to be part of those plans."

"Look, Lynette. I know you've had some incredible 'experience,' but you've gotta understand. I'm not interested in getting back into the church thing. You know? I played that game."

She looked offended. "So it was a game to you?"

"No, no. That was a bad choice of words. I'm just saying I've been there and done that. And it didn't work."

"Will you at least start talking to Him? Just ask God to speak to you. I know He will."

Owen stared at her for a moment. "I guess that 'preacher's wife' thing is still in you after all."

"Please, Owen?"

"I'm not making any promises. Just let me be, all right?"

She shook her head 'yes' reluctantly.

As Lynette thought over that conversation, she hoped and prayed that Owen would hear from God so they could share a renewed passion. Especially if a baby was coming into their lives, she hoped they would be on the same page. The baby. She remembered the pregnancy test that was lying in the bathroom, waiting to be read. "Oh, Lord!" Lynette stood from the window seat and walked to her room, hoping and praying. "Please, God. Please."

She laid her eyes on the testing strip. She gasped with excitement. "Positive! It's positive," she screamed. It seemed like forever since her last pregnancy. She could hardly contain herself. Tears flowed and she thanked God for the gift. She picked up the phone to dial Owen, but stopped herself. Lynette wanted to do something creative to surprise him. She was certain that he'd already given up on her becoming pregnant. The great reveal had to be an exciting one.

With the first pregnancy, she shared the happy news by wrapping up a stack of books about becoming a father. The second time, she wrote on the bathroom mirror with lipstick, 'Hello, Daddy.' Now, the third. *I know!* Lynette picked up the phone.

"Hey, Owen. I was thinking…for dinner tonight, how about going to Perry's Steakhouse in Marshall City?"

"Dang, woman. You're feeling rich today."

"Well, we've only been there once and I thought it'd be nice to get out and enjoy the evening. We never do anything like that. Please?"

"All right. That works. I wanted to talk with you about some exciting news, anyway. Might as well converse over a nice meal."

Her mind was so focused on the baby that she didn't stop to ponder what Owen's exciting news might be about.

That night, she walked to the hostess desk with Owen, grinning from ear-to-ear. "Hi. I called earlier today and made reservations for the Smith Family, party of three."

Owen piped up. "Party of three? Who did you invite?"

"You'll see."

"Whoever it is, I hope we're not paying for their meal, too."

"Sure we will. I already told them you're buying."

As they approached the table, Owen saw it. A candlelit table for two, with a highchair. "What?" He was stunned. "Really, Lynette? Are you…"

"Yes! Yes!" He hugged her tightly.

"This is definitely a surprise. I guess I'll be buying a lot of meals for this guest of yours." He chuckled. "Oh, shoot. I'd better sit down before I fall over."

She smiled, feeling hopeful. "Are you happy, Owen?"

"Of course, I am."

Lynette clasped her hands together in front of her, leaning her elbows on the table. "I can't believe it. I'm scared, but so happy."

He took her hand. "I have some exciting news to share with you, too."

"Wonderful. What is it," she smiled inquisitively.

"Do you remember how I used to talk about being a park ranger…or wildlife conservationist?" He grinned.

She looked surprised. "Yeah."

"I applied for a position in the Cascade Mountains in Oregon. I've already interviewed once and today, they called to schedule a second interview."

"Oh, my God." Lynette didn't know what to say.

"Babe, they'll completely train me and help me start a program so I can get certified. The job provides a two-bedroom cabin that we can live in. It's at 5,000 feet elevation with a spectacular view. The pictures are unbelievable."

"Wait a minute, Owen." She blinked her eyes. "This is all happening so quickly. First of all, why didn't you tell me that you applied for this job?"

"I didn't want to waste time having discussions that might not be worth having. I wanted to make sure there was even an opportunity before I said anything."

She tried to hide her disappointment. "I don't even know what to say. I...I don't know. We have a life here at the ranch."

"But this isn't the life I want, Lynette. This is my opportunity to do what I've always dreamed about."

"You never mentioned this 'dream' until after we were married. Why did you wait until then?"

"Well, I had lots of other things on my mind at the time, like being with you."

Lynette sighed. "I wasn't expecting this. I'm sorry. I know you're excited. I'm just in shock."

Owen touched her hand. "When we go home, I'll show you the pictures. I think you'd love it."

"But...5,000 feet? Is it near a town? Are there grocery stores nearby? What about medical care? With a baby, we'd need to be near doctors."

Owen laughed. "Well. Honey, what do you expect? This line of work usually requires remote living. We'd be learning to live a basic lifestyle. The nearest town is forty-five minutes away."

"Forty-five minutes! As in…that's the nearest place to get gasoline and food?"

"There's gas and a small general store twenty minutes away. But it's not that bad. We can adjust."

"You're talking long winters and possibly being snowed in. Owen, that might not be safe with a small child. What if there's an emergency?"

"That's why we'll learn the basics of living. First aid, and how to handle emergencies. That's all part of the adventure."

She shook her head. "I'm sorry, but I don't want to be so far away from everything. We have a child to think of now."

Owen sighed. "Look. We can talk about it more when we get home. You might feel differently about it later."

She tried to be somewhat supportive. "So when is this second interview?"

"Tomorrow."

"And if they want you, when would you have to start?"

"In three months."

She couldn't handle the thought. "Absolutely not! Owen, I'll be in the middle of my pregnancy." She began to cry. "After the miscarriages, there's just no way I'm going to move to some remote place. I'm not Mrs. Ingalls!"

"Calm down. Let's just enjoy this night. And enjoy the fact that you're pregnant. We'll revisit this tomorrow."

## Chapter Twenty-Eight

Kat pushed her way through the crowd in the Atlanta Airport. She randomly collected images in her mind of people's faces who passed by her. She wondered how many of them were also traveling long distances to be with loved ones who were dying. Her grandmother was always strong and healthy, especially for a 96-year-old woman. The family believed that "Mia" would most definitely surpass the 100-year mark, but things changed suddenly. Now she was here to say goodbye to Mia and help the family make funeral arrangements.

Kat hurried into the restrooms and found an empty stall. "Thank God," she whispered as she fumbled with her zipper in desperation. The quiet voice of a woman in the next stall caught her attention. *Is she talking to herself?* Kat listened. *Oh. She's on the phone.*

The woman began to weep, speaking in a hushed tone. "I can't do this anymore. I can't. I thought we were getting married, Jack. This always happens to me. Why? I don't understand. Please...please, can we just get together to talk?" A few seconds later, the woman dropped her cell phone to the floor and Kat listened to her muffled cry. Kat prayed for her silently, asking God to help the woman. She debated whether or not she should say anything to the distraught woman. *I don't have time for this. Ugh. Why is there always drama?*

As Kat prayed, pictures began to flash through her mind. *Father, what is this?* Some of them were like video clips playing on a screen before her eyes. A young, brown-haired girl running to her father for comfort after falling down. The father smacked her in the face. "I told you if you didn't stop, you'd get hurt! Next time, listen to me." The little girl sobbed. Another scene appeared in her head, vividly. The girl sat alone in her bed, frightened by thunder and lightning. She jumped up and ran into her parent's room, leaping onto their bed. The father sat up and grabbed her by the hair. "Dumb kid! You hurt my leg!" He forcefully picked her up and took her back to her bedroom. "This is where you belong, not in our room. Stay put."

Kat's heart began to break for the woman in the stall. She realized that God was showing her pictures of the woman's life as a child. Kat decided to linger for awhile to pray until the woman calmed down enough to leave. She kept her eyes on the woman's navy blue high heels and the cell phone that sat at her feet. More visions filled Kat's mind. The places those feet had walked…in and out of relationships with men…desperately seeking a man who would love and accept her. A little girl, desperate for a father. A woman, passionately pursuing the love of a man. As Kat prayed, she heard a faint voice. "Stepping into me." *What is that?*

The woman let out a soft whimper. A drop of red hit the floor next to the cell phone. And another drop. Blood began dripping quickly on the hard, cold floor. "Oh, my God!" Kat yelled. She ran out of her stall and began shaking the door to get to the woman. "Someone call for help! Call 911!" Kat banged on the door. "Ma'am! Open the door. Please open the door." The woman wailed, "Leave me alone!"

Kat pleaded with her. "Sweetheart, listen to me. You have so much to live for. You don't know it right now, but you do! Please open the door so we can help you." Kat laid flat on the dirty floor and slid herself into the stall. As she stood, she saw the woman slumped over against the wall, head hanging down and sliding off of the toilet. "Listen to me, sweetie. I'm here to help you." She reached down and lifted the woman's chin up. Kat gasped. "Oh, my God! Oh, my God. Fay."

Fay managed to open her eyes slightly. When she saw Kat's face, her chin began to quiver and tears streamed down her cheeks. "Please forgive me, Kat. I'm so sorry."

Kat leaned against the metal wall in stunned silence. Her knees weakened, her face went pale, and she struggled to stay conscious. Her eyes refocused on Fay's face. Emotions waged war against each other. Anger, bitterness and rage threatened to rise, but in the midst of the whirlwind, the images of the little girl played in Kat's mind. As she looked at Fay, slumped against the wall, blood dripping from her wrist, all she could see was the little girl. An unexpected compassion filled Kat's heart. From lungs that seemed to lack air, she mustered the words, "I forgive you."

Kat removed the scarf from around her neck. She held Fay's hand, carefully, as she wrapped the scarf around her wrist like a tourniquet. She pulled tightly, hoping to slow the flow of blood. She looked at Fay's face, pondering the irony that such weakness and frailty carried a seemingly overpowering strength to demolish a marriage and family. Kat had suffered the pain of haunting images of her husband being intimate with Fay, but now, it was all different. The woman who was once such a threat to her was merely a wounded child. A powerless, hopeless human being. She stared, wondering if this was even real. Fay whimpered, "I'm sorry, Kat."

Kat leaned forward, pushing Fay's hair away from her eyes. "You're forgiven, Fay. You have a good life ahead of you. God wants to be your Father. Let Him embrace you. I promise, you'll find what you've been searching for."

Suddenly, airport paramedics banged on the door, "Ma'am, let us in, please!" Kat quickly opened the door and stepped aside. As they tended to Fay, the women's eyes remained locked. Words rang in Kat's spirit, *I in you and you in Me. Christ in me, the hope of glory. Forgive, as I have forgiven you.* She pondered the oddity of the Spirit taking charge over her body. Her heart and mind that should have been offended, seeking justice, merely stood in a holy hush that was filled with utter peace.

She watched as Fay was placed on a stretcher. Fay reached her hand toward Kat. "Thank you," she whispered. Kat leaned over, and spoke into her ear. "You're free. Go fulfill your purpose." One of the paramedics looked at Kat, "Do you know this woman?"

The words pierced her soul. She wasn't sure how to respond. "I used to know her. But, no. I haven't seen her in years."

"Do you have any contact information for her family?"

"No, sir. I don't. I just happened to be here today."

"Thanks for your help today. We'll take it from here."

"Is she going to be all right?" Kat nearly shuddered at her own words. Her concern for the woman who nearly destroyed her marriage, family and identity was a surprise.

"Looks like she'll be fine."

Kat knew the moment was real, yet it seemed like a dream. The world that faded away from her at the sight of Fay's face was slowly emerging from the haze. She gathered her purse and carry-on, trying to remember why she was in the airport to begin with. The thought of her grandmother dying and the encounter with the woman that momentarily won her husband's heart overwhelmed her and she began to weep. Kat found a quiet corner and called Preston.

## The Holly Herald

Jackson and Dylan sat across from each other at a large, wooden desk. "Jackson, the article you wrote about us several years ago, when everything was falling apart, you found a way to honor and protect the hearts of people. Not only ours, but the hearts of this whole community. That's what I want to do. If we can change the way that our staff reports, we can literally transform the atmosphere of this town."

"Dylan, I know. And I hope I've demonstrated that well, but it's not everyone's style. Most reporters do what works best. Good, old-fashioned manipulation. It's the easiest way to get readers. It's the rumors, exaggerations, bad news and fear tactics that keep readers picking up the papers. The thing that bothers me the most is smearing people's reputations, though. That's got to be the worst of these evils."

"Yeah. This is the dilemma with the article we have to write. You and I have to create something positive about Sam Jones, and everyone hates the guy. The town womanizer, gambler, and drunk. He's cheated so many local businesses and made promises that he never intended to keep. Suddenly he has this turnaround and he's trying to raise funds to build a center for rehabilitating former drug users and prostitutes. This should be celebrated, but instead, you see how people are reacting. I'm afraid that if we can't shift their thinking, they're going to drive Sam right back into the hole he crawled out of."

Jackson sighed. "Dylan, do you trust Sam?"

"Well, honestly? No. But that's only because I know the Sam of the past. If he's truly made a change, though, I have to give him the grace to succeed. Everyone needs a chance to become who they were created to be."

Jackson raised an eyebrow. "You're saying that we have no choice but to trust him?"

"I suppose so. Isn't that what God does for us all the time?"

"Listen to you, Dylan Vanberg. You're still a pastor at heart." Jackson smiled at his friend. "I remember you saying that God's mercies are new every morning. That's starting to make sense to me now. Everyday, He's choosing to give us a fresh start."

Dylan smiled. "Yes! And that's exactly what we have to do for Sam. He needs the community to back him up."

Jackson bit his lip as he sunk into deep thought. "Why do you think it's difficult for people to accept something good from someone who's done so much bad? It's like, does the bad outweigh the good? Can their 'bad' contaminate the good that they do? Can a person truly change?"

Dylan's eyes widened. "Wow. Those are some good questions. I guess the answer to that can be found in how Jesus lived His life on earth. The disciples that He chose weren't perfect. They struggled with understanding what He taught them. They even lacked in belief. Jesus corrected them so many times, yet He never stopped walking with them and never stopped seeing them according to who He called them to be. God never gives up. It's the seventy times seven thing. It means to continually forgive." Dylan's eyes filled with tears. "I know that for sure. After my marriage fell apart, God put up with my doubts, fears, and accusations of Him. His mercy is mind-blowing. He could have struck me down, but everyday was another chance." Dylan looked down, trying to suppress his emotions. "I was cruel to Him at times. And all along, He was holding me."

Jackson patted his friend on the back. "It amazes me how you still talk about showing mercy to others. I know there were times you wanted to beat the heck out of Owen, but you never touched him and never drug him through the mud. I want you to know that people notice how you've handled things, and it says a lot to the community. You're setting a standard. And it's beautiful, my friend."

"Thanks, man." Dylan smiled. "So back to your question. Does bad outweigh good? You got me to thinking about how many Christians live as if it does."

"What do you mean?"

"Well, when I was a pastor, I remember reacting to negative things as if everything was thrown into a tailspin. How weak does that make God seem? I would get all up in arms over the bad stuff, and it blinded me to the truth. I'd get caught up with what was wrong, and then lose sight of who God really is. When bad news became the focus, it's like we, as a church, went blind." Dylan shook his head as he recalled his old ways. "My God. All that preaching on the negative stuff. Not that I shouldn't have addressed it, but, wow…I think I mentioned it every Sunday and it became the focus instead of Jesus. I think that I put it in front of the congregations' faces so often, that they eventually started doing and acting like the very thing we were upset about. It's no wonder we had so many issues to deal with."

"Wow, Dylan. I never thought about that."

Dylan continued. "Do you remember that group of witches that came through town several years ago?"

"Yeah. I remember it stirring things up pretty good."

Dylan leaned forward with intensity in his voice. "Think about it. Everyone became so afraid of being cursed. We exhausted ourselves over that, thinking we were fighting it in the spirit, but I think we reacted more in the flesh. Our own fears opened the doors to lies, paranoia and a witch hunt within the church. Now that I think about it, why was our worship to God and our praise of Him apparently ineffective against the darkness? Why did we walk in fear when we're clearly told in Scripture by God Himself, 'Do not fear, Do not be afraid, Just believe...and on and on?' We declare great faith and this 'mighty God' in our songs, but then we act like frightened little guinea pigs running around, looking for a place to hide. We lived life as if God wasn't enough."

Dylan slammed his fist on the table. "Jackson! I was so blind! I feel like I did a disservice to Hope Fellowship."

"No you didn't. You helped so many people."

"Maybe partially. But I'm afraid I harmed them in a way. I want to make it right."

"Well, you're a newspaper man now, so you pretty much have a platform to speak from." Jackson smiled. "How about a new column?"

"I'll have to think about this. I wish I could speak at the church, just to make some things right."

"You know, Dylan? The way you live your life in this town makes things right," Jackson smiled.

"Aw, man. You always do my heart good. How did I get such a great friend?"

Jackson joked, "Well, I guess you're one of the lucky ones to make my acquaintance."

"Yeah. Yeah. Back to Sam Jones. He's got this fundraiser coming up and we need to write something that'll move the community to get behind him. It would be tragic if no one wanted to support his vision. That would crush him."

"I wonder what inspired him to do this? I think I'll go chat with him and get some more information."

"Sounds good."


### At the Ranch

"Lynette, you've been a weeping basket case for two days. I'm not taking the job, so calm your butt down."

"You're not?"

"No, I'm not. I called and let them know we won't be coming."

Lynette ran to Owen and threw her arms around his neck. "Thank you, Owen. I know how much you wanted the job, but thank you for putting me and the baby first."

"It's not like I have much choice." He sighed.

"Why do you say that?" She looked at Owen, confused.

"I can't have an unhappy wife stuck in the mountains with a baby. I'm not blaming you. Honestly, I know it wouldn't be practical with a baby on the way."

Lynette looked concerned. "Will you resent me? And the baby?"

"Of course not. I'm not going to resent anyone."

She smiled. "Maybe a bit later down the road, we can revisit the idea of moving to the mountains."

"Perhaps." Owen looked down at his notebook.

"What are you working on today?" she asked.

"Nothing, really. I'm just writing out some plans and ideas."

She was curious. "What kind of plans?"

"I'm just throwing around the idea of selling the ranch in the future. Charlie's going to do an appraisal next week, so I'm gathering some information for him."

Lynette looked surprised. "When are you thinking of selling? And where would we go?"

"I don't know. After the little muffin arrives, we can think about putting the property on the market." Owen pulled some papers from his briefcase.

"Would we move into Holly? Or Marshall City? Where do you want to go?" Lynette was uncomfortable with the idea of change happening right after having a baby.

Owen looked at her as if she'd lost her marbles. "Where do I want to go? I told you. The mountains. But since you're not ready for that, maybe we can just rent something in Marshall City until you feel better about going."

"Owen, help me understand you clearly. When you say you want to move to the mountains, do you mean for the job that you just turned down? Or would we randomly be choosing a town in the mountains to move to? You're confusing me."

"My heart's set on the job. Whether or not this particular one is open when you're ready, I don't know, but there are other positions that I'm keeping an eye on."

Lynette felt knots growing in her stomach. "So what you're saying is that you're still pursuing this idea, whether or not I'm okay with it? What if I never want to live in a remote place like that?"

Owen sighed. "Well, then we might have a problem, but we'll just work it out. Don't worry about it right now. Nothing's happening yet, so relax."

"But, Owen. Our lives are about to change drastically. Don't you think we need some time to settle down after the baby comes? I don't think I'll have the energy for a major change while trying to adjust to being a mom. I'm enjoying the ranch and I'd like to be here awhile. I mean, I've envisioned raising our kids here, and I thought you wanted the same thing."

"Lynette, I did want the same thing. But I know that I'll regret it if I never take the opportunity to do what I've always wanted. I'm afraid that if we start raising a family here, we'll never leave. The sooner we make the change, the better. I'm not getting any younger."

Lynette stepped onto the front porch and sat in her white, wicker rocking chair. *God, please. I can't imagine making a change right away. I just want this baby to be born healthy. I want to stay here and raise a family. Please, Lord.* She rarely got to see her family as it was. Her parents were slowly warming up to accepting her new life with Owen. Lynette hoped to stay close enough for frequent visits with them and her sister. Moving to the mountains would mean no friends and no family. It would mean adjusting to a lifestyle that she never desired. It would mean that Owen would be fulfilling his dream while she learned to be a mountain woman. She envisioned scenes from the old movie 'Seven Brides for Seven Brothers,' and she began to cry. "I guess I'll have to learn to sing songs all the time and entertain myself."

## Chapter Twenty-Nine

Annie's Cafe was filled with the daily lunch chatter as Holly's people converged there to exchange thoughts and information. Marcy had called upon Miss Emma Gray and Beverly Watkins to help her plan a baby shower for Lynette. The women sat in a booth discussing details.

Emma wore her purple muumuu that Beverly enjoyed ridiculing. "Well, I sure hope you're not gonna wear that circus-dress to the shower, Emma."

"Oh, Beverly. The only reason I wore this dress today was to drive you nuts." Emma grinned. "And it worked!"

Marcy was amused by the two ladies and she appreciated the free entertainment.

Emma continued. "And at least I'm wearing something. Did you hear about my neighbor yesterday?"

"Nope."

Emma laughed. "Oh! It's the funniest thing ever. Ruthie lives a couple of doors down, you see? She's a big nag, always griping at the neighbors for various reasons. She makes it a habit of knocking on Mr. Peters' door nearly everyday to fuss about anything and everything. Well, yesterday, Mr. Peters was taking a shower and Ruthie kept knocking on his door. He got impatient with her, so he jumped out of the shower and answered the door, totally naked!" Emma slapped the table and roared with laughter.

Marcy covered her mouth as she giggled. Beverly leaned back in the booth and howled. "I guess that taught her a lesson!"

"I'd say so. I don't think she'll be bothering him again anytime soon. Beverly, you'd better thank the Lord God on high that I'm wearing my purple muumuu. Be thankful, because things could look much worse. I need a good ironing underneath this dress, and let me tell you…Victoria has no secret strong enough to handle these hanging baskets." Emma motioned toward her chest.

Marcy snorted as she broke into a belly laugh. "Emma, you're terrible!"

"That's what my daddy used to tell me. He'd say, 'Emma Jane, you're so bad, even the devil doesn't want you.'"

"Oh, that's horrible," said Marcy.

Beverly picked up her corn dog like a gavel, and smacked it on the plate. "Overruled! I call this court to order! Emma Jane, I hereby order you to keep your hands away from your chest and keep the purple muumuu on while ceasing all speech that describes what's underneath of it!"

Marcy lost herself in laughter. She was barely able to catch her breath.

Lucy approached the table. "It's evident today that Emma and Beverly are in the house." She chuckled. "You're definitely keeping the atmosphere light in here. I like it. Too bad I missed out on this conversation. Marcy, will you fill me in later?"

Marcy tried to speak through uncontrollable laughter. "Yes. Yes. I will. Oh my."

"Is the baby shower all planned out?" asked Lucy.

Marcy picked up her empty notebook. "We haven't even started! With these two ladies, I'm not sure if we'll ever get anywhere."

"Marcy, thank you for doing this shower for Lynette. It means a lot to me that you're doing something nice for her."

"Oh, Lucy. You're welcome. I know it's an awkward situation, but every baby should be celebrated, no matter what the circumstances are."

"Are you catching any flack for it?"

Marcy shrugged. "A little here and there, but it's trivial. I just ignore it."

Lucy smiled. "That's probably the best thing to do."

Emma piped up. "Beverly's done called us to order with her massive corn dog. Let's get busy."

Dylan approached the table. "What's going on over here today? When I walked in, I could've sworn there was a party happening in this corner."

Marcy was happy to see him. "Dylan! Oh, we're just visiting and making plans."

"What kind of plans?"

The ladies were unsure about mentioning Lynette's baby. They didn't want to open any old wounds.

"It's just a baby shower," said Beverly.

Dylan nodded his head. He wasn't naive. He heard that Lynette was pregnant again. "Lynette's baby?"

Marcy looked at Dylan with compassion. "Yes, dear."

He smiled. "Thank you for being kind to her. I know she's been through hell. I'm glad she's got something to look forward to."

"Dylan Vanberg, you are one incredible man," Beverly said. "If you weren't too young for me, I'd be asking you out."

He grinned.

Emma patted his back. "Oh, you won't be single for long, young man. I hear things around town. Several ladies have their eye on you."

Dylan was intrigued. "Well, they haven't told me about it."

Emma winked. "Soon enough. Soon enough."


### The Article

The Holly Herald was released with Dylan's new front page column, 'Snapshots of Holly.' Each week, he wrote about different facets of life in Holly. His goal was to go deep into the hearts of the townspeople. Dylan was prompted to write from the depths of his soul, and the first subject that he explored was love. He knew the whole community was aware of his failure in the love department, but he was determined to convince them that love was the only hope for mankind, and that it should be pursued despite repeated failures. He was captivated by watching people grow through trials and challenges. He was intrigued by the way they were transformed by victories and tragedies. He often sat on his front porch, pondering how love fit into the equation.

The morning greeted people with a warm, fall breeze. People all over town sat on their front porches, reading the paper. A peaceful, hopeful presence settled over the town of Holly.

---

### Snapshots of Holly
### Love: One of Life's Great Mysteries
### By Dylan Vanberg

Love. All have desired it. Some have tasted, touched and seen glimpses of authentic love while wading through the mire of self-discovery. Part of love's mystery is the way that it makes itself known in the midst of hatred, confusion and all kinds of darkness. Often, we learn what love is by experiencing what love is not. Many have experienced the outer core of love, but how much of humanity will be able to touch the core of love and be immersed in its fullness?

Being immersed in the fullness of love requires vulnerability, nakedness of the heart and soul, and a life without secrets. I once heard someone say, "You are only as sick as your secrets." And they were right. "Therefore, confess your trespasses to one

another, and pray for one another, that you may be healed."
(James 5:16) We are not to confess for the purpose of receiving
judgment, but rather to receive the prayers and support of others,
which brings healing. We are not to hear confessions for the
purpose of oppressing and ridiculing another, but rather to lift
them up.

Confession to a heart of authentic love brings healing, because
the hearer fervently prays for the freedom of one tormented by
secrets, and the authentic lover will never treat one according to
what they have done wrong, but according to their true identity
as a whole person. Once a person has stripped their heart bare,
their eyes become opened to see themselves clearly in the mirror,
and they are empowered to live a life of wholeness. This is what
love does. And I believe that love lives in Holly.

The vulnerability and revealing of ourselves that brings the face
of love into our vision and takes us deep into the heart, is a risky,
sometimes painful journey. But if one pushes past fear and
embraces even the difficult parts of the quest, there will be no
room for disappointment. Each of our journeys is different. I
have come to believe that no one's journey is easy. Along the
pathway created by our choices and the choices of others,
ultimately we will come to know that love is not a feeling or a
philosophy, but Love is a person. And He has been with us all
along.

And sometimes the purest of hearts are birthed in the darkest places. This is one of the mysteries of grace. This is the mysterious way of love. And love lives in the people of Holly.

## Chapter Thirty

The morning of November fifteenth, Owen and Lynette drove to Marshall City as Lynette labored. She breathed through each contraction, holding her belly to feel the movement. "You're doing well, Lynette." Occasionally, Owen would offer words of encouragement as she focused. The moments in between contractions were filled with silence. She seemed to go deep into herself, giving all energy and attention to her body and what it needed to accomplish. Owen stared straight ahead, fixated on the idea of how his life was about to change.

He was excited about meeting his son, yet he was filled with fear. He wondered if it was possible to be a good father...an adequate father. As Lynette moaned, he asked himself, *What have I done?* Fear and doubt made his hands shake. Thoughts swirled through his mind: *Lynette and I are so unstable. Why did I think that having a baby was a good idea? I think I want to have children, but I'm not really sure. Too late now. I have no choice. I mean, I want to see my son, but I don't know if I can do this fatherhood thing.*

"Owen." Lynette reached over and squeezed his arm.

"Yeah?" He glanced over at her.

"Can you drive a little faster? I feel a lot of pressure."

He pressed the accelerator harder. "What kind of pressure?"

She tried not to cry. "Just all over. I think the baby is moving down."

"Oh, shoot! Not yet!" He sped up.

Lynette couldn't speak anymore. She only groaned.

As Owen drove, his mind was filled with more doubt. *She's going to be livid when she finds out the job opened up again. How can I force her to move? And with a baby in tow. I just wanna get this over with. I'm done with Holly, done with the ranch, done with trying to make this marriage work. Keeping a woman happy is impossible. Why should I have to put my dreams on hold because of what she says?*

Owen battled thoughts of divorce throughout the whole pregnancy, but he couldn't find the courage to tell Lynette. He talked with a lawyer but he came to his senses, wondering what the heck he was doing. He knew he needed to make this marriage work and he knew he needed to be a good dad. He hoped to avoid becoming another broken family. The thought of proving himself to be a failure to his parents and community was more than he could bear.

In those moments of struggle, he would convince himself, momentarily, that he'd be doing Lynette a favor by setting her free. He thought his son would be better off having a different father. He was torn in two. Online articles and men's magazines evoked a sense of self-preservation and the pursuit of happiness, no matter what the cost. Owen's friend, Will, sowed doubt in his mind about remaining married. Will frequently referred to Lynette as being a spoiled little pastor's wife who had a princess mentality. Owen would try to shake those words from his head, but when Lynette complained about the old carpet and cabinets in the house, he'd lose hope of ever making her happy. Between Will and the poor advice in men's columns, Owen was confused.

He hoped she would change her mind about moving to the mountains. He told the man in charge of hiring that he could potentially move in one month. They agreed to hold the position open for him. The only problem was that Lynette knew nothing about it. When he learned of the opening, he decided to test the waters with Lynette. Owen hinted at putting the ranch up for sale, and she immediately became a puddle of tears. He told her he was serious, but she blew it off with, "Owen, I think you're going through a mid-life crisis." He resented her for calling his passion a 'mid-life crisis.'

He still cared for Lynette, but he often wondered if they needed to free themselves from each other. After reading Dylan's column, he wondered if he could ever be one of those who experienced the depths of love. Since marrying Lynette, Owen became more consumed with his former dreams as the years went by. He supposed that Lynette was something he had to conquer, or rather, gain to prove that he could do whatever he set out to do. When he was at his lowest point, winning the pastor's wife was a challenge that he welcomed, and it fed his ego. Now that he had a wife and a child on the way, he decided he'd have to force them to fit into his desired lifestyle.

"Owen! Don't park the car. Just pull up to the door," she groaned.

They made their way into the hospital and got settled in.

## At the Christmas House

Dylan stood in his living room, thinking about how quickly Christmas was coming. As he considered the placement of the Christmas tree and numerous decorations that he had thrown into boxes, he thought it might be a good idea to trash it all and start over. Eliminating the past, completely. He considered the 'Dream Door.' He decided to clear it out and start over with new dreams for his future, but that would have to wait until after Christmas. *I'll get to it later.*

Dylan loaded his car with the old, artificial Christmas tree and decor. He headed to the local thrift store and dumped the things of years gone by into the bin. "Au revoir!" He waved goodbye to the items. Dylan was infused with a new energy he hadn't felt in years. Purging and casting away items that reminded him of the past broke the shackles from his spirit. He wished he'd thrown them away long ago. *Letting go is such powerful liberation. Why did I wait so long?*

Dylan stopped at the grocery store to replenish his pantry. Something about this season brought him happiness and the fall breeze brought back good memories for once. Dylan was thankful for the sudden turnaround in seasonal familiarity. The Thanksgiving and Christmas season were always so joyful and filled with blessings, but when Lynette left him right before Christmas almost five years ago, sadness became his constant companion. Each year, the decorations, the feel and scent of the air, and the familiar songs served as a tormenting reminder of all things gone wrong. But the winds had shifted.

"Hello, Marcy!" Dylan ran into her on the bread aisle.

"Oh, Dylan! How are you?"

"Doing great. And you?"

"Very well. David and I are just stocking up on groceries. We're having company this week."

"Good company, I hope? No pesky in-laws or unwanted guests?" He chuckled.

Marcy smiled. "No. Well, it **is** in-laws, but they're not pesky, thank the Lord. I got lucky on that one. David's sisters are coming."

"Nice."

"Dylan, did you hear that Lynette's in labor this morning?"

He looked surprised. "No, I hadn't."

"I got a call from her early today and they were heading to the hospital. She asked for prayer. I thought you'd want to know."

"Yeah, definitely. Thanks for telling me. I'll be praying for her."

Marcy looked at him with great kindness and admiration. "I know it's not easy, Dylan, but I want you to know you're such an inspiration to this whole community. Especially after the article you wrote about love. Wow." She shook her head in awe. "It touched many people. Your words even found their way into

Pastor Dean's sermons. You may not be in the pulpit, but who you are still flows from it."

Dylan smiled. "Thank you, Marcy."

"Have you considered getting back into ministry?"

"I used to think about it, but honestly, I'm enjoying what I'm doing right now. I like the freedom I have. It's different. I can impact the community through the newspaper, and on a broader scale. I don't feel the invisible pressures that pastors deal with. You know, the high expectations that come from everyone? I'm free to be me. No one's analyzing my life, trying to see what brand of toilet paper I use." He chuckled. He turned to pick up a box of pastries. "And no one's going to talk about how sinful I am for eating these." They laughed. "I can do my job and earn a paycheck and buy a new car without people looking online to see how much the price tag was. I'm pretty happy with where I'm at. Being a regular Joe isn't so bad."

Marcy giggled. "Especially when that regular Joe is you. But I do worry about you not having a church community."

"I know I look like a backslider for not being in church all the time. I'd love to be at Hope Fellowship, but I'm not sure if that's a good idea or not."

Marcy shrugged her shoulders. "A lot of time has passed. Maybe you could come back now."

"I'd need to chat with Pastor Dean first. I do pop in and out of the Baptist church down the road and I've even attended mass at the Catholic church a couple of times."

Marcy looked surprised. "Mass? Wow."

Dylan nodded. "That's one thing that's been so eye-opening to me. I was wrapped up in my church bubble as a pastor. Being forced out turned into a good thing because I've been able to see that God is at work everywhere. I thought my church was the only light in the world. I was wrong. I experience Him when I go for long walks, and it's like He shows me how big He really is. I love being outside the box." He smiled, hoping Marcy would understand.

"Wow, Dylan. Maybe I should get out sometime." She giggled.

He explained. "I'm not saying that people need to leave their church, but I'd definitely encourage people to get out and see what God is doing elsewhere. It's so easy to get caught up in one person's vision and agenda. Not that the agenda is bad. It's just that people's expectations often distort the vision. I think God places dreams and visions in many people and if we can all walk in unity and bless each other, the world would be transformed. We're all just a piece of the big, beautiful puzzle. Churches should empower other churches. Individuals should empower other individuals. Organizations should speak well of each other and celebrate each other. That's what I want to see happen."

Marcy agreed. "That's so true. I have to say, young man…it won't be long before you're behind a pulpit again." She smiled.

"Maybe. But if not, I'm okay with that. One thing I've learned in working for the paper and getting out into the community is there are all kinds of callings on peoples' lives that go beyond the church walls. I mean, Marcy, you know how it is. Ministries get jealous of each other. Some think they're better than another because they believe their vision is the 'right vision.'" I wonder why it's hard for people to acknowledge that God gives different visions to different people, and they're all important. These are the things I'm feeling passionate about lately."

"Obviously," she laughed. "My goodness, Dylan. Pastor Dean might need to invite you to speak at Hope. These are such great thoughts!"

Dylan smiled at her kind thought. "By the way, I know I'm guilty of the things I just mentioned." He was quick to point out his own faults. He didn't want his observations to lead to making himself appear as if he had it all figured out. "Do you remember when I used to make fun of the Nazarene church in town because their focus was on the beautification of Holly? And that time we dove into fighting human trafficking…that other group was mad at us for not participating in their foster care event that was going on at the same time. Just like silly, little children. It's a good thing our Father is patient." He chuckled. "Each vision is important. Why do we get so silly? It's **all** important."

Dylan was on a roll with his thoughts. He opened his arms wide. "Aren't we all just God's children? Why can't we live as children that are loved by their Father and celebrate each other? I think that's what honors the Father. That's how I hope to finish out my life."

Marcy stood, shaking her head. She wore a grin on her face. "Dylan Vanberg. These last five years have certainly taught you a lot. I love how God brings good out of the most difficult situations."

Dylan agreed. "Yeah. It's ironic. Darkness is meant to blind. But God has this amazing way of using people's darkness to bring sight. That's just how good our Father is. He can win with any hand He's dealt." Dylan smiled. "I like looking at the stars at night. It reminds me that darkness makes them shine brighter." Dylan paused for a moment as Marcy stood, shaking her head in agreement. "Oh, my gosh! I'm sorry I've been talking your ear off, Marcy." He was slightly embarrassed.

"Not at all, Dylan. I love hearing what's on your heart." Marcy's phone rang. "Excuse me a second."

"Sure." He stood by, waiting.

"Hello? Oh, wonderful! And everything went well? What's his name? Good…good. Oh, thank you for calling. Give her our love."

Marcy hung up the phone, smiling. "Well, Lynette had the baby. She and her son are doing great. Seven pounds, nine ounces."

"What's his name?" Dylan asked.

"Asa Brooks. Isn't that lovely? Asa Brooks Smith."

Dylan was stunned. He put his hand over his heart. "Asa?"

She nodded. "Yes."

"That's the name I picked for a boy. I told Lynette I wanted a son named Asa someday." Dylan's eyes moistened. "I can't believe she used that name. I thought she didn't care for it much."

"Oh, my goodness, Dylan." Marcy touched his arm, hoping he wasn't sad. "That's not a very common name. What does it mean?"

Dylan felt emotional, but he contained his feelings well. "Asa means 'healer.' It's from the Bible."

Marcy thought for a moment. "Asa Brooks. Beautiful. It's like 'healing river' or a 'healing stream.' What a beautiful name."

"I can't believe she chose that name. I'm just…I'm surprised."

"Dylan, it obviously meant something to her, and I think that's wonderful." Marcy hugged him.

"I'd better be going home, Marcy. I'm glad I ran into you. It's so fitting that I got to hear this news with you." He smiled.

Dylan got in his car and brushed away tears as he drove home. His heart ached, yet with hope. He was in awe of the paradox of hopeful aching. He wondered why Lynette's baby name choice was affecting him so strongly. "Asa." He spoke the name out loud. The sound of it melted his heart. *God, You are my healer.*

As Dylan pulled into the driveway, he admired his house. Yes, it needed painting and the shutters were still damaged from a storm several years ago, but he liked the way it reflected who he was. The structure was slightly battered, yet strong and it carried the promise of restoration. He thought of the dreams that lay beneath the old porch. Like the house, he still carried those dreams in his heart, yet he submitted them to God and chose to believe in goodness and hope, despite their death.

The Christmas House once carried laughter, light and a joy that brought healing to others. Dylan was determined that it would become a place of hope again. And he was confident that he himself would be filled with light and laughter. As he stared at the home, he envisioned fresh, white paint and red trim. "All things new," he said to himself. Dylan stepped onto the lawn and threw his arms wide open. "Come and paint me, God!"

## Chapter Thirty-One

Owen opened the front door, carrying Asa in his car seat. "Well, here we are. Your mother has a room all set up for you." He set the car seat on the living room floor and went to the kitchen, returning with a beer. He plopped down on the sofa and sighed. "Hopefully we can get some rest tonight. Trying to sleep in a hospital is like being tortured. I swear, that nurse woke us up every two stinkin' hours."

Lynette sat next to him. "Excuse me, but I actually pushed a seven pound watermelon out of a lemon. What do you have to complain about?"

He patted her leg. "And you did it well. Way to go."

She looked confused. "Am I being complimented or insulted? I can't tell."

"Take it as a compliment." He reached for the remote control and turned the television on. Lynette sighed.

"Owen, can we please turn it off for a minute? We just got here and it's our first time being alone together as a family, in our home."

He clicked the television off. "What is it you want to do?"

Lynette looked disappointed. "Well, it's kind of a special moment. Can't it be sacred for at least a few minutes? Maybe we can pray together?"

He chuckled. "Pray together? You can pray and I'll listen."

"But Owen, it would mean a lot to me if you would pray over our home. At least speak some blessings over your son."

"Blessings? That old preacher's wife lingo is coming up again. Ever since that experience in the car, you've acted and talked differently."

"Is that a bad thing?"

Owen shrugged. "It's not bad, but it's…different. That's not the person that I married."

"Is that a problem for you?" Lynette waited for his answer.

"I don't know."

Her pulse quickened. Lynette had envisioned that bringing Asa home would change everything. She believed she and Owen would somehow be supernaturally unified. Even the baby's name meant 'healer.' Surely this child would be a part of their restoration and completion. Lynette was certain that her encounter with God promised change for Owen. But now, Owen's words shook the solid foundation she had created in her mind.

"So, we can't pray?" she asked.

Giving in, he sighed and leaned forward. "Here, take my hand." She put her hand in his. Owen closed his eyes and struggled for words. "Lord, thank you for this baby boy. I ask that you bless his life and keep him strong. I would like it if he didn't have to experience too much pain, so please protect him. Bless his mother and help her to raise him well. Amen."

She added, "And Lord, bless his daddy, too. Amen."

Lynette hugged Owen. "Thank you." She looked around the room. "Christmas is right around the corner. I think you'll need to be my decorator this year. I'm not sure how much I can get done with the baby.

"Why don't we skip it this year? That way you don't have to mess with putting everything away."

"Owen, you know how much I love Christmas! And this is Asa's first. Please? Will you help me set everything up?"

"All right. I suppose."

The doorbell rang. Owen stood to answer the door. "Oh, I forgot to mention that Will was stopping by."

"Oh? I'm going to lay down for a bit. Can you keep an eye on Asa?"

"Sure."

Owen opened the door for Will. "Hey, man. Come in."

Will grunted as he entered. "So where's the little bundle of boy?"

Owen pointed at Asa in the carrier. "There he is. Asa Brooks Smith."

Will leaned over to peer at him. "He sure is cute. Looks just like his mother. How much did he cost you?"

"Oh, don't even get me thinkin' about that. I'm hoping those bills won't come in for awhile."

"You don't have to worry about that, Owen. The sale of the ranch will take care of the bills."

Owen's eyes got big and he ran toward Will, motioning for him to shut his mouth. "Shhh. What the heck are you trying to do, man?"

Will quieted his voice. "You still haven't told her? Dude. You'd better start communicating."

"I can't deal with that right now. I'll talk to her later."

"You're kinda getting down to the wire, don't you think?"

"Later, Will!"

Asa began to cry. "Oh, shoot. I don't know what to do with a crying baby." Owen started unbuckling the straps on the car seat and he lifted his son onto his shoulder. "Shh. Shh. Not yet, little man. Your mother's sleeping."

Will watched, amused. "Well, look at you. Never thought I'd see you bouncing a baby." Will chuckled. "That's a sight, for sure."

Owen rolled his eyes. "You should try it. Wanna hold him?"

Will puckered his face in a sour fashion. "While he's cryin'? Do I look like a fool?"

Owen grinned. "Yep." He felt something warm on his arm. Looking down, he realized that Asa's diaper overflowed.

Will roared. "Dookie alert! Who looks like a fool now?"

Owen held Asa away from his body. "Why don't you make yourself useful and hand me that diaper bag before I smear it on you?"

Lynette walked in the room. "What's going on in here?"

Will laughed. "Dookie alert! Asa got 'em good."

She giggled. "Here. Give him to me."

As Will continued laughing, Owen glared at him. "I swear, you're just like a two-year-old. When are you going to grow up?"

"And I'm the best friend you've got," Will chuckled. "So what does that say about you, Owen?"

Owen left the room to clean up while Lynette tended to the baby on the floor.

"Lynette! You're gonna change his diaper on the floor?"

"Will, I've got a changing pad under him. Calm down."

"Still, what if it gets on the carpet?"

"Well, it can't hurt this carpet much."

"Yeah, Owen says you don't like this house."

"I like the house fine. It's the old decor that I don't like."

"Well, good luck with that."

Lynette looked at Will. "What do you mean, good luck with that?"

Will smirked. "I'm just sayin' that I doubt Owen's going to put any money into this place. Especially now. He'll have all those hospital bills to pay."

Lynette didn't respond. She finished changing Asa and took him into the bedroom.

Owen, fresh out of the shower, opened the dresser to get some clean clothes. Lynette looked surprised.

"A little baby poop on your arm and it requires a complete shower?"

"Wouldn't you do the same? That's nasty." He rustled through the drawers.

She laughed. "Oh, Owen. You'd better get used to it. I hear it happens a lot with babies. Spit up…leaky diapers…you name it."

"Wonderful," he sighed. "That's what I've got to look forward to?"

Lynette stared at him. "Did you seriously not think about the fact that babies poop?"

"Of course. But it's supposed to stay in the dang diaper!"

She watched as he pulled the shirt over his head. "I have a question for you, husband." She sat in the rocker next to the window.

"What's that?"

"Do you think Will is a good influence?"

"We've been friends since high school. He's always been there for me."

"I know. But do you think he's good for you?"

Owen slammed the dresser drawer closed. He turned toward Lynette. "So, is this what happens? You get married, have a kid, and then your wife starts complaining about your friends? Is this how it's supposed to go?"

"Owen, I don't mean to make you angry. And I'm not attacking Will. I'm just saying he doesn't sound very supportive of us."

"He's fine, Lynette." Owen left the room.

## Hope Fellowship Staff Meeting

Pastor Dean sat at the conference table with his church board. "The Christmas program rehearsals begin the weekend after Thanksgiving. I'm really excited about this one. Over the last year, I've had several people come to me, telling about some really intense, meaningful dreams they've had. This started happening so frequently that I finally made the connection. I really believe God is visiting people in their sleep, and I noticed there's a common theme. Every dream has to do with grace and our union with God."

One of the elders spoke up. "What do you mean by union with God?"

"Well, one example is found in John 14:20. It's probably the most significant verse I can find regarding union with Him. Jesus said, **"In that day you will know that I am in My Father, and you in Me, and I in you."** I never paid much attention to it before. I had to read it a dozen times before it started sinking in. Let me read to you what He said before that. You can follow with me in John 14:7-11.

**"If you had known Me, you would have known My Father also; from now on you know Him, and have seen Him. Philip said to Him, "Lord, show us the Father, and it is enough for us." Jesus said to him, "Have I been so long with you, and yet you have not come to know Me, Philip? He who has seen Me has seen the Father; how can you say, 'Show us the**

Father'? Do you not believe that I am in the Father, and the Father is in Me? The words that I say to you I do not speak on My own initiative, but the Father abiding in Me does His works. Believe Me that I am in the Father and the Father is in Me; otherwise believe because of the works themselves."

Pastor Dean looked at his team. "Guys, Jesus reiterates several times that He and the Father are one and the same. Then in verse twenty, he clearly says He is in us and we are in Him. Have you ever thought about that? These dreams that people are having lately are about stepping into Christ and being one with Him. I think it's significant and we're supposed to pay attention. Especially with the Christmas season coming up, I don't want to preach the same, typical, old Christmas message. There's something more that God wants us to see. I believe if people realize they are unified with Christ, crucified with Him and raised with Him as He said, peoples' lives will be changed. Think of the freedom that's found in knowing that. It changes everything. It changes how we see ourselves and others."

An elder cleared his throat and interjected, "Pastor Dean, this sounds dangerous to me. What if people start running around thinking they're God?"

"No one's going to actually think they're God. But hey, He said we are created in His image and after His likeness. So we're supposed to be **like** Him. My goodness, Jesus Himself said 'Be perfect as I am perfect.' How ridiculous is that? All I know is that we can't ignore this 'in Him' thing. Look up that phrase in the Bible and you'll see how serious Paul was about it."

"Pastor, don't you think people might get lazy in their walk…maybe slack off in living right? I've heard grace preachers go there."

"I've never heard a grace preacher say it's okay to sin. If anyone preaches that, they're missing what grace is." Pastor Dean leaned back in his chair with a look of revelation. "Oh, my goodness. Every preacher is a 'grace preacher.' If we preach Jesus, then we're preaching grace." He chuckled, shaking his head. "So, where did you hear that? Who's saying it's okay to sin?"

"Well, I've heard people talk about it."

"The answer to that is found in Romans 6:15. Paul talked about being dead to sin…being under grace and not law. He said, **'What then? shall we sin, because we are not under the law, but under grace? God forbid.'** Grace is about having the freedom **not** to sin. Have you ever been so in love with someone that you wouldn't do anything to hurt them? I think that's why this union with God thing is so important. When you know God in His fullness, you won't want anything less."

Elder David chimed in. "I love this, Pastor Dean! I've seen how grace frees people from their prisons and I've seen it restore. Marcy and I have discovered what it means when the Bible says **'Love covers a multitude of sins.'** Love is powerful.

I agree with you. I'm behind you one hundred percent in getting this message out."

Pastor Dean smiled. "Thank you, David. I appreciate your support. This brings me back to the Christmas program. I called upon the people who've told me about their recent dreams. I asked them to share the dreams with the director so we can weave it into the theme of the program. I really think this will be the most powerful message that's been conveyed since I've been here."

David leaned forward, "Well, let's get busy then."

## Chapter Thirty-Two

On the first of December, Jackson spent several minutes trying to convince his eyes to open. Deep sleep, he thought, was like a drug that connected him to another world, and at times the trip was delightful. This dream world captivated him and he wondered how his subconscious self had experienced the things it did. Who were the people he encountered and where did these crazy ideas come from? He spent the entire night in a forest with an intriguing, passionate painter who allowed his living, breathing creation to consume him.

Jackson lay next to Lucy as she slept. He turned to face her, admiring her pregnant, sunlit form and the peaceful contentment that enveloped her. Images of the dream returned to his mind. He thought about the painter opening his arms to the angry, raging canvas that he awakened with his breath. Once beautiful and pulsing with life, the canvas became thick with darkness. The man opened his arms to embrace its hatred and it consumed him, for a moment. The man inhaled, pulling its violence into his lungs.

Jackson remembered screaming at the man to stop because he feared for his life. But the man was focused on his mission and he wasn't afraid of death. He submitted himself to the raging canvas as it poured its anger into its creator's body. Jackson watched it go inside of him, piercing him to death and the earth groaned. Jackson screamed and wept at the death of the creator, but what happened next pierced his heart with a truth he would never forget.

The painter began to move. He reached into his own chest and pulled the painting from himself. A towering pine tree that stood before him opened its arms like an easel, and the man rested the painting there. "Now, you and I are one," the man said. He touched the dead canvas, admiring the textures and designs he had created. As he ran his fingers over every inch of the painting, beauty returned. Darkness faded away. Color appeared and it returned to its original form. Light was in his mouth and Jackson heard the man's voice saying, "You have died with me. Now you will be raised with me." The man breathed into the canvas as he had in the beginning.

Once again, life and beauty were living and moving, breathing within and from the canvas as it took its place in the forest. Instantly, the earth had calmed. Birds of every kind filled the trees. Jackson heard sounds in the woods that surrounded him. He turned to see what it was. Moving through the trees were many animals, walking toward the scene, in joyful awe of the man and his painting. "This is unbelievable," he said to himself. All of nature seemed to celebrate what took place.

Now awake, Jackson lay next to Lucy, pondering the things he had seen. *Crazy dream*, he thought. He sat up in bed, rubbing his eyes. He peered outside his window at the old house across the street. He studied the faded shutters that still hung, waiting for Dylan's craftsmanship...and the screen door that woke him every morning as Dylan Vanberg left for work. *Is he ever going to fix those shutters?* The house seemed to stare back at him, threatening to remind him of the disappointments of the past. His friend lived there, but it wasn't the same as it was in the beginning. The house used to be full of life. Jackson longed for those times, for Dylan's sake.

Here it was, the first of December. He thought about what happened at the Christmas House exactly five years ago. He remembered the preacher man on his knees, weeping as his wife drove away. He wished that Dylan wasn't alone.

Lucy stirred, waking up next to him. "Hey, sweetie. What are you looking at?"

Jackson turned and smiled at Lucy. "Oh, hey. Good morning, beautiful. I was just looking at Dylan's place. I wish he'd fix those shutters. Maybe I should offer to do it."

"Maybe. He's been working on things over there, little by little. I'm sure he'll get around to it."

Dylan nodded. "I hope so. He kinda let it all go after his marriage ended. I was just thinking about it. Can you believe that was five years ago? At least he's finally starting to clean up over there."

Lucy wrapped her arms around her husband. "It takes time for people to rise out of the valley. You know? I admire you. You're part of the reason that Dylan's doing as well as he is. You've been a really good friend to him." She kissed Jackson's cheek.

Jackson and Lucy spent the next hour getting showered and dressed, chatting about the day's agenda. As they headed downstairs for breakfast, they sat in their "tea spot" in front of the window. Jackson looked lovingly at Lucy. "I can't believe we're going to have a baby."

"I know, right?" She smiled at him.

"You'll be the best mom ever. Our kid is so lucky."

"Thanks, love. This baby will have the most incredible father, and that makes me happy." The couple gazed into each other's eyes, beaming with happiness.

"Now that Lynette has a baby, I'm sure she can give me some advice. Speaking of Lynette, oh, my gosh, little Asa is so adorable!"

Jackson nodded in agreement. "He sure is. Cute kid."

"When we saw him yesterday, it kinda hit me, you know? We're actually going to have one of those! He's only two weeks old. That's the youngest baby I've ever seen. I had no idea they were so tiny. It freaks me out a little. I don't want to break our baby."

Jackson laughed. "You won't break our baby."

She smiled. "I hope not. Hey babe, I just had an idea! Maybe you could start writing a column for fathers. That would be cool."

Jackson shook his head and shrugged. "I don't know. I've got a lot to learn before I start writing about that."

"But seriously, think of how practical it would be. There are moms and dads all over town who need advice and encouragement. You should talk to the Herald about it."

Jackson raised his eyebrow. "You have a point there. I'll think about it."

As he sipped his tea, he looked outside at Dylan's place, and something caught his eye. Jackson gasped. "Oh, my God."

Lucy was startled. "What? What's wrong?"

His eyes were fixed on Dylan's front porch.

"Lucy, look." He pointed at Dylan's house.

She turned her gaze to the window and clasped her hands over her mouth, in shock. "Dear Jesus. Oh, Jesus."

Across the street, Lynette was sitting on the porch swing with Asa strapped into a baby sling on her belly. Next to her was a stack of papers and some other items. She held a letter in her hand, and she wept as she read it.

"Jackson, what is she reading?"

"I'm not exactly sure, but it looks like there are several papers sitting next to her, but it's hard to see from here."

Jackson and Lucy watched as Lynette opened envelopes, one after the other, reading the notes inside. Tears flowed down her cheeks.

Jackson suddenly remembered Dylan talking about the Dream Door. "I think I know what she's looking at. Years ago, Dylan told me about this spot on the side of their porch. It's like a little door, or something. They called it their 'Dream Door.' He said they found an old love letter in it after they bought the house. I think it was from the nineteen-thirties or forties. Dylan and Lynette made that spot their special place to store their dreams and ideas. Like a time capsule, I guess. I'd bet you anything Lynette just pulled that stuff out of there!"

"Should we call Dylan?"

"I don't know. Let's wait a few minutes and see. She's got a lot of stuff to go through. Let's just keep an eye out."

"Jackson, this is so unbelievable."

"I know. It's ironic. This morning I was thinking about what happened five years ago. It's exactly five years ago today that she left. The first of December…I could never forget that. I always remembered that date because I had a deadline that day for the Christmas article. December 1st."

"Oh, my gosh." Lucy leaned her head over on Jackson's shoulder. "Keep the curtains pulled a bit. I don't want her to see us watching. I feel like we shouldn't look, but I can't help it!"

The day after Lynette left Dylan, he started writing daily letters to her until she married Owen. Each letter was filled with his feelings, regrets, memories of happy days together and the dreams he still longed to share with her in the future. Some notes were long and others, only one or two words. Now, as Lynette read them, she was overcome with the pain that Dylan expressed on certain days, and her heart broke for him.

Jackson peered out once more to be sure Lynette was still there. "I can't believe Dylan hasn't heard her out there. He must be sleeping late."

"I know," Lucy responded. "Should we call him yet?"

"Wait a few more minutes. She probably needs this time to herself."

Lynette stood from the swing and walked down the steps.

Lucy panicked, "I think she's leaving! Call Dylan!"

"Hold on. Watch."

Lynette turned and went to the side of the porch.

"Yep, it's the Dream Door I told you about. See? She's getting stuff out of it."

"I wonder where Owen is. Do you think he left her or something?" Lucy asked.

Jackson shrugged. "We just saw them yesterday. Seemed okay to me."

Lucy shook her head. "I thought he was awful distant."

Lynette walked back onto the porch, carrying a rectangular package. Jackson and Lucy watched as she tore through the tape and wrapping. A canvas emerged. Lynette dropped to her knees, holding her hand over her mouth, trying to stay silent. But her cry was visible. Dylan had painted a beautiful field of flowers. In the field was a pair of blue baby booties. The sky overhead was filled with puffy, white clouds that formed the name 'Asa.'

Inside the Christmas House, Dylan was sleeping deeply. He was caught up in a dream in which he was suspended above the earth, as if weightless. Jesus stood before him, face-to-face. "I'm in you and you're in Me. Step into Me, Dylan, and you can see. Don't be afraid. We are one." Dylan trembled with fear and ecstasy as he placed his hands into Jesus' hands. "Closer. Step into Me."

Dylan spoke to Jesus. "But I can't go further. We're as close as we can get. My toes are touching yours."

Jesus smiled. "Step into Me."

Suddenly, Dylan understood what was being asked of him. He wondered if he might die if he chose to step into Christ, but he wasn't afraid to die. Dylan had nothing to lose. He lifted his right foot and stepped forward into Jesus, pressing his face into the chest of Jesus. As he melted into the heart of God, his eyes were opened to an awareness and knowledge he had never experienced. His heart was filled with a love so immense and deep that he was sure it would rip him in two. But this love was life, and he would live. He looked down at the world below him. Compassion poured from his soul like a waterfall.

"You can do all things through Me. Nothing is impossible."

Dylan's spirit merged with His Father's and his body pulsed with bliss at the tangible reality of being His son. Dylan remembered a verse from long ago: "The Lord is good to all; he has compassion on all He has made."

"I in you and you in Me."

The voice lingered in his mind as he descended to the earth, into his bed, and he awakened. Dylan sat up immediately, catching his breath. "Whoa!" His body still tingled with a heavenly presence.

"Get up, Dylan."

He heard an audible voice that drew him to his feet. He grabbed a robe and wrapped it around himself before brushing his teeth. "Dylan, go now." The voice prompted him to exit the house. He quickly ran to the front door and pushed the screen door open. In front of him, Lynette was on her knees, holding the canvas and weeping. Baby Asa slept quietly in the baby sling.

"Lynette!"

She looked at him with swollen eyes. "Dylan." She could barely speak his name, but she reached her hand out to him. "Dylan," she sobbed.

He began to weep as he knelt in front of her.

Jackson and Lucy watched in awe, crying. Old Emma Gray sat on her front porch, wiping her eyes with a handkerchief.

Lynette wrapped her arms around Dylan's neck, holding him tightly. "I'm sorry I ever let go. Oh, Dylan. I still love you. I love you so much."

Her words took his breath away. A million pounds lifted off his chest. He pressed his face into her neck, releasing hot tears. "I never stopped loving you, Lynnie." After a long embrace, Dylan stepped back. "Can I see Asa?"

She nodded and gently pulled the sling fabric away from his face. "This is Asa Brooks."

Dylan lovingly stared at the sleeping baby. "He's beautiful. What a perfect little face." He looked at Lynette. "You're a mom," he smiled.

She shook her head, chin quivering. "Yeah. And I'm in a mess. I don't know what to do. Owen left me. He filed for divorce without telling me and he took a job in Oregon. That's what I woke up to this morning. Divorce papers and a letter from him, telling me he has a buyer for the ranch and that I have two months to get myself settled somewhere. Nice, huh?" Tears spilled from her eyes.

"I'm so sorry. You don't deserve that."

Still breathless from the intermittent cries, she replied, "Oh, but I do deserve it. I was such a fool. I can't believe I was so blind." She pointed to the letters strewn on the swing. "All of these letters you wrote…" sobs interrupted her. "The painting, Dylan. I don't know what to say."

He took her by the arm. "It's chilly out here. You and Asa need to come inside."

He opened the door for her. They stepped in the house.

Across the street, Lucy squealed with excitement as she wiped tears from her face. "I can't believe this. Oh, Lord, be with them."

Jackson took her by the hand. "I'm pretty sure we just witnessed a miracle."

Emma picked up her notebook and jotted down, 'December 1st. Grace and Mercy visited the porches of Holly.' The old woman's face was wet with joyful tears. *I can't wait to tell Beverly.*

As Dylan and Lynette stepped into the house, she immediately noticed the painting over the fireplace. "Oh, my gosh. Where did you get that?"

"I did it." Dylan smiled.

"You mean…you painted it?"

He nodded. "I sure did. I have a lot more to show you. I regretted not taking that art class with you, so I decided to give painting a try. Mrs. Elliott gave me a few lessons and it just kind of flowed. I couldn't believe it myself."

Lynette smiled at him. She turned her attention to the painting again. "This is incredible. Dylan Vanberg, you're a natural artist. Who would have thought?"

He motioned for her to follow him. "Come check this out." They walked into the bedroom and Lynette gasped when she saw the paintings. "What do you think?" Dylan was overjoyed that she was finally seeing the work that was born out of his dreams.

Tears rolled down her cheeks as she studied his paintings. "Unbelievable. They're captivating. And so deep." She saw her river painting, still hanging near their bed. "You kept my painting!"

"Of course. Why wouldn't I?"

"Dylan, I painted that after a dream I had. I heard this phrase several times, 'His grace is sufficient.' And recently I keep hearing this other one. 'Stepping into me.'"

His eyes widened with wonder. "Seriously?" He was intrigued. "I've been hearing that phrase over the last few years. In fact, I woke up from a dream this morning. You've got to hear the dream.

Dylan told her the detailed dream about his encounter with Jesus and becoming one with Him. "And I realized that we've been one all along. And you're one with Him. We're all connected, you know? All my life, I've lived as if there was great separation between me and God, and I had to work hard to get near Him. All it took was one wrong thought, and I'd feel like I fell away from God and I had to start all over, trying to claw my way up a mountain. Ironically, it was when I felt like I reached the pinnacle that everything fell apart. It was self-righteousness. In my pride, I was so blind that I couldn't even love you the way that Christ loved the church. And I lost everything."

Lynette's eyes leaked as she listened to him.

Dylan continued. "But those circumstances helped to wake me up. I've felt things and seen things that I never would have known if I had stayed in that place of blindness. The pain was nearly unbearable at times, but I'm thankful for it because God used it to open my eyes." Dylan's eyes were wet. His voice trembled. "And He was so faithful to me through it all, even when I doubted Him and blamed Him." Dylan's voice cracked. "God is so much better than we think."

Lynette shook her head in agreement. Asa stirred and opened his eyes. "It's almost time for him to eat." She took him from the sling. Dylan watched in awe. Seeing his ex-wife, the only woman he ever loved, nurturing such a little life made him smile. His heart was pierced with a sadness, though, that the child wasn't his own. He figured it was part of the awakening…part of the journey that he had no choice but to be grateful for.

"He's so perfect. Can I hold him?"

Lynette was pleasantly surprised. She considered how Dylan must feel, knowing that Asa's father had betrayed him. "Are you sure?" she asked.

"Yes."

As Asa yawned and stretched, she placed him in Dylan's arms. He gently held him close to his chest. "Oh, my goodness. So tiny. Hi, Asa. I'm Dylan. How are you, buddy? You're the most perfect baby I've ever seen." Lynette's eyes released more tears as she watched. Dylan looked at Lynette. "I can't believe you're a mom. So, what's it like?"

"Well, it's indescribable. He's just over two weeks old, so I'm pretty sleep deprived. That's the hard part, but it's wonderful, really. There's nothing quite like bearing a life inside of you, feeling the movement and then getting to see his face. I didn't know I could love a baby so much."

"What about Owen? I mean, if he wants a divorce and all? How will that work with a baby?"

She shook her head with disgust. "I don't know. He's been so distant throughout the whole pregnancy and I've felt like a single mom. He checked out a long time ago. I thought that seeing Asa would help things. Owen apparently had this life-long dream of being a park ranger-slash-wildlife conservationist and he got a job offer right when I got pregnant. I told him I didn't want to go because we'd be living up in the mountains, far from civilization and I didn't think that was a good plan with a baby on the way. Honestly, even if we didn't have a child, I don't think I could handle that kind of life. Owen didn't take the job and I thought things were back to normal. But obviously, I was wrong."

Dylan looked pained for her. "So he just took a job where?"

"In Oregon. It's the job he wanted before. It came open again, so he took it."

"Did he ask you to go?"

"No. Not this time. He knew I wouldn't go. Not with a little baby." Her eyes overflowed. "It's hard to believe that a man would choose a job over his own son."

Dylan shook his head. "You mentioned he's selling the ranch?"

"Yes. I have a few weeks to figure out where to go. He mentioned in the letter that he already had a lawyer draw up documents stating that I'll get twenty percent of the sale. Can you believe that? Twenty percent? That's all I'm worth to him. At least it's something, though. That should get me through until I find a job."

Dylan stared at her. "Lynette?"

"Yeah?"

"You don't need to get a job. This is still your home. Come home." She put her hand over her mouth as her eyes squinted with deep emotion. "Lynnie, I'm serious. You and Asa belong here."

"Oh, my God, Dylan." She wept. "I don't know."

"What's your hesitation?"

Lynette spoke through sobs. "I can't do that to you. After what I put you through, I can't be a burden anymore."

Dylan leaned close to her. "You're not a burden. You're my wife. In my heart, in my eyes, we never divorced."

His words struck her heart. "After all I've done, why would you still want me?"

"I don't see you according to your past. I see you for who you are, and who you were always meant to be. Look at me. I'm not perfect, so don't think that I'm any better than you. It's only being in Christ that makes us perfect. That's something I'm beginning to see."

She smiled through her tears. "I see that the preacher man is still in there. And I mean that in a good way."

"Well, I'm no preacher man. I'm just a son who's come home to his Father."

They sat quietly for a moment.

"Lynette, will you consider moving in? You can have the master bedroom and I'll take the guest room for now."

"I'll consider it. I just don't want to become a burden to you. And, honestly, Dylan. Being around a baby…the nighttime feedings and crying…I'm not sure you know what you're asking for. And there's the fact that Asa's father is who he is. I'm worried that could become an issue."

Dylan stared deeply into her eyes as he cradled Asa in his arms. "Do you see me holding your son?"

"Yes."

"Do I look as if I'm struggling to love this child?"

"No."

"Lynette, he's part of you. And I love you. I know exactly what I'm asking for. I'm asking you to marry me again. And I want Asa to be my son."

She held her hand over her heart and sobbed. "Your kindness is killing me. I don't understand this grace, Dylan."

"You don't have to understand. I don't understand it, either. It just is."

She worked hard to get her words out between the tears. "When I left you, my heart was cold and hardened. But I thought about you a lot and I knew I still loved you. I regret the pain that I caused you. Not long ago, I had a moment with God. He absolutely drenched me with His love and presence, and my heart felt alive again. I just haven't had anyone to share it with. I would think about you, but I tried to redirect my thoughts to Owen because he's my husband, you know? He separated from me in his heart a long time ago. In fact, I don't know that he ever fully gave me his heart. Neither one of us did. I guess what I'm trying to say is that my heart has always been for you, and there were times when I wanted to come home, but I knew I had made a choice that I couldn't change." She sobbed once more. "I really do want to come home, to be your wife, and live life with you. I want that. But what will people think? What will it look like?"

"Lynette, I don't care what people think. They can think what they want and say what they want, but if they're smart, they'll see that it's redemption for both of us. If they have eyes to see, they'll know that we've always loved each other."

"I want that, Dylan. I really do. But maybe we shouldn't talk about it until things become more clear."

"Lynnie, I think it's clear as can be. You said you want this. And I want it, too. The dreams and visions…the things we've experienced. God has been in the mix all along."

She smiled. "He has. Well, what can I say? Owen wants to be a single man again. That's his choice, so I guess I'm free to make mine. The divorce papers speak volumes. He's had this in mind for a really long time."

"Then you're free."

She nodded and smiled. "I suppose I am."

Asa began to cry. "I'd better feed him now." Lynette took him from Dylan's arms. "I breastfeed. I can go in the other room if this is weird for you."

Dylan chuckled. "No way. I'm comfortable with it if you are."

She smiled.

"I'll go make some tea. Would you like some?"

"Thanks, Dylan. I'd love some tea."

He made his way into the kitchen, marveling over the goodness of God. For a moment his heart ached for loved one's whose stories had not turned out to be as beautiful as his own. *God, I know You're faithful, even to them. You have a way of turning the ugliest things into beauty. Lord, I can't thank you enough for bringing my wife back to me. And Asa. Help me to be a good father to that little guy.* Dylan remembered a phrase he had written in a newspaper article. He didn't understand when he wrote it, but it suddenly made sense. *And sometimes the purest of hearts are birthed in the darkest places.* Dylan pondered the way that God can use darkness against itself to purify hearts. When darkness tries to destroy, God uses its supposed power to bring light instead. *Oh, my God. You are so good. Surely, there's nothing to fear.*

Dylan returned to the living room where Lynette was feeding Asa. He found himself staring at her. *How is it that the things I hoped for long ago have come true? But in such a horrendous way?* He smiled at the irony. *God, she's a beautiful woman.*

Lynette looked up. "Why are you staring at me with that grin?"

"You're so beautiful. And honestly…just watching you is making me feel things I haven't felt in a long time, if you know what I mean." He winked.

"Dylan Vanberg!" She laughed. "You **have** changed!"

"Can you blame me? It's been five long years, woman."

They laughed as he left the room.

# Epilogue

Owen stood in the snow outside of his cabin. He breathed in the cold air, smiling at the view across the valley. The sound of frozen tree branches crackling behind him settled his soul with peace. This was the solitude he had long desired. Holly was always a reminder of his brokenness and failures. Now he had the clean slate he longed for. Guilt and shame convinced him that he wouldn't be a good father, and his calloused heart persuaded him that he was doing Lynette a favor by setting her free. He cared for his son, but he hoped that Dylan would accept him as his own.

Fay Lockley sat in Sacred Heart Chapel in a small town in Idaho, listening as the choir sang. She wept, overwhelmed with gratitude for old friends who took her into their home while she got her life together. For the first time ever, she felt loved and welcomed with a father's embrace.

Emma Gray, Beverly Watkins, Mike and Curt shared a table at Annie's Cafe, visiting with Emma's daughter and grandchildren. Laughter and joyful conversation filled the air. Marcy and David sat together in a booth, discussing Christmas plans with their family. Jackson and Lucy Sawyer laid in bed, settling in for an afternoon nap. He wrapped his arm around his wife's pregnant belly, feeling the movement of the life to come.

In Marshall City, Preston and Kat embraced each other next to the fireplace while their children decorated the Christmas tree. O Holy Night echoed through their home as the kettle whistled.

At the Christmas House, Dylan strung lights across the front porch while Lynette watched through the window as she rocked Asa. She was in awe of who he had become. Unconditional love penetrated her entire being, opening her eyes to the goodness of God. Lynette turned her attention to the painting above the fireplace. She admired the diamonds in the veil and the brushstrokes of Dylan's hand that caused light to come from within. *Let the Spirit and the Bride say come.* Tears filled her eyes. She was captivated by the man who had chosen her, not just once, but twice.

**Other books by Traci Vanderbush**

**Walking with a Shepherd** (2006) This was Traci's first book, written as encouragement for ministers' wives. She shares her own stories of the early days of her husband's ministry as a senior pastor, and the difficulties that many women secretly deal with behind the scenes as they live in the "house of glass."

**Mr. Thomas and the Cottonwood Tree** After several recurring dreams about a tree where children would encounter God, Traci felt led to write a book for children that would release emotional healing, based on some of her personal experiences with the Father. Within the dreams, she kept hearing "Mr. Thomas and the Cottonwood Tree." She began researching cottonwoods and found that they exude a resin that some refer to as a "Balm of Gilead." This confirmed to her that there would be healing within the story.

**Vignette: Glimpses of Mysterious Love** (2014) Love is an indefinable mystery. This is Traci and her husband's attempt, after learning the art of falling in love with each other once again, to articulate the limitless depths of the human soul. Through various journal entries, thoughts and poetic expressions regarding love, mercy, grace, and sexuality, join them on this journey of glimpses into mysterious love.

**The Magic of our Forefathers** (2015) The Magic of Our Forefathers speaks of the hidden gifts of past generations and how they affect our lives and future generations. Traci creatively unwraps the revelation of our ability to experience "time travel" through becoming aware of the value of our connection with the older generation. Through personal recollections and short stories, life lessons are revealed and hope-filled strength is given to the reader to overcome life's challenges.

**Life with Lummox** (2015) Lummox is a cuddly, bubbly, bouncy, happy, lovable character that's full of fun and wonder. The hard part about being a Lummox is that the world is filled with stuff to trip on, knock over, and break. So to be a happy, hairy fellow means you smile with every smiley smile you've got. The story of Lummox encourages children to embrace and find treasure in the seemingly awkward and eccentric. Life with Lummox is written by Traci Vanderbush and delightfully illustrated by the love of her life, Bill Vanderbush. The rhythm and rhyme combined with jolly pictures will bring smiles and laughs to all who read. Perfect for reading to pre-schoolers. Early elementary students would also enjoying reading this delightful story. Adults of every age also find themselves smiling over Lummox.

Visit www.tracivanderbush.wix.com/mrthomas

www.tracivanderbush.blogspot.com